Praise for Daryl Wood Gerber's
Cookbook Nook Mysteries

"There's a feisty new amateur sleuth in town and her name is Jenna Hart. With a bodacious cast of characters, a wrenching murder, and a collection of cookbooks to die for, Daryl Wood Gerber's *Final Sentence* is a page-turning puzzler of a mystery that I could not put down."

—Jenn McKinlay, *New York Times* bestselling author of the Cupcake Mysteries and Library Lovers Mysteries

"In *Final Sentence*, the author smartly blends crime, recipes, and an array of cookbooks that all should covet in a witty, well-plotted whodunit."

—Kate Carlisle, *New York Times* bestselling author of the Bibliophile Mysteries

"Readers will relish the extensive cookbook suggestions, the cooking primer, and the whole foodie phenomenon. Gerber's perky tone with a multigenerational cast makes this series a good match for Lorna Barrett's Booktown Mystery series . . ."

—*Library Journal*

"So pull out your cowboy boots and settle in for a delightful read. *Grilling the Subject* is a delicious new mystery that will leave you hungry for more."

—Carstairs Considers Blog

Books by Daryl Wood Gerber

The Cookbook Nook Mysteries

Final Sentence
Inherit the Word
Stirring the Plot
Fudging the Books
Grilling the Subject
Pressing the Issue
Wreath Between the Lines
Sifting Through Clues
Shredding the Evidence

The French Bistro Mysteries

A Deadly Éclair
A Soufflé of Suspicion

The Fairy Garden Mysteries

A Sprinkling of Murder

Suspense

Girl on the Run
Day of Secrets
Desolate Shores
Fan Mail

Writing as Avery Aames

The Long Quiche Goodbye
Lost and Fondue
Clobbered by Camembert
To Brie or Not to Brie
Days of Wine and Roquefort
As Gouda as Dead
For Cheddar or Worse

SHREDDING THE EVIDENCE

A Cookbook Nook Mystery

Daryl Wood Gerber

BEYOND THE PAGE
PUBLISHING

Shredding the Evidence
Daryl Wood Gerber
Copyright © 2020 by Daryl Wood Gerber
Cover design and illustration by Dar Albert, Wicked Smart Designs

Beyond the Page Books
are published by
Beyond the Page Publishing
www.beyondthepagepub.com

ISBN: 978-1-950461-44-8

~ Cast of Characters ~

Main characters

Bailey Bird Martinez, assistant at shop
Bucky Winston, husband of Cinnamon Pritchett and a firefighter
Cinnamon Pritchett (Winston), chief of police
Cary Hart, Jenna's dad, owns Nuts and Bolts
Flora Fairchild, owner of Home Sweet Home
Gran, Gracie Goldsmith, regular customer, now assistant at the shop
Jake (Old Jake) Chapman, wealthy retiree
Jenna Hart, co-owner of Cookbook Nook and Nook Café
Katie Casey (Landry), chef at Nook Café
Keller Landry, Katie's husband, ice cream entrepreneur
Lola Bird, owner of Pelican Brief
Marlon Appleby, deputy
Pepper Pritchett, owner of Beaders of Paradise
Rhett Jackson, owner of Intime and Jenna's fiancé
Tina Gump, former assistant at the Cookbook Nook
Tito Martinez, Bailey's husband, reporter at the *Crystal Cove Courier*
Vera Hart, Jenna's aunt and co-owner of Cookbook Nook and Nook Café
Z.Z. Zoey Zeller, mayor of Crystal Cove

Additional Characters in *Shredding the Evidence*

Alexa Tinsdale, fitness studio owner and personal trainer
Audrey Tinsdale, wife of Eugene Tinsdale
Brianna Martinez, Bailey's daughter
Eugene Tinsdale, *Crystal Cover Courier* owner/editor
Harmony Bold, wedding planner
Kylie Obendorfer, reporter at the *Crystal Cove Courier*
Marigold Martin, Midge's daughter
Midge Martin, owner of Shredding, a restaurant
Min-yi, Katie's ten-month-old adopted daughter
Mrs. Garofalo, receptionist at Crystal Cove High School

Principal Baker, principal at Crystal Cove High School
Reynaldo, assistant chef at Nook Café
Sasha Appleby, Marlon Appleby's adult daughter
Savannah Gregory, baker at Latte Luck
Shari Gregory, owner of Latte Luck and Savannah's mother
Steven and Sue Appleby, Marlon Appleby's adult son and his wife
Viveca Thorn, Alexa Tinsdale's assistant

SHREDDING
THE
EVIDENCE

Chapter 1

"Help, Cinnamon!" I shouted. "I can't stop."

Cinnamon Pritchett skated in front of me, grabbed me by the shoulders, and jammed her toe stops into the ground. "Breathe, Jenna. Toe stops. Remember? Toe stops."

"Yes," I said, teeth chattering. It had been ages since I'd skated. Catching a downhill had nearly done me in. "Why did I think it was flat along the coast?"

Cinnamon laughed. "Nothing in the area is flat."

"The ocean is."

We lived in Crystal Cove, California, a seaside community consisting of three crescent-shaped bays. A range of modest mountains defined the eastern border and trapped ocean moisture, blessing our sweet community with a temperate Mediterranean climate. The boulevard that ran parallel to the ocean was rife with shops and restaurants. On the southernmost end of town stood the Pier, a boardwalk boasting carny games, a theater, and other fun activities. That was where we'd been going until I nearly took a header.

"Next time you say we need to bond," I rasped, "let's go for coffee at the Nook."

With my aunt, I owned the Cookbook Nook, which was a culinary bookshop, and the adjoining café. The Nook Café was known not only for its fabulous meals but also for its midmorning and afternoon treats. It was a perfect spot for a get-together, sans injuries.

"Doesn't a scone sound good?" I asked.

"Nope. Now that I'm pregnant," Cinnamon said, "I need to work doubly hard at keeping my weight down."

Cinnamon was four months pregnant and didn't show a whit. At the start of our skate, she'd announced she was *with child*. I was thrilled for her. She and her adorable fireman husband had been trying since the day they got married. Pushing forty, she was no spring chicken in baby-bearing years.

"I've been eating like I'm having quadruplets," Cinnamon groused. "I never used to be hungry. I could go all day on an energy bar. But now?" She released me. "Good to go?"

1

"Yes. Toe stops. Got it." I adjusted the strap on my helmet and drank a sip of water from the bottle I carried in a bottle holster. "Race you back."

"You'll lose."

Cackling, Cinnamon tore off. I tried to keep pace but failed. I knew I would. I had no delusions about being a speed skater, and she had been skating since she was a girl. When taking midday breaks from her job as our chief of police, Cinnamon would often skate around town. Not many people knew she was off the clock then. Some felt a loop of skating was her way of keeping an eye on the locals.

"Speaking of weight," Cinnamon said, slowing her pace so she could skate beside me as we neared town, "how is —"

"Faster," a woman barked. "Faster, Priscilla. Watch out!"

I whirled around just in time to miss being plowed down by a trim woman in leggings and a black-and-white T-shirt featuring a crossword puzzle. Behind her ran Kylie O, the thirty-something food critic for the *Crystal Cove Courier*. The *O* stood for Obendorfer, which was a mouthful. If my surname had been that instead of Hart, I'd have shortened it to a single letter, too.

"Sorry, Jenna." Kylie slowed near me. "Got to keep up the pace." She also wore leggings, but her black-and-white T-shirt featured a raccoon and read *I work out so I can eat garbage.* Her locket bobbed as she jogged in place. So did the timer hanging around her neck. "Keep going, Priscilla. Don't slow down." Kylie sprinted off.

Cinnamon rolled her eyes. "Who knew a runner could be dangerous? As I was saying, speaking of weight, how's Bailey doing with hers?"

"She's got five pounds to go."

Bailey, my childhood pal and coworker at the bookshop, had given birth over six months ago, but she hadn't lost all the weight she'd put on. She was not happy about that, but she was madly in love with her daughter, Brianna, who resembled Bailey with short spiky hair and big eyes and an affinity for brightly colored clothing; the clothing was Bailey's doing, not Brianna's, of course.

"Bailey should skate with us," Cinnamon suggested.

"She will, once she finds a steady babysitter." The search for someone reliable had been endless. Bailey's mother, Lola, was pitching in when she could, and Bailey, who had switched to half days, was bringing Brianna to work for her morning shift. I loved having the baby there. She was so easygoing. No tears. No squalling. She lit up whenever Bailey read books to her, cookbooks in particular. Something about the word *teaspoon* made Brianna giggle nonstop. Plus, she adored Tigger, my rescue ginger cat, who nuzzled her whenever he got the chance. Luckily, she wasn't allergic to him.

"How's Tito doing?" Cinnamon asked.

"Great." Tito was Bailey's husband. "He adores Brianna."

"No, I mean work-wise. I heard Eugene Tinsdale is having financial difficulties at the paper and might be retiring. Does that mean the newspaper will fold?"

Eugene Tinsdale owned the *Crystal Cove Courier*.

"I don't think so." Tito was a stalwart reporter for the *Courier*. When we'd first met, he'd been stubborn and mulish and hard to like, but then he'd met Bailey and had turned to mush. "As far as I know, Eugene is looking for a buyer."

"Is Tito interested?"

"Doubtful. He doesn't have the funds, and he likes being a reporter."

Cinnamon swerved into the parking lot of Fisherman's Village, the quaint two-story shopping mall where the Cookbook Nook and Nook Café were located, and drew to a perfect stop on the cobblestone.

Me? I nearly took another header. I tried my toe stops, but they skidded. To save myself, I grabbed hold of a column. My feet kept going. I slid down the poll and landed on my rump. "Well, that was elegant, don't you think?" I chuckled. My ego was more bruised than my behind.

Cinnamon bit back laughter and helped me up. "Got to be careful on irregular surfaces."

"Fair warning."

"What's going on up there?" Cinnamon hitched her chin.

A lot of customers were climbing the stairs to the second floor of the mall.

"The Cameo is screening episodes of *Shredding* over the next few days." The Cameo, a petite movie theater, usually showed classics, but this week it was offering a binge-worthy selection of foodie television shows as well as foodie-themed movies.

"What's *Shredding*?" Cinnamon asked.

"Where have you been? It's a popular cooking show featuring Midge Martin. It's named after her restaurant. Midge tapes the show once a week in San Francisco. You must have eaten at her place. You like salads."

"My sweet husband is a devotee of steak and barbecue." Cinnamon winked. "Those are the places we go for dates. For the Food Bowl, we'll be taking in the All Star Barbecue."

"Nice," I said.

Our quirky mayor made it a point to create theme weeks for Crystal Cove, which thrived on tourism. The more themes the merrier. For nearly a week, from Thursday to the following Tuesday, restaurants and independent chefs were celebrating our annual November Food Bowl. It was one of Crystal Cove's greatest and most attended celebrations. Throughout the event, many of the restaurants in town were offering specialty meals.

"Rhett and I are planning on going to the barbecue event, too," I added. "Five barbecue chefs dishing it up in one venue sounds like heaven." Rhett was my fiancé and part owner of a new bistro, Intime.

I'd set a schedule, with and without Rhett. Tomorrow, I would go to Intime, which would be open to the public for the first time and would be offering a seven-course meal with wine pairings. On Friday night, Bailey and I would tour Buena Vista Boulevard, our main drag, which would be open only to pedestrians so people could taste wares from pop-up vendors. On Saturday, Rhett and I would stroll the Pier, which was featuring appetizer vendors, and then we'd return to town to dine on barbecue. On Sunday, restaurants would focus on family meals; my family would skip that night to enjoy our weekly meal. On Monday, the Nook Café was dishing up six hours of lunch choices. And on Tuesday, the final night, the Pelican Brief Diner, which belonged to Bailey's mother, Lola, was featuring a prix fixe fish fry. Lola had invited chefs from all over the Central Coast to participate. They would serve the event on the restaurant's rooftop.

"I've got to get these skates off before I break my neck," I said.

"I'll give you a hand." Cinnamon steadied me so I could bend down and remove my skates. "Between you and me, I'd prefer attending the More Bubbles Brunch."

The brunch was being held at the Crystal Cove Inn, a charming bed-and-breakfast and one of the original establishments in town. Pairings of champagne with cheese, meats, omelets, and desserts were on the menu.

"Of course I won't be able to imbibe," Cinnamon added. "But I'm sure they'll have mock mimosas."

"Maybe we could do a ladies morning out," I suggested. "On Tuesday. My day off. Think you could swing it?"

"I'm on duty for the next six days straight. I won't have a morning to spare."

"C'mon. Get your deputy to cover you."

"We'll see."

When Cinnamon and I had first met, we were at odds. She thought I was guilty of murder, and I didn't trust her because she was officious. Over the years, thanks to the fact that my father had been her mentor, way back when, we'd bonded and become friends.

"If you can't do the brunch," I said, "see if you can break free on Monday evening. I'll be going to Shredding for its Food Bowl. I promised to take Bailey. They have a blue cheese and bacon salad to die for, and I heard Midge is going to make a shredded tandoori chicken salad."

"Sounds good." Cinnamon glanced at her watch. "Oh, gosh, it's late. Gotta go." She blew me a kiss. "This was fun."

I unlocked the front door of the Cookbook Nook and strolled inside. Tigger, the adorable ginger cat who had introduced himself to me the day my aunt and I were remodeling the shop, charged me. Before heading off for my skating adventure, I'd dropped him at the store. "Yes, I'm back, fella. I didn't abandon you." I caressed his head, stowed my skates and paraphernalia in the stockroom, changed into a pair of capris, a pumpkin-colored sweater, and sandals, and returned to the register.

As I was sorting ones and fives, I heard a whimper and searched for the sound. Bailey, in a blue peasant blouse over jeans, was crouched by the display window.

"Whoa. Did you slip in before me?" I asked.

"Yep."

"What are you doing here so early?"

"Brianna couldn't sleep."

The baby was lying on a colorful blanket-style play gym, an arc of animal-shaped toys dangling overhead. She was reaching for the critters and missing—hence the whimper. At six months, she was starting to understand failure.

"Why did you lock the front door?" I asked.

"I didn't want customers coming in"—Bailey brandished a hand—"especially while I was dressing the display case with unwieldy tools."

Beside her on the floor lay a dozen items, including an orange rotary cheese grater, a yellow veggie slicer, a red food processor, a stainless steel mandoline, an old-fashioned potato peeler, and half a dozen sharp knives.

"Wow," I said.

"Food Bowl week is challenging. I can't do something that will represent all the tastings in town, so I settled on shredding and chopping gadgets, you know, to go with the binge-watching upstairs and to complement Midge's upcoming demonstration."

On Saturday at noon, Midge and Chef Katie, the chef at the Nook, were going to give a class for our customers showing how to shred with confidence. They planned to make a variety of salads, appetizers, vegetarian pizza, and more.

"What else do you think I should add?" Bailey asked.

"How about *The Chopped Cookbook*?" The full title was *The Chopped Cookbook: Use What You've Got to Cook Something Great*. It was written by the Food Network chefs and featured some delectable recipes, including salsa-marinated skirt steak soft tacos and chilled peanut chicken noodle salad. Thinking about food made my mouth water. A protein shake for breakfast wasn't cutting it. "And since we're nearing Thanksgiving, let's get in the spirit and add some fall leaves, those beautiful brown paisley oven mitts, the ceramic turkey cookie jar, and the magnetic ceramic turkey salt- and pepper shakers."

"Don't you want to save those for next week's display?"

I frowned. "Yes, you're probably right."

"Don't worry. I'll add an apron and a few other goodies."

In the Cookbook Nook, we offered not only cookbooks and fiction about food but also unique culinary and kitchen items. Many of our aprons were one of a kind.

"And let's ditch the knives," I said.

"On it." Bailey bounded to her feet, removed the knives from her assortment, and went in search of other items, allowing me some one-on-one time with Brianna.

I murmured to her and tickled her under her chin. She cooed and offered big smiles.

"How's it going with wedding planning?" Bailey returned with a handful of decorative porcelain vegetables—eggplant, radishes, red lettuce, and such—and set them alongside the slicing and dicing items before moving off again.

"So far so good." Rhett and I had found a beautiful bed-and-breakfast with gorgeous gardens in Napa Valley, and we'd set a date for an evening wedding next June. "Not much to do yet. We're considering a menu, but nothing is written in stone. We've browsed invitations online. We're wondering whether we need to send out *Save the Date* cards."

"Yes, and don't think you have all the time in the world. The months will fly by." Bailey patted her post-pregnancy belly. "Trust me, I have a baby to show for my nine months."

With my aunt, father, and Bailey giving me advice, I was sure the months would *not* fly by.

"If I were you, I'd take Cinnamon up on using her wedding planner," Bailey said.

"Good idea." I gave Brianna a tickle and got to my feet. "Hey, did you see the line heading up the stairs to the *Shredding* screenings?"

"I did." Bailey set a pair of orange kitchen mitts on the floor. "Can you imagine watching foodie-themed shows every day? I'd be eating everything in sight."

"I told you I took one of Midge's classes, didn't I?" I was a foodie, but I wasn't a gourmet cook. I didn't learn how to cook until I'd joined my aunt in this venture. My mother had been the chef in our family. Now, whenever I had some free time, I watched cooking shows on television, plus Chef Katie, a longtime friend, had made it her mission to teach me one recipe at a time. Rhett, also a gifted chef, was guiding me, too. I loved how patient they both were.

"I want to take a class soon," Bailey said. "Do you think Katie will do one on making natural baby food?"

"Ask her. You never know."

Bailey knelt down, gave her baby a kiss, and started creating the display case. Arranging everything took time, but I knew I could trust her. She had a great eye for color and design. When we'd worked at Taylor & Squibb, an advertising agency in San Francisco, she had been the product person, and I had served as a concept person.

"Hey," Bailey said over her shoulder, "did I tell you about Midge's set-to with Kylie O yesterday?"

"No."

Bailey let out a stream of air. "She is such a prima donna."

"Midge or Kylie?"

"Kylie, of course." Bailey wrinkled her nose. "I can't remember the last foodie recommendation she made that I agreed with. Octopus with Brie? Squid ink on avocado toast? Blech. She does like to review the exotic."

"You mean *weird*." I giggled. "I don't know her well, but I've seen her around town. Rollerblading, surfing, running. In fact, she and a jogging mate almost knocked me over earlier."

"You're kidding."

"Kylie was yelling, 'Faster! Faster!'"

"Taskmaster," Bailey carped. "I think she runs to work off all the calories she takes in tasting food for her reviews."

I popped to my feet and started tweaking the array of specialty cookbooks on the round table near the entrance. After a day of customers, these displays ended up wrecked. "She's quite a zealot."

"You're telling me." Bailey whistled. "I took a group pilates class with her before I got pregnant. Alexa Tinsdale was the instructor."

Alexa owned Your Wellness, a fitness studio in town, and was considered one of the premier pilates instructors in the Central Coast area. Clients came from as far away as San Jose and Carmel. *Be brave, be bold* was her motto.

"Kylie was in Alexa's face throughout. 'You don't know what you're talking about.'" Bailey imitated a high-pitched nasal voice. "And 'Why should I take orders from you? You're a hack.' It was intense."

"Poor Alexa."

"Nah. She dished it right back." Bailey snickered.

"Alexa loves paleo cookbooks" — I held up a book — "like this one."

"I know. I delivered *The Big 15 Paleo Cookbook: 15 Fundamental Ingredients, 150 Paleo Diet Recipes, 450 Variation* to her home last week. She was throwing an impromptu party for friends and wanted something new to serve."

I faced Bailey. "Aren't you and Tito taking private lessons with Alexa now?"

"Good memory. Yes. Not together. Separately." Bailey placed a porcelain tomato into the front window display. "Anyway, back to my story about the pilates class. As it turns out, Kylie and Alexa have been friends since childhood. The in-your-face antics were all for show, but I've got to tell you, everyone in the class was sweating bullets until we found out." Bailey placed a green pepper beside the tomato. "As for the set-to between Kylie and Midge at Shredding, I was there picking up dinner to go, and man, it wasn't pretty."

Brianna rocked and rolled herself onto her belly. Bailey cheered and replaced Brianna on her back. She wasn't crawling yet. *Late bloomer,* her grandmother had said. I happened to know some babies never crawled. They went straight to pulling up on a piece of furniture and cruising. I had been that baby, my father often reminded me. Always on the go and curious to a fault.

"What happened?" I asked.

"Kylie questioned the originality of one of the recipes in Midge's latest cookbook," Bailey said.

"She didn't."

"She *did.* Kylie called Midge a phony. To her face. In front of a restaurant full of people. Knives and mandolines" — Bailey lifted the stainless steel one — "were involved."

"That doesn't sound fun."

"It wasn't."

After finalizing the tweaks to the display table, I crossed to the vintage kitchen table where we always had a jigsaw puzzle set up for customers to toy with. To honor the Food Bowl, I'd found a food-themed, cat-themed jigsaw puzzle in which mischievous kittens were scrambling on a baking counter, messing with cookie preparations. Every time I glimpsed it, I smiled.

"Kylie pushes buttons," Bailey added. "Tito can't stomach her."

Daryl Wood Gerber

Tito loved food and wished that he could write restaurant reviews in addition to his regular reporting. His grandmother had been an exquisite cook and had interested him in all of the world's cuisines.

"Speaking of Tito," I said, "how's it going at the newspaper? I heard Eugene Tinsdale might sell."

"Tito's worried. He's afraid a new owner will ruin everything, or worse, that no one will buy the business. I can't imagine Crystal Cove not having a newspaper, can you?"

"No." I liked reading my news via paper, not online. If we didn't have a newspaper, then the local news would come from as far away as Santa Cruz or even San Jose.

"Needless to say, tension is high at the office, and Kylie O hasn't made it easier for Tito."

"How so?" I roamed the store double-checking that all of the moveable bookcases were anchored in place. I didn't want a customer to lean against one and have the shelf and the customer go sailing.

"Kylie is demanding that she and she alone cover the Food Bowl."

"But that's ridiculous. There will be too much going on for one reporter to report it all."

"That's what Tito said, but would Kylie listen? No, she would not. She's deaf. Obstinate. A real piece of work." Bailey leaned in and lowered her voice. "Between you and me, I think my sweet husband would like to clock her."

Chapter 2

"Who's getting clocked?" Gracie Goldsmith asked as she waltzed in and hung her pashmina on a hook by the register. "It had better not be me," she added, stashing her Dolce & Gabbana purse beneath the counter. "I'm right on time." Most everyone in town referred to Gracie as *Gran* because, when she wasn't working at the Cookbook Nook — she had been dying to help out three days a week — she was grandmother to three adorable girls. She'd been a clerk for two months, but I swear, she knew more about our stock than I did. Her personal assortment of cookbooks would rival a collector's. "And Bailey, please don't say your darling baby."

"Don't be silly. No one will be clocking Brianna." Bailey lifted her daughter off the floor and moved the play gym to the stockroom.

"Good to know. Babies need all the love and attention you can muster." Gran fluttered her fingers in my direction. "Morning, Jenna. I'm ready for duty. Want a cup of coffee? I'm getting some for myself."

"Sure. I could use a cup."

Gran slipped into the stockroom and returned with a mug for each of us. "Now, who's getting clocked?"

I took a sip and said, "Kylie O, the foodie reporter."

"Oh, that woman." Gran set her mug on the counter. "She walks around with such airs. And does she ever go a day without whisking that blonde hair of hers over her shoulders? I'm sure she does it so people will pay attention." Gran mimed Kylie's snooty hair-tossing gesture, which made me laugh.

I never understood long hair. Too much work. I wore mine in a shoulder-length blunt cut.

"And that body," Grant went on. "Honestly! Have you ever seen the woman eat? She's so toned it's disgusting."

"Jealous much?" I asked.

"Not a whit." Gran smoothed the bows of her silk blouse. "I'll have you know that back in my day I was a looker." She was in her seventies and quite vivacious.

"You still are."

"Get out of here. By the by, have you seen the signs announcing the

Food Bowl around town? They're beautiful. Z.Z. has done it again."

Z.Z. Zeller was our mayor. Talk about vivacious. The woman never slowed down.

"Yesterday, I went online to make my plan." Gran moved to the computer and entered a website address in the browser. "Have you girls done so? If not, you'd better. I don't know how anyone will visit all the venues, of course, but at least you'll be able to pick and choose. And by the way, be prepared to laugh. Whoever wrote the schedule should be commended for his or her wit."

"Bailey's mother contributed."

Gran winked. "I thought so. Lola is so clever. Listen to this. 'All right, folks. Reschedule birthdays, anniversaries, quinceañeras, or whatever you were planning on doing. You're going to be busy this week.'"

"Aw." Bailey bounced Brianna on one hip. "Your Nana put that in for you, *bebe*. Your daddy can't wait to throw you your quinceañera."

A quinceañera, or *fiesta de quince años*, was a celebration of a girl's fifteenth birthday, celebrated widely around the world.

"Read another one," Bailey said.

Gran chuckled. "Okay, here we go: 'Pour a cup of strong coffee and start texting friends to see what they're into, and then coordinate. Do you want to see some cool food movies? Do you know somebody who's going to be very upset if they miss out on Midge Martin's shredded chicken salad? Mark up your calendar. And then have another cup of coffee.'"

I laughed. "I've bought tickets for a few things."

"Good girl," Gran said. "Here's one more. 'You're set, right? Now it's time to go to the gym and get in shape for all the food bowling you're about to do.'"

Bailey kissed her baby's cheek. "That sums it up for me. I'm going to the gym a lot."

Gran smiled. "You look wonderful just the way you are."

"I'd like to lose this." Bailey swiveled and showed Gran her hind side.

"Take in the dancing at Azure Park. That's what I plan to do with the girls. Dance, dance, dance. Every night there will be DJ's from coastal radio stations."

"And food vendors throughout the day," Bailey said. "Way too many food vendors. Selling ice cream and cookies and cotton candy."

"And salads and healthy foods," Gran said.

"Grant me willpower!" Bailey raised a fist.

"Good morning, everyone." My aunt Vera sauntered in wearing a copper brown caftan. She was carrying the matching turban and had applied her makeup with a deft hand.

"You look nice," I said.

"Thank you."

"Got a hot date?" I asked.

Aunt Vera didn't respond. I noted she was stroking her phoenix amulet.

"Is everything okay?" I asked.

"Too-ra-loo," she crooned and disappeared into the stockroom.

Okay, that was weird. She'd looked worried. Why?

When my aunt returned, she sat at the vintage kitchen table and began shuffling a deck of tarot cards using a handheld method, sliding cards out and reinserting them.

I joined her. "Do you have a client coming in?"

Occasionally, Aunt Vera told people's fortunes. Though I didn't believe in tarot and such, she did, and I didn't buck her enthusiasm for it. She believed in dispensing as much good news as she could.

"Mm-hm," she mumbled unenthusiastically, again causing me to be concerned.

"Want me to shuffle those for you?" I asked.

"As if." My aunt believed that shuffling was a way to bond herself to the deck. By handling the cards, she allowed the conversation with the spirit world to begin.

"You don't do a reading without someone asking for it," I said. "What's going on?"

"Nothing."

"Liar."

Aunt Vera frowned. "Fine. I'll confess. I did a telephone reading for a friend last night."

"And you didn't like the outcome?"

"Not in the least."

"Are you hoping you can redo it now and change the result?" I asked.

"It doesn't work that way."

I clasped her wrist. "Who did you read for?" Someone special, that was for sure. For her to break her own steadfast rules and not do the reading in person meant the caller had to be a really close friend. "Who?"

"Me." Eugene Tinsdale strode into the shop. Forty years ago, Eugene had given up his dream of becoming an Olympic hurdler and had followed his father into the newspaper business. He'd never looked back. How he loved a good story. I knew him because he also enjoyed good food and was a regular at the Nook Café. Usually, he was an elegant man with an easy smile and a jaunty spring in his step, but not today. The lines around his aging eyes were deep, and his gait was sluggish. Even his seersucker suit seemed lackluster.

I rose to greet him, my hand extended. "Sir."

Eugene didn't shake. Instead, he sat in the chair I'd vacated and stared at my aunt. "Well, Vera?" My aunt and he had gone to school together. They'd never dated. They hadn't had that kind of relationship. They'd bonded over politics and chats about history. Years ago, when the newspaper was flagging, my aunt had helped Eugene out financially. Did he need her help again?

My aunt handed Eugene the deck of tarot cards. He shuffled like a professional gambler and gave the deck back to her. Slowly, she turned over the top card. The Ten of Swords. I didn't know much about tarot, but I could identify each of the cards and its apparent meaning. This one featured a man lying facedown with ten swords in his back.

My aunt moaned softly. Yes, the card was startling, and yes, it was an indicator that the person for whom the reading was being done, in this case Eugene, might suffer an unwelcome surprise, but it could also mean that something bad had already happened. However, even if that were the case, it could also signify that Eugene would have to brace himself because something worse could be on the horizon.

"Ahem." My aunt's gaze said *Leave.*

I blew her a kiss, flipped the front door sign to Open, and returned to the register.

Bailey sidled over to me. "*Psst.* What's Eugene doing here?"

I told her briefly. "His tarot reading didn't start very upbeat. In fact, it's —"

"Don't worry." Bailey batted the air. "You know your aunt. She'll put a positive spin on it. She never says anything negative."

That all sounded well and good, but this time I wasn't sure Aunt Vera could.

• • •

A half hour later, Eugene left the shop looking disheartened, and my aunt headed to a meeting. What kind of meeting, she didn't say. She was rarely so vague, which made me even more curious.

Doing my best not to worry about her, I focused on the business at hand. Customers arrived in droves. We'd ordered many of our local restaurants' cookbooks—many printed by independent presses—so visitors attending the Food Bowl event could find the recipes to meals they'd enjoyed during the week.

In addition, our supplier showed up with a number of boxes filled with other new cookbooks I'd ordered.

"About time," I said.

"Sorry." He was a freckle-faced man who blushed easily. "The distributor's truck got held up in customs."

A load of books came from a printer in Canada.

"This is the one I've been waiting for." I pulled *My Street Food Kitchen: Fast and Easy Flavours from around the World* from one of the boxes. Gran had recommended we offer the title. A renowned food writer had written the cookbook because she'd wanted to share recipes from her travels around the globe. Everything in it sounded intriguing to me. Icy ceviche. Dirty burgers.

"Don't miss this one," the supplier said. "It's my favorite." He held up *Tacolicious: Festive Recipes for Tacos, Snacks, Cocktails, and More.*

"You read what you bring?" I asked.

He grinned. "If the cover catches my eye, sure. Plus, I knew the name. I've been to the restaurant in San Francisco. Mexican flavors with a California twist. What's not to like?"

I signed his freight bill and bid him goodbye.

At one p.m., Bailey and Brianna left for the day. Throughout the afternoon, Gran and I scrambled to keep up with purchases. Lots of tourists had arrived in town for the start of Food Bowl. By the end of the day, I was beat. I texted Rhett and asked what time he would be heading home. He didn't respond right away. I didn't expect him to. He had invited six discerning chefs to taste test the seven-course meal that he would serve tomorrow night. He was relying on them to give him their honest opinions.

Years ago, long before I'd met Rhett, he'd served as the chef at the Grotto, a restaurant that had been situated on the second floor of Fisherman's Village. When it burned down, due to arson, he left the business and opened a sporting supply store.

"It's you and me, cat." I scooped up Tigger and we strolled home, my rollerblade bag looped over my shoulder.

Home was new to both of us. In the spring, Aunt Vera had purchased the California ranch-style house across the street from her house and my cottage, both of which she owned—she'd invested well in the seventies—and she'd presented the house to Rhett and me as an early wedding gift. As much as I'd loved living directly on the beach, I knew that owning a larger house as a couple would be ideal for us. My cottage had been teensy; the house was spacious. Rhett hadn't moved in yet. He was still living in his cabin in the hills because he felt opening Intime would require crazy hours, and he hadn't wanted to wake me in the wee hours of the morning. Even after we were married, he didn't plan to give up the cabin. He enjoyed communing with nature. Mini solo vacations, I assured myself, would be healthy for our relationship.

Rhett and I had agreed on a neutral color scheme for our new home. We hadn't completed everything yet. The living room, master bedroom, and guest room needed painting, and the two bathrooms needed retiling—the previous owner had loved blue everything—but the kitchen was done, thanks to Keller Landry's expert craftsmanship. Keller was Katie's husband, whose occupation as an ice cream entrepreneur couldn't pay all the bills, especially in cooler months, so he'd taken over his father's trade and had turned out to be quite adept at woodwork. I loved the beveled cabinetry, granite counters, and massive island he'd installed. A separate crew had put in the hardwood floors.

I stowed my rollerblades in the hall closet, set Tigger on the floor, and queued up some jazz music on my iPhone. "Loud?" I asked the cat.

He mewed.

"Loud it is."

I switched on the Bluetooth portable speaker so music would blast through the house, and then threw together a platter of salami, Gruyère, and olives, and poured a glass of sauvignon blanc. When I finished my quasi-dinner, I would set to work. Keller was going to do most of the regular painting as well as retile the two bathrooms, but I wanted to paint the master bedroom. I'd envisioned a seascape mural on the wall behind the king-sized bed. If I were diligent, I'd be done in a couple of weeks. Granted, I wouldn't be painting when I was enjoying Food Bowl events, but I'd accounted for the missed days.

My cell phone jangled. I muted the music, grabbed the phone off the counter where I'd set it beside my purse, and answered.

"Hey," Rhett said. "Did I disturb you?"

"Nope." How I loved the sound of his voice, sexy and warm and filled with confidence. The day I'd met him, I'd fallen for him. Of course, I hadn't let him know that until a long time after, but something about his calm self-assurance had captured my heart instantly. "How is tonight's run-through going?"

"So far, three courses have passed the smell test." He chuckled. "What are you doing?"

"Eating dinner and then painting."

"Nice. You've neglected your art for a while."

That was another thing I loved about Rhett. He thought about my needs, my wants. Oh, he had a healthy ego, but he considered me an equal and was always making sure I took care of myself.

"Not that kind of painting," I said. When I was younger, I'd dreamed of becoming a famous artist. I'd painted a lot of ballerinas. "I'm tackling the master bedroom mural."

"What's that?" Rhett said to someone in the background. "Jenna, sorry, I've got to go. Disaster strikes. The minced chicken salad is a bust. Love you."

"Love you."

The moment I ended the call, my cell phone rang again. My aunt's name appeared on the screen. I answered. "What's up?"

"Are you busy?"

I grinned. No painting for me tonight. "I'm free. Want to have dinner with me?"

"I'll be right over."

When I'd lived in the cottage, my aunt had rarely visited. I'd usually gone to her house. Now that I was in a larger home with a four-season palette of plants in the backyard—camellias in the winter, azaleas in the spring, honeysuckle in the summer, and brilliant blue sage in the fall—she enjoyed coming to me.

"I'll bring wine," she said.

Quickly, I threw together a chopped salad using the items I'd set on my appetizer platter and added avocado, Roma tomatoes, and cucumber. I topped it with a honey-lemon vinaigrette dressing that I'd made last week, threw a baguette and a round dish of butter into a basket, and filled large goblets with ice water.

The rear patio off the kitchen and adjoining living room faced east and was a perfect place to barbecue or enjoy a cup of coffee or glass of wine. I set the patio table with place mats and place settings and then moseyed to the front porch, which was the ideal location to watch the sun set. A sliver of open space between Aunt Vera's house and the cottage allowed for a direct view of the ocean.

Fifteen minutes later, my aunt appeared with a bottle of the same sauvignon blanc I'd poured. *Like minds,* I thought. She'd changed out of her caftan and was wearing flowing silk pants with a royal blue sweater.

"Don't you look pretty," I said. "Going on a date later?" My aunt and Deputy Marlon Appleby, a widower, had been seeing each other for quite a while.

"No."

"Why are you dressed up? Not for me." I took the wine and led her into the kitchen.

Tigger scampered to her and rubbed his back against the hem of her pants. She scratched his head.

"I was going to have dinner with Z.Z.," my aunt said, "but it turns out a client is backing out of a deal, so she canceled."

Our mayor, when not running the town, also sold real estate. Her grown son had gone back to college, and Z.Z. was helping him out financially so he wouldn't be burdened with enormous debt when he graduated.

"Okay, but that's not why your forehead is pinched, is it?" I twirled a finger at her face. "You're worried about Eugene Tinsdale."

"How did you—" My aunt sat on a stool at the island. "Are you finally tapping into your extrasensory perception?"

"I don't have ESP, and I never will, but I could tell you were concerned about Eugene at the shop earlier. What's up?" I opened the wine, poured her a glass, and after setting our salads, bread, and water on a tray, led her to the patio. Before I sat, Tigger swatted me with his tail.

"Sorry, buddy." I hurried inside, fetched his bowl of tuna, and returned. I set the bowl near the patio table. He chowed down before I even took my seat.

My aunt took a bite of her salad and congratulated me on the homemade dressing.

"Did the meeting you attended earlier have to do with Eugene?" I asked. "I heard he's thinking of putting the newspaper up for sale."

"Yes. I met with a banker. They're not willing to extend him a loan."

I sipped my wine. "I'm sorry. So, the reading you gave him. Is that the problem? Does he want to know how to proceed?"

"No. He's worried about Audrey." His wife of thirty-eight years.

"Is she sick?" I asked.

My aunt shook her head. "No."

"Is her business suffering, too?"

Audrey owned a fine art studio. She taught classes and often took students to the beach to paint *en plein air*, outdoors. Occasionally, she came into the Nook Café for a bite to eat, although she didn't venture into the Cookbook Nook. According to a customer who knew Audrey well, Audrey wasn't much of a cook.

I said, "The testimonials on her website are incredible." I'd checked Audrey out because I'd considered taking a few art classes to up my game.

"They should be." My aunt set her fork down. "She's talented, insightful, and caring. No. Her business is fine. Eugene is worried because she's not her typical happy-go-lucky self. I went online to see if someone had written something negative about her. You know how cruel people can be on Facebook and the like. Nothing."

"Perhaps she's concerned that Eugene is thinking about selling the newspaper. Maybe she's worried he'll be underfoot if he retires."

"Perhaps."

"Lots of couples need space when one or the other retires," I said, sounding like a seasoned retiree. I tore off a piece of bread and slathered it with butter—one of my guilty pleasures. A thought occurred to me. I tried to tamp it down but couldn't. "Um, is it possible Audrey has met someone else?"

"As in a lover?" my aunt gasped. She wasn't a prude. The notion must have taken her aback.

"You know, maybe she's fallen for a student or an art dealer."

"Oh, dear, I hope that's not it. Eugene and Audrey are the perfect couple. And their daughter Alexa is such a doll. She would be heartbroken if anything happened between her parents. She dotes on them, and they dote on her. You know Alexa, don't you? Of course you do. She comes into the store." Aunt Vera sighed. "I remember how eager Alexa was after college to show her parents her worth. When she opened her fitness studio and made it a success in less than a year, she was glowing with confidence."

"She's got a great reputation. I've taken a couple of group classes. Both Bailey and Tito take private lessons with her."

Tito had gone to Alexa for years. He said that as a reporter he needed his body to be in tip-top shape in case he needed to chase a story. Bailey had started up recently because she'd wanted her pre-baby body back.

Aunt Vera pushed her plate away.

"Are you sure Eugene doesn't have a clue about what's depressing his wife?" I asked. "He should."

Aunt Vera threw me a stern, judgmental look.

I pressed my lips together. She was right. Who was I to talk? I hadn't known what my former husband had been up to, not even after he'd done a disappearing act by pretending to be dead—may he now truly rest in peace.

"No," my aunt said. "Eugene seems clueless, and I believe him."

"You've told me the tarot cards never lie," I said. "What else did they reveal?"

Aunt Vera moaned.

"Is it that bad?" I asked.

"Intense love or intense hate could be involved."

I placed my hand on my aunt's. "Maybe this time the cards are wrong."

Chapter 3

I woke the next morning weighed down by a feeling of foreboding. I hated whenever that happened. Sure, I could pinpoint the cause. My conversation with my aunt had set me on edge. If I were to admit it to myself, I was a bit of a Pollyanna. I wanted everyone in Crystal Cove to be happy and thrive. I didn't want anyone to struggle. But life wasn't like that. I'd struggled, and overcoming those challenges had made me who I was—a strong, confident woman.

Tigger followed me into the kitchen and did a figure eight around my ankles as I brewed a pot of strong coffee. After drinking a cup, I took a brisk walk on the beach. The salt air cleared my head and a refreshing shower energized me. Donning my favorite aqua sweater and jeans and flip-flops, my preferred footwear, did the rest. I left the house feeling empowered.

The moment I arrived at the Cookbook Nook, I sat at the register and sent Cinnamon a text asking her for her wedding planner's contact information. At least I could start that ball rolling. That would set my mind at ease about the next few months. She responded in less than a minute and warned me: *Don't delay.*

Taking her advice, I contacted the wedding planner, and she, like Cinnamon, responded in less than a minute. She could meet tomorrow morning as long as I filled out her questionnaire first. *Give a busy woman a job and it gets done,* I mused. I responded in the positive and texted Rhett with the appointment information, then I pushed my cell phone aside.

"Good morning!" Bailey trotted in with Brianna and baby items in tow. Dressed in a hooded jacket and slouchy pants, she resembled a Sherpa loaded for a trek up Mount Everest. "You won't believe it! I found a sitter . . . a nanny . . . a *whatever* . . . and you'll never guess who it is."

"Who?" I rounded the counter and helped her unload the baby's blanket, play gym, diaper bag, and sit-me-up floor seat—a darling owl-styled chair with eating tray and flipper toys.

"Tina."

"Our Tina?"

Tina Gump was the twenty-something clerk we'd hired a little over a year and a half ago. She'd quit during the summer so she could attend culinary school full-time. She dreamed of becoming a chef.

"Has she given up on school so soon?" I asked.

"No, she's taking a full load, but all her classes are in the morning. Her father is still helping her, but she would really like to make some extra spending money. Plus, she loves Brianna, and Brianna loves her. So Tina can attend classes in the morning then take Brianna home for me and, while Brianna naps, Tina can do homework. Win-win. I'm back on full-time three days a week, boss, if you need me, that is."

"You won't miss being with your baby?"

"I'll miss her, but I really do need some *me* time." Bailey placed her hand on her chest. "And *me* time is time spent with you and customers and—" She faltered.

"Adults."

"Exactly." Bailey let out a long sigh. "Am I a horrible mother?"

"You are exactly what you're supposed to be. Your daughter is well-adjusted. Your marriage is fine and dandy. Tina will complement your needs perfectly."

"If she lasts a few months, at least it will get me over the hump. I'll even have time to work out without a baby on my hip!" Bailey did an arm-pumping dance with Brianna in her arms. "Alexa, here I come."

"Baby?" Chef Katie Landry, née Casey, swooped into the shop from the breezeway that connected the Cookbook Nook to the café. "Do I hear a baby?" She hadn't donned her chef's jacket over her clothes yet. She was just coming on duty. Her unruly curls bobbed as she took Brianna from Bailey. "Who's my best girl?" Katie cooed, lavishing the baby's neck with kisses. "Want to fly?" She held Brianna overhead. The extension made her navy blue dress rise up. "Fly, baby. Fly."

Brianna wiggled her arms and legs as she giggled with delight.

"Katie, that's enough. Put her down," Bailey ordered.

"I won't drop her." Katie and I were both tall, but thanks to her work as a chef, she was eons stronger. She pulled Brianna to her chest and kissed her once more before handing her off to Bailey. "She's so pretty. Who does she get that from? Tito?"

"Ha-ha." Bailey mock-scowled.

Bailey, Katie, and I had grown up together, although we'd hung out with different crowds during school. Now, we were best of friends.

Bailey set Brianna into the sit-me-up floor seat, told her she'd be right back, and carted the rest of her items into the stockroom.

Katie watched the baby in earnest. I wondered if she was regretting working now that she and Keller were the proud parents of Min-yi, an adorable Korean girl. By the time they'd taken custody, Min-yi had already been crawling. Did Katie worry about missing other milestones? She caught me staring at her and smiled broadly.

"I'll be baking muffins today, Jenna," she said. "Pumpkin with chocolate and shredded coconut. Don't miss them. It's a new recipe I'm trying for Thanksgiving. I'll have them out by ten." Daily, she set treats for our customers on a tiered tray on the table in the breezeway.

"I can't wait."

"And don't miss today's lunch special. I'm cooking up a variety of salads and grilled sandwiches as practice for our Food Bowl event. A bacon with macaroni-and-cheese grilled cheese sandwich is on the menu."

"Heaven help my hips," Bailey said as she returned from her chore. "Why do you torture me?"

Katie guffawed. "Eat half. Everything in moderation."

"As if I had that kind of self-control." Bailey glowered at her.

"Jenna, darling, it's awful." Gran hustled in, the tails of her cocoa-colored sweater flapping wildly. "On the street. He . . ." She huffed, clearly out of breath and distraught. "He . . ." She tried again but failed.

"He who?" I put a hand on her shoulder. "What's wrong?" I peered past her but couldn't see anyone on the walkway beyond the parking lot.

"Tito," Gran said.

Bailey whirled around. "What about him? He's due here in an hour for the magic presentation."

A long time ago, when Tito had stepped in for a magician who'd taken ill, I'd grown a new appreciation for him. He'd never struck me as the suave and charming type, but he'd been wonderful. So, to launch Food Bowl week at the shop, we'd decided to have a gathering for our customers. Tito was going to make apples and saltshakers and all sorts of foodie-related things disappear.

"Tito and that other reporter," Gran said. "On the street. They're going at it."

"Which reporter?" Bailey asked.

"Kylie O."

"Oh, no!" Bailey raced out of the store.

Katie said, "I've got Brianna, Jenna. Go with her."

I dashed out.

Running in flip-flops was always a challenge. "Bailey!" I shouted.

My pal might not have lost all the baby weight, but apparently carrying the baby around had given her extra thigh strength. She was shorter than I but outdistancing me by at least six strides.

Farther up Buena Vista Boulevard, across the street from the Pelican Brief Diner, near what we liked to call mini San Francisco, an octet of aqua blue, two-story bayside structures, stood Tito and Kylie and a flock of people. Tito was dressed in chinos and a collared shirt. Kylie was wearing a skintight black outfit and inch-high fashion boots. Her long blonde curls, the same that Gran had made fun of, cascaded down her back.

I couldn't hear what the two were saying, but their intention was clear. Kylie was blocking Tito's access to the Chicken Kebabs cart vendor. Tito tried dodging right and left to cut around Kylie, but to no avail.

Putting on speed, I caught up with Bailey before she reached her husband. I grasped her elbow. "Hold on. Let's form a plan."

"No time to plan." Bailey wrested her arm free. "If Tito throws a punch, he could lose his job. It will be Kylie's word against his as to how the argument started."

"There are plenty of witnesses," I said. "And the vendor must know what's going on."

Bailey didn't slow down, so I didn't either. We arrived at the fracas at the same time.

". . . my territory," Kylie shouted, clearly in the middle of a tirade. "I'm the foodie reporter. Not you."

Tito said, "I have every right."

"It's my assignment," Kylie rasped.

". . . Food Bowl week," Tito countered. "Too many events for you to cover by yourself."

How long had they been arguing? Both of their faces were beaded with perspiration.

Bailey rushed to Tito, ducked under his flailing arm, and injected herself between him and Kylie. How I admired her pluck. She pressed her hands to his chest. *"Mi amor,"* she said calmly. "Calm down. Back away."

"But—"

"No, *caro mio.* Do this. Now. You will discuss this with Eugene. He will get her to agree."

Kylie hissed. "I'll never agree. The Food Bowl is mine to cover. Mine."

I drew near to the cart vendor, a petite woman who owned a small diner at the north end of town, and whispered, "Are you okay?"

"Rattled," she murmured.

"Who started it?" I asked, taking note of what she was selling—fried chicken that smelled divine, in four different flavors: Cajun, Asian, regular, and garlic.

"Who do you think?" The vendor rolled her eyes. "It's always Kylie. Tito was already here, ready to rave about my food. How could I tell him no? He's a regular. A good guy. Kylie has visited my restaurant once. *Once,"* she emphasized. "And her write-up wasn't stellar. But then she shows up and yells that she wants to make it up to me. Tito claimed first rights, but . . ." The vendor threw her arms wide.

"Enough!" Kylie pushed Bailey out of the way. "Leave this spot, Tito Martinez. I'm warning you."

Tito broke free from Bailey and aimed a finger at Kylie. "You will not have the last word here."

"Until I change professions or take my last breath, food in Crystal Cove is my territory." Kylie folded her arms. "Eugene will support me."

Bailey, using all the muscle she had, steered Tito away from the cart and vendor.

"Magic show," Bailey said. "One hour."

I drew alongside but kept mum.

Tito grunted. "Kylie's right. She has a power hold on Eugene. I've seen her with him. He's putty in her hands."

"It's not fair," Bailey cooed, "but let it go."

"I'm the cook." Tito thumbed his chest. "Kylie isn't. She doesn't know food or flavors. She's a hack."

"Talk to Eugene," Bailey coaxed. "After the magic show. Maybe you can convince him to change his mind."

Tito scrubbed his hair with a hand. "What if he sells the paper? What if it goes under?"

"Is that what's really driving this set-to between you and Kylie?" Bailey asked.

I suggested Bailey and Tito go to the Nook Café to grab a coffee. Chill before the magic show. I promised Brianna would be fine. They agreed.

Kylie smirked as my friends trudged away. I shot her a look. She raised her chin defiantly and mimed for me to *run along*.

On my way back to the shop, I pushed thoughts of Kylie aside and drank in the festivities signaling the onset of Food Bowl week. Gran had been right about the bevy of signs. There were posters in store windows and hand-painted banners crisscrossing the street. Anyone visiting for the festival had to be torn by all the choices.

Best Burgers Anywhere: featuring chefs from Cheesey Burger, Beans and Burgers, Love Me Burgers. Rhett and I had eaten at all three of the diners. Delicious.

All Star Barbecue: 5 chefs. 5 entrées. 5 ways to have a saucy time. This was the one Cinnamon, her husband, Rhett, and I would attend.

Rooftop Fish Fry: Come on up Tuesday and sit a spell. Lola had gone all out with gourmet photographs of heaping piles of fried fish. I started to salivate.

Cameo Theater Film Festival: the new TV sensation Shredding *plus popular movies like* Secret of the Grain, The Hundred-Foot Journey, Chef, Julie & Julia, *and* Babette's Feast.

I'd seen every one of the movies and had savored the array of foods. *Chef* was a delightful story about a guy who quit his high-end position at a restaurant and reignited his passion for cooking as he launched a food-truck business.

Near Fisherman's Village, a glitzy banner emblazoned with green and gold and doused with glitter caught my eye. *Scientific*

Minds: a panel will discuss the future of food. Smart move, I thought. The festival wasn't all about dining. Some of it had to do with sustainability. Apparently, the event was going to be popular. A *Sold Out* placard blocked out the word *Tickets.*

I didn't spy a banner for Intime. Most likely it was strung closer to the center of town, near the dolphin statues, where the bistro was located.

"Hi, Jenna." Flora Fairchild, owner of the specialty shop Home Sweet Home and a regular at the Cookbook Nook—she loved any cookbook that featured chocolate—jogged toward me and kept running in place. Her jogging outfit complimented her toned shape. Her thick long braid bounced on her back. "I intend to eat at every event. How about you?"

"A few. Not all."

"Don't deprive yourself," she said. "It merely takes a little extra effort to keep the pounds off. If we don't use it, we lose it."

I was one of those rare birds who'd never fought my weight. My height had something to do with it. My metabolism, as well. Plus, I exercised daily. Not heavy aerobics but I walked, ran, and rode. Dad had drilled into me that I had one body in this life, and I was in charge of making it work.

"I saw your father," Flora said, as if reading my mind. "At the Pelican Brief with Lola. Smooching. Those two are such lovebirds. Someday," she added wistfully and ran off.

My father and Lola had been dating for a while. My mother had died years ago and my father had mourned mightily. When he'd allowed himself to love again and he fell for Lola, I'd been happy for him. He deserved someone wonderful.

"Jenna, hold up!" Z.Z., aka Zoey Zeller, bustled to me as I veered into the Fisherman's Village parking lot. Like Flora, Z.Z. was wearing a jogging outfit, although hers was baggy and made her appear even squatter than she was.

I bit back a smile. Had the whole town gone exercise crazy?

"I wanted to chat with you about your aunt," Z.Z. said.

"What about her?" My insides snagged with concern. Surely Aunt Vera hadn't been talking out of turn about her reading for Eugene Tinsdale.

"It's regarding her sweet deputy's children."

Deputy Appleby had two grown children in their thirties.

"Go on," I said.

"Sasha isn't being nice to your aunt."

"You're mistaken. Sasha adores her."

"Not any longer. I saw the two of them just now. At the café. They were having coffee. You know Sasha had a baby three months ago."

"I do. A baby girl."

Z.Z. peeked over her shoulder. "Well, you'd have thought your aunt had the plague or something. Sasha wouldn't let Vera hold the baby."

"Really?"

"She refused. She said the baby would cry." Z.Z. batted the air. "Why not give the poor kid a chance? She might like your aunt, right?" She huffed. "It made my blood boil."

"What did my aunt do?"

"You know Vera. She doesn't like to make waves. She smiled and said she understood. But honestly, I don't think she did. Her eyes were brimming with tears. Do something."

"I can't—"

"Yes, you can. Insert yourself. Your aunt needs you." Z.Z. trotted away.

I slogged into the shop worried about my aunt. When had Appleby's daughter become rude? Would her rudeness drive a wedge between her father and my aunt? I sure hoped not. My aunt deserved a world of happiness, having been denied love so many years ago.

Gran was sitting at the children's table, tending to Brianna in her floor seat, while chatting with two little girls I recognized. Both were coloring. Tigger weaved between their legs and the table's legs.

"Miss Hart." The mother of the girls waved to me. She reminded me of a hummingbird, flitting from bookcase to bookcase. "Help me pick out the perfect gift for my mother-in-law."

Knowing I couldn't solve my aunt's or Tito's problems, I slapped on a smile and said, "Let's talk about her likes and dislikes."

The woman toyed with tendrils of her white-blonde hair. "Sweets. Scones. Bread. Like me."

"As if," I joked. Given her trim figure, I doubted she ate anything more than celery.

For fifteen minutes, I guided her through the pastry section. When we found *Taste of Heaven*, the independently published cookbook for Taste of Heaven Ice Cream Shoppe, she whooped with glee. Her mother-in-law adored ice cream. The owner of Taste of Heaven had included over fifty recipes for her renowned ice creams. My favorite was chocolate-caramel swirl.

As the happy customer exited the store with her girls, Aunt Vera waltzed in.

"If you're hungry," I said to her, "don't miss Katie's pumpkin coconut cupcakes."

"I'll pass. I just had a lovely coffee." Her skin shone and her eyes glistened. She was dressed in normal everyday clothes and not a caftan—unusual for her but not troublesome, seeing as she'd had a coffee date with Sasha. "We're quite busy, aren't we?"

"The town is abuzz with good vibes. Z.Z. has a knack for luring people to Crystal Cove."

"She certainly does."

Seeing as my aunt wasn't acting as though her boyfriend's daughter had dissed her, I decided to ignore Z.Z.'s entreaty and let the event pass. If and when my aunt wanted to bring up the subject, I would be all ears.

"Is everything all right with Bailey?" Aunt Vera asked as she roamed the shop, tweaking things—the jigsaw puzzle on the vintage table, the array of aprons.

"Bailey?"

"Don't be coy. I heard about the fracas with Kylie O and the street vendor, and I saw Bailey and Tito enter the café. She was close to tears."

I drew my aunt to the register. "Bailey's worried about Tito's job status. If Eugene fires him—"

"He won't."

"But what if Kylie presses him to?"

Aunt Vera *tsk*ed. "Do you think that young woman holds sway with Eugene?"

"Bailey thinks so."

"What do I think?" Bailey strode into the shop and made a beeline for her daughter.

Gran waved to the child, ceding her rights. Bailey lifted Brianna from the floor seat and balanced her on one hip.

I glanced at my aunt. "We were discussing Eugene and whether Kylie had him wrapped around her pinky."

"And whether he'll sell," my aunt added.

"If he doesn't and the paper folds, Tito's sunk." Bailey's voice cracked. "There aren't any other newspapers in Crystal Cove. In order for him to continue doing what he does, we would have to move."

My aunt clucked her tongue. "If Eugene actually puts the *Courier* up for sale, someone will buy it."

"Who?" Bailey spread her arms. "Tito would love to, but he doesn't make that kind of money. Who else in town has that kind of capital?" She gazed at my aunt.

I wagged my head. "My aunt can't own everything." In addition to her house and the cottage, my aunt owned Fisherman's Village and a number of other properties in town.

Aunt Vera gawked at me. "Why can't I?"

Chapter 4

As we set up the shop for the magic show, Aunt Vera discussed the possibility of buying the newspaper. She had the means. On the other hand, she was confident that Eugene would figure out how to keep it afloat.

When customers started taking their seats and Tito appeared in his magician's costume, we tabled the discussion.

"Let the magic begin!" Tito proclaimed, all evidence of his quarrel with Kylie vanished. Looking dapper in his red cape and top hat, he introduced himself and said he'd be entertaining the crowd for forty-five minutes. "Now, who have we here?" He extended his hand to a young redheaded girl who was sitting cross-legged on the floor.

Shyly, the girl reached toward him.

From his hand popped an apple, as if it were a bouquet of flowers.

"How did he do that?" Bailey asked, Brianna still braced in her arms.

"Magic," I whispered.

"He won't reveal any of his secrets," Bailey groused.

"Good for him." I patted her back.

"For my next trick," Tito said, his eyes sparkling with enthusiasm, "I'll need help from a young gentleman. You, sir."

Gran's granddaughters and their mother were in attendance. Accompanying them was the daughter-in-law's nephew, a sullen, shaggy-haired fifteen-year-old.

"Rise," Tito commanded.

After a gentle prod by his aunt, the boy got to his feet.

Tito laid a piece of newspaper on the floor. "Stand on this, young man, and face the audience."

The teen obeyed.

"I'm going to teach you the disappearing bandanna trick. Here we go." Tito reached inside his cape and pulled out a blue bandanna. "Now, I have to admit I haven't done this trick in a while, so please be patient with me." He handed the bandanna to the boy. "Show the audience there's nothing there."

Jaded beyond his years, the teen displayed the front and back of the bandanna.

"Now, let's take this other bandanna . . ." Tito reached inside his cape and pulled out a bright yellow banana. "Uh-oh. This isn't a bandanna," he said, looking perplexed, his stage charm in full gear.

The audience laughed. The boy rolled his eyes.

"Oh, well," Tito said, "it's Food Bowl week. Some magic fairy must have swapped this banana for the bandanna in fun. Let's give it a try." Tito stuck out his hand. "Young man, give me the bandanna, and you take the banana." They swapped items. "Now, this next step will be tricky. Fold the banana in half and then in half again."

The teen gaped at him. "Really, dude?"

"Do you want me to do it?" Tito winked.

"Yeah. I'm not grossing out my hands."

Bailey whispered, "Is my husband adorable or what?"

I said, "Adorable."

Tito draped the bandanna over one arm and took the banana from the boy. In a goofy manner, he folded the banana. It popped open. The audience roared with delight. He folded it again. The insides spilled onto the newspaper. More laughter and a few groans.

"Okay, for the next step, I need to palm the bandanna . . . I mean, banana." Tito hid it behind his left hand and frowned. "Hmm. You can still see it, can't you, young man?"

The teen nodded. "I'm not blind."

"Oh, well, I guess I'm not very good at this. Let's continue." In a boisterous stage-style voice, Tito said, "I will make this bandanna . . . I mean, banana . . . disappear. First, I will fold the other bandanna, the *real* one, in quarters to create a makeshift bag. Like so." Tito did. "Now, I will set the second bandanna—in this case the banana—in the first bandanna, and squish it into a small ball." He dropped the mess of a banana into the folded bandanna. "Of course, I won't really drop the banana in. I'll palm it."

"But you did drop it in," the boy said, clearly exasperated with Tito.

"You're right, again. I did." Tito scratched his chin, working the schtick. "Okay, well, let's see what happens. Next, I squish the bandanna—I mean banana—into a small ball."

The audience uttered hushed *Uh-ohs*, reacting the same as I. The real bandanna was doomed.

"And then I'll open the bandanna and show you the banana has disappeared," Tito said.

"Good luck with that," the teen said dryly, eliciting chuckles from the crowd.

"I think I should say some magic words," Tito said. "Got any?"

"Honestly, dude?"

"Three will do."

"Yeah, fine. Magic, please work."

More laughter.

"Good enough." Tito repeated the boy's words and waved his right hand over the folded bandanna. Then he released the corners of the bandanna, and *voilà*, the banana was gone.

The teen gawked. "Whoa, man. Awesome. How did you do that? Will you teach me?"

"Not today, but thanks for being a good sport. Fold the newspaper and make the remainder of the banana disappear . . . into the trash."

For the next half hour, Tito regaled the crowd with other disappearing acts and sleights of hand. In his spiel, he kept reminding them that they were being deceived and misdirected.

When Tito concluded, although the crowd shouted, "More," he ceded the floor to me.

I thanked the crowd for coming, directed them to browse the various books we offered for sale. For the younger fans of the presentation, we'd stocked a few books, including the adorable Magic School Bus story *Food Chain Frenzy*. And then I reminded each to have a tasty Food Bowl week.

As Tito left with Bailey, I noted they both looked happier, as if the set-to with Kylie had magically disappeared.

One could hope.

• • •

The rest of the day went smoothly. We sold a number of salt-and-pepper sets, two apple-shaped cookie jars, a couple of foodie jigsaw puzzles, and dozens of books. Food Bowl traffic was a boon. At closing time, I was exhausted, but my day was not yet over.

I took Tigger home, dressed for dinner, and arrived at Intime at seven p.m.

Rhett greeted me with a kiss and stepped away. A swizzle of

desire swept through me as I took him in, so commanding in his chef's coat and slacks, his eyes glistening with pride.

"Well? What do you think?" he asked.

"Of you? Stunning."

"Very funny. You don't look so bad yourself."

I'd worn a simple black sheath and chunky gold jewelry, and I'd pinned one side of my hair back in a flirty way with a decorative clip. "Thank you, kind sir."

"What do you think of the restaurant?" Rhett flourished a hand like a TV model.

He hadn't wanted me to see the bistro until it was complete. It had taken all my reserve to stay away.

I turned in place, drinking in the ambiance, and said, "It's gorgeous."

Like his parents' restaurant in Napa, it was a classic French bistro, its walls lined with mirrors and deep mahogany paneling. Bronze-finished, candelabra-style chandeliers provided a warm glow.

"Everything I expected," I went on. "The music is nice, too." A rendition of "Claire de Lune" was filtering through speakers. "And the aromas are divine. Are you pleased?"

"Yep."

"Do I smell onion soup?"

"What's a bistro without a good *soupe aux oignons*?"

"Heavy on the melted cheese?"

"*Absolutement.*" Rhett kissed his fingertips. "Follow me." He grabbed a menu and led me to a table draped with a white tablecloth and adorned with a single white rose in a crystal vase. Over his shoulder he said, "Your father and aunt aren't here yet."

"Dad texted. They're running a half hour behind. Hope that's okay."

"It's fine."

The three of us had agreed to enjoy the first night at Intime by ourselves. No deputy accompanying my aunt and no Lola accompanying my father.

"Did you come up with a replacement for the minced chicken salad?" I asked as I sat.

"I did. It's a secret." Rhett unfolded my napkin and handed it and the menu to me. "See you in a bit." He signaled a waitress to bring me a glass of pinot gris and strode toward the kitchen.

Before Rhett disappeared into the kitchen, Kylie O sashayed into the restaurant. She clasped him on the arm and said something while whisking her long locks over her shoulder in the dramatic way Gran had described. In her tight shimmering blue dress, Kylie reminded me of a mermaid, the wicked kind. Rhett guided her to the table next to mine, set for four. He opened her napkin for her and handed her a menu. Kylie set the menu aside and scanned the restaurant. When she caught sight of me, she grimaced. Why? Because she associated me with Tito? Because I'd witnessed their altercation?

I smiled broadly. *When facing the enemy, disarm with charm,* my father would say.

Kylie didn't react, and I realized I hadn't been the target of her disapproval. She was gazing past me toward the front of the restaurant. I swiveled to see who was there. No one had entered. A few people were standing by the pane-glass window, apparently studying the menu. A woman in white ducked out of view, as did a man in black. For a moment I wondered if the man could have been Tito until I remembered he had convinced Bailey that, despite all the tasty temptations that might interfere with her diet, they should take Brianna to Azure Park.

The front door opened, and Eugene Tinsdale strode into the restaurant, his smile as strained as it was yesterday, although he appeared more robust in an expensive navy suit, white shirt, and bold red tie. His wife, Audrey, and their daughter, Alexa, followed him in — Audrey in a stylish floral frock and Alexa in a black sheath. Both were wearing stud earrings and necklaces; Audrey was carrying a bright pink shawl. Despite the mother and daughter's thirty-year age difference, they looked similar. Both had styled their short dark hair in feathery wisps around their faces. Both had exotic eyes and high cheekbones. Of course, Alexa, thanks to her profession as a personal trainer, was much more fit than her mother.

Intime's hostess, a willowy brunette, guided them to Kylie's table. Audrey kissed Kylie on the cheek before sitting down. Alexa gave Kylie a hug. Eugene patted her shoulder and took the seat next to her. He spied me and nodded. I responded in kind.

The waitress showed up with my wine and asked if I needed anything. I told her I was fine and perused the menu, each item explained in detail within parentheses: *hors d'oeuvre* (minced artichoke tartlet), *potage* (French onion soup), *poisson* (blue crabs), *entrée* (braised lamb shanks), *sorbet, salades* (salad), *fromage* (a variety of cheeses), *desserts* (apple tartin), *café* (coffee). I couldn't wait to taste everything. I knew each morsel would be seasonal and top-notch. Quality and consistency mattered most to Rhett.

"Kylie, tell me about the National Newspaper Association convention," Audrey said.

Kylie laughed coyly. "What happens at the NNA stays at the NNA."

Eugene's wife cut him a look.

"She's kidding, sweetheart," Eugene said. "We did what we always do. We addressed business objectives of community newspaper owners, publishers, and staff. We had a few educational sessions and a few peer-sharing activities."

Audrey stifled a yawn.

"What do peer-sharing activities entail?" Alexa asked.

Kylie said, "I attended one with upper management to help figure out how to create meaningful jobs. That's the best way to keep employees engaged. You went to that one, too, didn't you, boss? Cajole employees. Make them feel as if they're part owner, even if they're not. Plus, I won an award for best restaurant review."

"Right," Alexa said. "Congrats on that."

Eugene signaled their waitress. "A bottle of the Louis Jadot Chassagne-Montrachet, please."

That was an expensive wine, I noted, for someone who might be struggling financially. Maybe Eugene wasn't; perhaps he purely wanted out of the newspaper business.

"Four glasses," he added.

"I'm not drinking," Kylie said.

Alexa leaned toward her. "Why not? Are you pregnant?"

Kylie coughed. "Get real."

"You're looking a little puffy down there," Alexa teased.

"Who's talking smack?" Kylie cuffed Alexa's arm. "You're the one who's put on weight."

"As if."

"Girls," Audrey chided.

Kylie and Alexa sniggered. Audrey rolled her eyes. Eugene studied his menu, staying well clear of the minefield.

I recalled the friendly-though-heated exchange Bailey had witnessed between Kylie and Alexa at a group pilates class. In our twenties, Bailey and I had taunted each other. Now, in our thirties, we'd stopped hurling personal insults. We didn't have fragile egos; we'd simply grown up.

Rhett appeared at my table and set down a plate with two onion tarts. "Catching any good gossip?" he whispered into my neck.

"Hard not to since we're all sitting so close."

"Ah, the beauty of a French bistro. In France, it is intentional. Everyone likes to know each other's business."

"Liar."

"Are you a Francophile?" he kidded. *"Non, mademoiselle."*

I swatted his arm teasingly and lifted one of the tarts. "These aren't on the menu."

"For you, anything. *Bon appetit.*" Rhett caressed my shoulder and moved on.

I bit into the tart and nearly swooned. The creaminess of the filling was divine, and the flaky pastry, perfection.

My father strode into the restaurant and made a beeline for me. "Sorry we're late." As always, he looked neat and put together. The blue in his plaid shirt complemented his tan skin. He kissed my cheek and sat opposite me. "Your aunt couldn't decide what to wear."

"Don't blame this on me, Cary Hart." Aunt Vera slid into her chair. The crepe de chine fabric of her print dress swished against the leather seat. "I was completely dressed when you showed up."

"You were not. You needed your earrings. Which took you ten minutes to hunt down," my father added.

"It was your car that made us late, little brother." My aunt whisked her napkin open and set it on her lap. "His tires were low."

"It took all of four minutes to add air."

"Stop." I held up a hand. "You're here. Order a glass of wine. Peruse the menu. I want this evening to be perfect for Rhett. No brother-sister spats."

"Comes with the territory." My father brushed a thatch of his silver hair off his forehead. "Familiarity breeds contempt." He winked at me.

"Sorry, dear." My aunt squeezed my hand. "I suppose we can't help ourselves."

My father adored my aunt, but he was younger by a few years, so at times they could snarl at each other. He once told me they had always vied for their parents' affection.

Movement outside the restaurant's front window caught my eye. Savannah Gregory, a marshmallow of a woman, was peering inside. She was the baker at Latte Luck Café. How I adored her cinnamon buns and nutmeg cookies. She loved browsing the Cookbook Nook for dessert cookbooks. One gem she'd purchased was *Layered: Baking, Building, and Styling Spectacular Cakes*, in which the author created wonderfully unique combinations, like pink peppercorn cherry or bourbon butterscotch. If only I could bake like that.

"How's business, Jenna?" my father asked.

"We had a bunch of fun today," I replied. "Tito gave a magic show."

Aunt Vera snorted. "He was a stitch. He did this thing with a banana, making it disappear after he'd mushed it. I can't explain the whole trick, but it was a hoot."

My father smirked, less than impressed. A former FBI analyst and currently the owner of Nuts and Bolts, a hardware store, he preferred life to be systematic. He had a sense of humor, but he didn't tend to appreciate the lighter side of life.

"What are you looking at, Jenna?" my aunt asked.

Savannah Gregory was pressing her hands against the window. What was she looking for? She wasn't dressed for work. She was wearing a frilly long white dress. Even from this distance I could tell she'd been crying.

"Aunt Vera, Dad." I rose to my feet. "I'll be right back."

I hurried outside. Savannah must have seen me coming because she changed course abruptly and started shuffling toward Aunt Teek's, the antique shop next door.

I caught up to her and said, "Hey, Savannah."

She pivoted. Her face was flushed, mouth trembling.

Choosing to downplay her sadness, I said, "I saw that Alice in Wonderland birthday party cake you were making yesterday at the café. Amazing. Just gazing at the many layers and icing made me gain weight. You are so talented."

"Thank you," she mumbled.

"Is something wrong?" I touched her arm.

She flinched and drew into herself, tucking her fleshy arms beneath her ample bosom. "I don't want to talk about it."

"I saw you outside Intime." I gestured. "Did someone stand you up?"

Savannah squeezed her lips together as if she were working hard not to burst into tears.

"Did you hope for a reservation?" I asked. "I know they were hard to come by."

A few tickets had been available online for the event and went like hotcakes. Luckily, Rhett had seen personally to my family's reservation.

"No. I couldn't afford . . ." Savannah shook her head. Curly tendrils of her blonde updo wafted with the movement. "No."

"You're all dressed up."

"I'm meeting my mother. Later."

Her mother, Shari, owned Latte Luck Café. Unlike Savannah, Shari was slim, trim, and filled with confidence.

Savannah shivered, even though it wasn't in the least cold.

"Was there someone inside Intime you were hoping to talk to? A former boyfriend, perhaps?" Maybe he was one of the diners in the bistro. Or one of the staff.

"No."

Suddenly, it dawned on me that Savannah might have been the person on the receiving end of Kylie O's disapproving glare.

I said, "Were you hoping to talk to Kylie?" Maybe Savannah had hoped to ask Kylie to review Latte Luck, but she'd missed nabbing Kylie before she'd entered Intime.

Savannah didn't deny it.

"Want me to fetch her?" I asked. "She ought to be thrilled to tout Latte Luck in the *Courier*."

"No. Please don't. She's with her family."

"The Tinsdales aren't her family. They're friends."

"They're like family," Savannah said. "She always talks about them. Alexa is like a sister. Audrey is like a mother. Yada-yada." She blinked, clearly realizing how snarky she'd sounded. "Kylie's parents were always in absentia and, with no siblings to keep her company, she latched on to the Tinsdales. Now that her parents are dead . . ."

"I'm sorry to hear that."

"They died in a helicopter crash when she was a senior in high school."

My eyes widened. "You know a lot about her. Are you two friends?"

"We were. Once. We used to run ten-Ks together," she murmured.

Given her size, I found that hard to believe, but said, "I like to run," in an attempt to bond.

"I used to, too, until Kylie . . ." Savannah worked her lip between her teeth. "Kylie runs fast. She likes to sprint." She twisted the toe of her right foot.

"Pretty shoes," I said, admiring her ballerina slippers.

"I can't wear heels anymore. My feet are ruined. Because of running. That's why I let myself go."

"You look fine."

"No, I don't. I eat too much."

I grinned. "Because you're such a great baker."

Savannah blushed at the compliment. "I know I should see a weight specialist, except the doctor will tell me what I already know. Eat less. Work out. I . . ." She didn't continue.

I felt awful about the way she was berating herself, but I didn't know how to console her.

"I'm not strong. I don't have self-control. It's Kylie's fault." Savannah peeked over her shoulder. Had she expected Kylie to be listening in? Was she afraid of Kylie's response? "She was always goading me. Faster. Faster."

I flashed on the day before when Kylie and another runner had nearly knocked me down. Kylie had been yelling, "Faster, faster," to the woman.

"Kylie forced me to do more than my body could," Savannah went on. "One time, I tore a calf muscle trying to beat her. It took a year to heal and now" — she outlined her body with one hand — "this is what I have to show for it."

"Why did you surrender to Kylie's wishes?"

"Because . . ." Savannah chewed her lower lip. "Because . . ." She blinked rapidly.

Mental slap to forehead. Because Savannah had been in love with Kylie. Maybe she still was.

I said, "If you tell Kylie how you feel—"

"No. Never. She hates me. She taunts me. She says I'm weak. And I am. I wish I weren't, but I am." Savannah sucked in a breath and lumbered away.

Chapter 5

When I returned to the restaurant, my aunt asked, "Is everything okay?"

I murmured, "Yes," and steered the conversation toward our respective days.

Dinner was incredible. My father couldn't stop raving about the blue crabs in lemon butter. My aunt was partial to the lamb shanks.

After dessert, when Rhett approached the table to bid us goodbye, he was on cloud nine. Kylie was going to write a five-star review. She and the Tinsdales had loved every morsel. I congratulated him on a job well done, kissed him good night, and reminded him we were meeting with the wedding planner in the morning at the Cookbook Nook. He promised to be there.

• • •

At seven a.m., Tigger and I took a slow run on the beach. I felt sluggish and a bit emotional. As my feet hit the sand, I realized why. I couldn't stop thinking about Savannah and the bitterness she'd felt toward Kylie. Strolling into my new house, I decided that I'd stop by Latte Luck Café later and check in on her. We weren't close friends, but I could show that I cared.

After showering and eating a quickie breakfast of melted Brie on toast slathered with jam, I rode my Schwinn to the shop with Tigger in the basket. Halfway to work, I realized Keller was coming to paint the guest room.

"Shoot," I muttered. I didn't need to let him in, he had a set of keys, but I'd offered to move all the furniture to the center of the room. Oh, well. Best laid plans. Keller was big and strong. He could manage.

I locked the bicycle in the bike rack near Beaders of Paradise, a charming craft store catty-corner from ours, and strode into the Cookbook Nook. I set my sweet cat on his kitty condo, and then after throwing open a window to let in fresh air, I fetched my folder with the wedding planning notes from the office desk in the stockroom. For months I'd been cutting articles and photos out of magazines and downloading décor tips I'd found online.

Harmony Bold, the wedding planner who had handled Cinnamon's wedding, had agreed to meet Rhett and me prior to opening. She did not disappoint when it came to confidence. She breezed in carrying a navy blue portfolio that matched her navy blue sheath. The simple strand of pearls and stud pearl earrings she was wearing suited her perfectly. Her face was serene, her smile beatific. If I'd searched every actress in an online acting directory, I couldn't have cast a woman who radiated more calm.

"Where shall we lay out everything?" Harmony asked. Even her voice was free of angst. "We have quite a checklist to go over."

I breathed easier knowing that the next few months, under her capable guidance, would go smoothly. On the other hand, Rhett was late. I checked my cell phone. No text message.

"Let's sit here." I indicated the vintage kitchen table. "Will it be enough room?"

"We'll make it work."

I offered Harmony coffee but she declined. While she pulled item after item from her portfolio, I texted Rhett: *Where are you?*

He responded with a quick: *Stuck. Work. Sorry.*

Drat. Okay, I wouldn't waste the woman's time. We'd get started. Rhett would catch up.

For thirty minutes, Harmony and I flipped through *Save the Date* cards and invitations and discussed fonts. I didn't think Rhett would mind if I made the selection on the latter since we'd viewed so many together a week ago. To ensure his approval, I decided to go with the same font he'd used on Intime's menu. When I needed to open the shop, Harmony and I made another appointment for Tuesday to go over the guest list and the wedding day timeline. I apologized for Rhett's absence.

"Don't worry." She smiled. "Happens all the time."

As I was writing my fiancé another text, Cinnamon strolled in. "I see you took my advice," she said. "Didn't you love Harmony?"

Cinnamon's mother, Pepper, trailed her. Both were carrying to-go cups from Latte Luck Café and wearing leggings, sweatshirts, and tennis shoes. That was where the similarity ended. I still found it hard to believe Cinnamon was Pepper's daughter. Though Pepper was happier than when I'd first met her, she had a taut face and somewhat stern demeanor. Cinnamon, with her camp counselor attitude and girl-next-door haircut and complexion, had to have been born from a completely different batch of DNA.

"Wasn't Harmony wonderful?" Cinnamon went on.

"Wonderful."

Cinnamon drew near and peered into my eyes. "What's going on? Is everything okay?"

"Everything's fine."

"Don't kid a kidder, Jenna Hart." Cinnamon twirled a finger in my direction. "Out with it. Were Harmony's suggestions over the top? Not to your liking? She can be flexible."

"It's Rhett." I sighed. "He didn't make the appointment. I saw him last night at the opening of Intime. He promised . . ." I screwed up my mouth. My friend didn't need to know what was rollicking around in my head. "He got hung up with something at work."

"Being a restaurant guy isn't easy." Cinnamon spoke from experience. She and Rhett had dated when he'd worked at the Grotto. When it went up in smoke, Cinnamon had suspected Rhett of the arson. Once she'd solved the crime and Rhett had been absolved, they were able to renew their friendship, but the love had fizzled.

"Enough about me. Harmony and I are on the same page. How about you two?" I swung a finger between mother and daughter. "Did you go for a run?"

"A walk-jog," Pepper said. "I can't do more than that." She was my father's age. "My knees are getting brittle. Ugh. Speaking of which, Cinn, I'm going to the shop and take a load off." Pepper owned Beaders of Paradise. "Stop by before you leave. I made you something."

As Pepper left, Cinnamon rolled her eyes. "I can only imagine what my mother made. A sweater with a beaded neckline? Not my style."

We shared a laugh. Pepper was a gifted beader, but her taste was definitely not her daughter's.

Cinnamon took a sip from her cup. "Mm-mm. Latte Luck makes the best coffee."

"Was Savannah there?" I asked.

"I don't recall seeing her. Why?"

"I ran into her last night, outside the restaurant. She was . . . upset."

"About?"

"Nothing." I moved to the register.

"C'mon, don't leave me hanging." Cinnamon followed me. "You were concerned enough to mention her. What gives?"

"I think she's in love, but the love isn't returned."

"You and I both know how that goes. Don't worry. She'll survive." Cinnamon paused. "Hold on a sec. You aren't thinking that she might do something to hurt herself, are you?"

"No."

Cinnamon crooked a pinky at me. "You can't help yourself, can you? Everyone in need becomes your pet project. You're a natural born fixer."

"Not true."

"*True.* A fixer knows another fixer."

I unlocked the register and checked the till. Plenty of cash for today's business. "It's just . . . Savannah seemed quite shaken, bordering on angry."

"Maybe she's hormonal. It's going around, I hear." Cinnamon patted her not-yet-showing baby bump. "If you don't watch out, you might find yourself with one of these, too."

"Bite your tongue."

Cinnamon tilted her head. "Why the fierce response? Are you saying you're not having babies before marriage, or not ever?"

I stared at her, unsure of the answer. Rhett and I hadn't discussed children. We would have to at some point. I was closing in on thirty-five.

Katie bounded in from the breezeway, not yet in her chef's coat, the bold vertical stripes of her dress swishing right and left. "When you have a moment, Jenna, can you come to the Nook? Midge Martin has stopped by and wants to talk about tomorrow's demonstration."

"Go." Cinnamon hooked her thumb. "I've got to clean up so I can do the city's business. Keep the peace and all that rot." She backhanded my abdomen. "You want one of these baby thinga-mabobs. You know you do. I've seen you doting over Brianna and Min-yi. Soon, my friend. Soon. Bye!" She ran out, cackling.

My aunt rushed in. "Sorry I'm late. Lots of traffic today."

"No worries," I said. "I'm going to the Nook for a few minutes."

"Tigger and I will hold down the fort," my aunt assured me.

"So will I!" Gran hurried in. "Traffic," she added, echoing my aunt.

"If Rhett calls," I said, "tell him where I am. Katie, let's go." I followed her into the café. "Nice dress. Is it new?"

"Hoo-boy, this old thing?" Katie plucked at the skirt. "I've had it for ten years, and I'll have it for another ten. Who knew a baby could be so expensive? Keller and I are saving every dime for Min-yi's college education." She pointed ahead of her. "There's Midge! Yoo-hoo, Midge."

Midge Martin, a wiry forty-something in a slimming floral sheath, was sitting at a table with a view of the ocean, although her back was to it. She rose and waved, her biceps steely from all the slicing and dicing she did at her restaurant. A self-made chef and a bit of a micromanager, she enjoyed doing most of the prep and plating herself.

"Hi!" Katie called.

The café wasn't busy yet. The first diners were allowed in at nine, but most wandered in around ten. The Nook didn't serve breakfast, only coffee and sweets until noon. Lunch and dinner were the primary meals. All the tables were draped with white linens and, like at Intime, boasted a single flower in a dainty crystal vase. Simple but elegant.

Beyond Midge, I spotted Audrey and Eugene Tinsdale sitting at a table for two. Lola and Z.Z. were seated at another table, bent forward and whispering. Were they discussing Z.Z.'s umbrage with how the deputy's daughter had treated my aunt? They both adored Aunt Vera. Were they devising a way to make Sasha relent?

"Jenna, so good to see you," Midge said as we arrived at her table. She rose to her feet and hugged me.

Definitely steel. I let loose with an *oof.*

"Sorry." Midge released me and primped her frizzy honey-blonde hair. "Don't know my own strength."

"Yes, you do," I said.

Midge guffawed. "Okay, you're right. I do. Sit." She resumed her seat.

Katie and I took the chairs opposite her. A seagull flew by, dipping sideways as if peeking in the window to say *hello.* A feeling of well-being swelled within me. To me, seagulls were good omens.

"How's your daughter, Midge?" I asked. I'd seen the teenager come into the store with Midge once or twice. "Her name is Marigold, right?"

"Good memory. She is a beauty. The light of my life." Midge tattooed the edge of the table with her thumb.

"Is she a chef like you?" I asked.

"She has promise." Midge beamed with pride.

Katie said, "Don't be modest, Midge. Marigold excels at everything she does because of your dedication to her."

"Don't give me the credit," Midge murmured. "I'm afraid I've been spending way too much time on my career lately. Luckily, Marigold is quite talented in her own right."

"How old is she now?" I asked. "Thirteen? Fourteen?"

"Fifteen."

Katie moaned. "Fifteen. The boy-crazy age."

"Tell me about it." Midge jokingly poked her fingers in her ears and sang, "La, la, la." She removed her fingers and drummed the table again. *Rat-a-tat.* "Now, to business. Regarding the demonstration—tomorrow—life is zooming at us. As I told Katie, I'm thinking of showing our audience how to make vegetarian pizza, salads, and appetizers."

I bobbed my head. "Katie mentioned that. It all sounds good, but will you have enough time to do so much? Maybe you should choose one?"

Katie fanned the air. "We'll have things prepped, and we'll have created the final products for tasting. The whole reason for the demo is to show how easy it is to put meals together by shredding, chopping, and julienning." She eyed Midge. "Is that a verb?"

"If it's not, it should be." Midge's eyes crinkled with humor. One of her great gifts, and the reason why her television cooking show was such a hit, was that Midge chatted animatedly while cooking. She made the audience feel like they were all her good friends. "How many have signed up?" Midge asked.

"We've got fifty so far," I said.

"Terrific."

"Um"—I clicked my tongue—"I saw a name on the list that I wanted to run by you."

"Who?"

"Kylie O is planning to attend."

Midge scowled. "Ooh, that woman. What is wrong with her? What did I do to deserve her wrath?"

I screwed up my mouth, hesitant to blurt it out. "Someone told me that she believes a recipe in your cookbook was not yours."

"She's wrong. It's mine. It's a Chinese chicken salad recipe." Midge frowned.

"Why would she claim otherwise?" I asked.

"Why?" Midge squawked. "Why, you ask?"

Katie rolled her eyes at me. Apparently, she'd heard Midge's rant before.

"Because Kylie is vindictive." Midge blew out a stream of exasperated breath. "Honestly, there are plenty of recipes that contain the same ingredients. Take sugar cookies, for instance. How many ways can you change up that recipe? When it comes down to it, a recipe is all about the voice of the chef and the way the tips and preparation are conveyed. I'm big on tips. Shredding is not as easy as it sounds." Midge swatted the air. "Don't worry, if Kylie shows up, I will be the epitome of grace and decorum. She will not rile me. I will not embarrass you or your store in front of the attendees. I promise." Midge drummed the table again, rose to her feet, and held up three fingers to certify her vow. "Now, if you'll excuse me, I've got to get cracking. I'm giving another opening statement upstairs at the theater before they screen more episodes of *Shredding*. Ciao." She blew kisses to both of us and scurried out of the café.

"Whew," Katie said. "She is a bundle of energy."

"She sure is."

"Let me know if you need anything further. I'm heading into the kitchen." Katie hooked her thumb over her shoulder. "Busy day ahead."

I weaved through a couple of tables and stopped when I heard a chair screech and a woman say, "You can't trust her."

I pivoted and spied Audrey Tinsdale on her feet, aiming an accusatory finger at Eugene. In a shirred smock top, leggings, and a minimum of makeup, she looked ready for a day of teaching art.

"Sweetheart, sit down," Eugene ordered. "I told you. She's going—"

"That's not what you said."

"Yes, it is. But . . ." Eugene spread his arms.

"*But?*" Audrey shot a hand into the air. "That's your answer? *But?*"

"What I was going to say is *but* she needs more time to get her affairs—"

"*Affairs.*" Audrey grunted. "Honestly, Eugene, for a man of words, you come up short all the time." She grabbed her cross-body purse off the chair, slung it on, and swept past me.

"Hi," I said.

Audrey mumbled a response and pushed through the exit door.

Eugene threw money on the table and hurried after his wife.

As he neared, I said, "Eugene, is there anything I can do to help?"

Eugene's face flamed red. Hadn't he realized everyone in the restaurant had heard the exchange? "No, Jenna. It's a long story. I . . ." He smoothed the lapels of his jacket. "I need to downsize, and Kylie Obendorfer has agreed to leave."

Kylie was the *she* in question? That surprised me. The Tinsdales and Kylie had seemed to have had such a lovely dinner last night. Audrey, in particular, had enjoyed chatting with Kylie. Savannah had said Kylie thought of Audrey like a mother. What had provoked this morning's outburst? Money? Hard times? If Eugene let a few people go, would the savings in salary help him keep the newspaper?

"In order to downsize," I said, "will you need to fire others? Like Tito?"

"I'm not firing Tito. He's solid."

Phew. I breathed easier. Even though my aunt had drawn Bailey and Katie into the fold by giving them a small limited partnership in the Cookbook Nook and café, Bailey and Tito needed both of their incomes to raise a child.

"This all pertains to the coverage about food and restaurants," Eugene went on. "Other than during this one special week, people want real news, not fluff. Kylie understands. She told me she has another future in mind."

Chapter 6

The morning sped by at the shop. Dozens of customers came in asking for Midge's cookbook, *Shred to Your Heart's Content.* We'd ordered fifty for the demonstration. Usually attendees each purchased a copy, but at this rate, we were going to sell out before the event. I telephoned the publisher that had issued the cookbook and asked if we could get a rush delivery on another twenty to thirty copies. The publisher agreed and would make a special delivery Saturday morning. I thanked him profusely, ended the call, and crowed. How I loved independent companies. So little red tape to cut through.

At noon, Bailey rushed into the store dressed in leggings and a mesh insert tank. "Tina has Brianna. I'm going to a private pilates class with Alexa. Want to come with me?"

"It won't be private if I come."

"That's okay. I can use all the support I can get. If I don't get rid of this baby tummy, my self-esteem is going to plummet." Bailey rubbed the small bulge.

I thought of Savannah, who had a real reason to suffer low self-esteem.

"Gran and your aunt will watch the store," Bailey said. "Please? Be brave, be bold!" she shouted like an Alexa convert.

Seeing as the rush from the morning had subsided, and knowing my pal was wound up with pent-up energy, I said, "I could use a good stretch."

I disappeared into the stockroom and changed into a pair of jogging shorts and a *Crystal Cove is Cooking* T-shirt that featured our logo on the back—advertising was all about getting the word out there—and then I walked with my pal to Your Wellness, Alexa's studio, which was located on the second floor of the Boldine Building, one of the mini San Francisco bayside structures. I'd visited the studio for group classes but never for a private workout. Alexa had spent a fortune putting it together. The space boasted distressed brick walls and sleek light mahogany floors. In addition to six pilates machines, there were two ballet barres, a floor-to-ceiling pole, multiple mirrors, and a wall between the glass-enclosed office and restroom filled with resistance bands, loops, and barbells.

Bailey tried to open the glass door leading to the building's foyer. "It's locked. Looks like the stores are closed. Now what?"

On the bottom floor of the building was an eclectic set of three shops: a china and crystal shop, a jeweler, and a florist, all owned and operated by members of the Boldine family.

"Maybe the shop owners took a vacation because of Food Bowl week," I said. "None of their businesses are tourist stops or particularly good draws for foodies."

Bailey stepped back and peered up at the second floor. I did the same.

Yesterday, as I'd passed the townhouses after Tito's dust-up with Kylie O, I'd noticed a *For Rent* sign in one of the upper-story windows. It was gone, which made me smile. I loved how prosperous our little town was.

"I'm right on time." Bailey checked her watch. "Alexa is never —"

"Hi, Bailey." Alexa Tinsdale, dressed in sleek black leggings and a long-sleeved shirt, a hefty tote bag slung over one shoulder, appeared behind us. "Hi, Jenna. Where's Tito?"

"Tito?" Bailey shook her head. "He's not supposed to work out with me."

"No. You have a private."

"And we never schedule back-to-back sessions," Bailey added.

"Yours was impromptu," Alexa reminded her.

"Right." Bailey stabbed her temple. "Baby brain."

"Tito has a standing appointment at ten thirty," Alexa continued. "I texted him that I was running late. Flat tire following a home session." She finger-combed her short hair. "Of course, my client drove off before she realized my situation. Long story short, I tried Triple A, but my phone kept cutting out, so I had to change the darned tire myself. Not fun. Let's hear it for hand sanitizer."

"Car trouble must be going around," Bailey said. "Tito's fan belt busted last night. He's driving a loaner. Maybe that's where he went. To the repair shop."

Alexa pulled her cell phone from her tote bag and scanned her messages. "Aw, yeah, Tito texted me. He thinks I forgot our appointment. He must not have gotten my text. Weird. I'll make it up to him." Alexa tapped a code on a keypad beside the glass door.

Something *clicked* and the door swung open. "After you, Bailey. Are you joining us, Jenna?"

"If you don't mind."

"Great."

As we ascended the stairs to the second floor, Alexa said, "I heard about Tito's run-in with Kylie the other day. Poor guy. She can be so — " She held up a palm. "No, I won't say it."

"Bullish," Bailey offered.

"No, that's not the right adjective." Alexa smiled. "Kylie and I might be lifelong buddies — rivals in fact, competing for the same top grades and the same cute boys — but it's because we have been competitive that I know all her quirks, and bullish isn't quite the word. She can be" — she tapped her cheek — "audacious and demanding. But I love her."

Alexa stopped outside the door to the studio, punched in a code on the keypad, as she had downstairs, and pushed the door open. A gentle breeze wafted out. "Hope you don't mind a cool space, Jenna," she said. "I know hot yoga has taken off, but I like to keep the windows open. Fresh air invigorates the soul."

"That's another of Alexa's mottoes," Bailey said.

As Alexa switched on the overhead lights, she gasped. "What the — "

Paper, both crumpled and shredded, was scattered everywhere. On the floor. On the machines.

Alexa let out a wail. "Who's that?" She dashed toward the reformer workout machine near the far window.

Bailey and I followed her, dodging the mess.

"Kylie!" Alexa shrieked. "Oh, no. Help me, Bailey. Jenna. Help."

But it was no use. Two lengths of rope with pull handles — fixtures of the tower-style pilates machine — had been wrapped around Kylie's neck. Her head lolled to one side and her feet dangled above the floor, as if she'd been hung from the gallows. She wasn't flailing. Not even a pinky spasmed.

Bailey gagged. I did my best not to. Sad to say, I'd seen my share of dead bodies.

Alexa reached to unbind Kylie.

I said, "Alexa, don't."

"But — "

"Don't. This is a crime scene." Without a doubt, Kylie had not become entangled accidentally. Someone had strangled her. The retractable rope system was taut, the raised mat platform positioned to the far end. "The police . . ." I didn't continue.

Alexa jammed the knuckles of her right hand into her mouth and wrapped her left arm around her body. Tears pooled in her eyes.

While I dialed 911 on my cell phone and reported the incident, Bailey clasped Alexa's shoulder and cooed something. After the emergency operator promised a quick response, I ended the call and surveyed the studio.

Were the crumbled and shredded papers significant, or had they blown in through the opened window? I bent down to examine one of the crumpled ones, pulling a tissue from my pocket so my prints wouldn't get on it—not knowing whether the killer's fingerprints might be. Without unfurling it, I could see it was a newspaper article about Savannah and the beautiful Alice in Wonderland Cake she'd made. Kylie had panned it in a review. Had Savannah killed Kylie? *Off with her head?*

I examined other papers. One, a freelance article by a reporter in Santa Cruz, described Tito and Kylie's feud over who would write the piece about the chicken kebab vendor. A second, posted in the *San Jose Mercury News*, discussed Midge and the set-to she and Kylie had engaged in. Mandolines—not the musical kind—had been involved. A third article detailed the events that had occurred during the National Newspaper Association convention. A photo of Kylie and Eugene Tinsdale appeared in the upper right corner. Kylie was holding a gold medal.

I lifted some shredded paper, but before I could study it, Bailey said, "Jenna, look!" She pointed.

On the mirror on the left side of the studio, someone had written: *You should have reformed.* The letters were tinged pink and greasy. It wasn't lipstick. Maybe lip gloss?

I released the shredded paper and eyed Alexa, who stood fixated on her friend's corpse. Her lower lip was quivering. "What was Kylie doing here?" she whispered. "We didn't have a private appointment. We haven't had one in a few years."

"Maybe she came to work out," Bailey said lamely.

"She has a reformer at home," Alexa said. "She doesn't . . .

didn't . . . need to use these. Sure, she liked coming to group classes to socialize, but to come here on her own? That's not like her."

"How did she get in?" I asked.

"She knew the code to the studio." Alexa brushed a tear off her cheek. "Like I said, she used to come to classes. The bigger question is why was she here now?"

"Perhaps she wanted to talk to you," I offered.

"About what? There's no text from her on my cell phone asking to meet." Alexa held out her phone to me and glowered in the direction of the entrance. "When will the police get here? What's taking them so long?"

Two short minutes had passed, but I knew from experience that, in a disastrous situation, every minute felt like an hour.

"Tito," Alexa whispered.

"He didn't do this," Bailey said.

"No, I'm not saying he did, but he must have come by, seeing as he didn't respond to my text about running late. Maybe he caught sight of whoever followed Kylie inside." Alexa sucked back a sob and inched closer to Kylie. "We shared everything, Kylie and me. Everything. Did you know she . . ."

I waited for Alexa to finish, but she didn't, so I said, "Did I know she *what*?"

"Kylie said she was quitting her job as a reporter. She said she had big dreams and had persuaded an investor to help her out. From the clues she dropped about what she was planning to do, saying she was going to keep whatever it was in the family, I assumed . . ." Alexa sighed. "I assumed she hoped to bail my father out at the newspaper."

"Aw. That would've been so nice." I wrapped an arm around her. "I'm so sorry for your loss."

Alexa shuddered.

• • •

Chief Cinnamon Pritchett, clad in her official brown uniform, could be intimidating. Gone was the snappy smile. Gone was the teasing and bantering. Grimly, she and her staff reviewed the scene. So far Cinnamon had limited her questioning to Alexa because it was her studio and she understood the equipment, not to mention that she'd spotted the body first. Plus, Alexa had had a long-standing relationship with the victim. Cinnamon had requested that Bailey and I hang to one side until she got around to us.

Bailey was allowed to call her husband. I was permitted to call my aunt, who told me not to worry. She would make sure everything at the store ran smoothly. Aunt Vera asked how I was doing. I mumbled that I was shaken but holding strong. I asked if Rhett had called. He had and he'd apologized profusely for messing up this morning's appointment with the wedding planner.

"Do you want me to touch base with him?" Aunt Vera asked.

"Yes. Thank you."

"I'll tell him you're with the police."

Swell. Rhett wouldn't be pleased that I'd stumbled upon another body.

Deputy Marlon Appleby drew alongside me. "Was that Vera you were speaking to?"

I raised my chin to meet his gaze. "Yes."

"We had a date scheduled."

"Don't worry. I told her you were on duty. By the way, I heard through the grapevine that your daughter isn't happy with my aunt."

"Who told you that?"

I filled him in.

As Appleby listened, he worked his moose-shaped jaw back and forth. "Sasha can be quite protective with the baby. Like her mother was, rest her soul. Don't worry. She adores your aunt. She'll warm to the idea."

"Maybe she thinks that my aunt, who has never had children, might drop her."

Appleby grinned. "Vera held you, didn't she? You ended up okay."

"Some might question your assessment." I winked. "You might want to set my aunt's mind at ease."

"Will do."

The deputy moved to have a word with the coroner, who was still taking pictures of Kylie. At first, the coroner had snapped various angles of her trapped in the reformer, clicking his tongue repeatedly as he'd moved to another viewpoint. I was pretty sure he'd never seen this method of murder. Now, after instructing two police technicians to remove the body from the contraption, he was photographing Kylie, who was dressed in black leggings and a black long-sleeved T-shirt, lying prone on the floor. The EMTs were standing by the entrance to the studio, ready to slip Kylie's corpse into a body bag and take her away whenever the coroner gave the signal.

To the morgue. My stomach lurched at the thought. Toe tags. Embalming fluid.

Alexa, who was sitting on the raised platform of a nearby reformer, elbows on her knees, head propped up by her fists, was green at the gills. Cinnamon perched beside her, mouth moving, notebook open, and pen poised.

Bailey slipped alongside me. "I couldn't reach Tito. I left him a voice mail." She pointed toward the mess of paper strewn on the floor. "What do you make of that?"

A ponytailed technician was gathering each piece carefully, looking as if she was trying to keep related pieces together.

"I don't know," I said. "I'm not sure if the killer brought all of it or Kylie did. Some are articles, each related to Kylie in some fashion. The shredded paper was sort of mixed media. Photo paper and regular paper."

Bailey motioned to the message on the mirror. "Why did Kylie need to reform?"

"I expect that's for the killer to know and the police to find out." I swallowed hard. "As we both know, Kylie wasn't well liked around town, but for the killer to write that message, suggesting she deserved the punishment of death? It takes a vicious mind."

A petite black woman in her early twenties, sporting intricate blonde ombré Ghana braids, rushed into the studio and gasped. Appleby blocked her advance.

"That's Viveca," Bailey whispered to me. "Alexa's assistant."

"What happened?" Viveca asked, struggling to peer past Appleby, her voice nearly a shriek. "Who's that lying on the floor? Is it Kylie? Kylie O? She's dead?" Viveca was dressed in a one-piece navy blue workout suit that looked painted on. Every contour of her perfect abs showed.

Appleby confirmed the identity. "What is your name?"

"Viveca Thorn. I'm Alexa's associate."

Associate, I mused. That held more rank than assistant. Was Viveca trying to give herself a boost, or was she nervous?

"What happened? Please, tell me," Viveca stammered. "Alexa, I'm here! I'm back!"

Alexa didn't acknowledge her.

"I got a text message from Alexa to pick her up a wrap for lunch," Viveca continued, "since she was running late. I went across the street." She held up the bag she was carrying from Latte Luck Café. "The line took forever, so —"

"Did you know Miss Obendorfer?" Appleby asked.

"Not personally," Viveca said, her voice tinny and tight. "I was hired a month ago, and she hasn't been in. And I'm not a foodie, so I don't follow her reviews. I've heard Alexa talk about her, though, in glowing terms." Viveca scanned the studio. "Did Tito Martinez do this?"

"No!" Bailey broke free of me and darted toward Viveca. "No, no, no. Why would you think that?"

"Tito was here. I saw him leave." Viveca shot out a hand. "I didn't think anything about it, but looking back —"

"Did you see Kylie with him?" Bailey asked.

"No. I didn't say that. I —"

"Were you witness to each person entering this building every single minute?" Bailey demanded. "Of course not," she snapped. "How could you be? You were standing in line at the café, probably with your back to the door. You don't know anything."

Viveca's eyes flooded with tears.

"Mrs. Martinez," Appleby barked. "Stop. Now."

"This woman doesn't know what she's talking about," Bailey persisted.

"Back away," Appleby said. "We will get to the bottom of this."

I rushed to my pal and braced her shoulders. "Calm down. Viveca is not accusing Tito."

"Yes, she is." Bailey sniffed.

"Ladies, please." Appleby eyed Viveca.

The young woman wiped a pinky beneath her beautiful eyes. Her lips parted, waiting for Appleby to continue.

"Miss Thorn, I'll need a statement," he said.

Viveca said, "Of course. May I give Alexa her lunch?"

"No." Appleby took the bag from her. He moved to a bank of cubicles where students could deposit their personal items and set the bag into one.

Tito burst into the room. "Bailey, I am here."

I gawped. Hadn't the police set a perimeter yet? First Viveca and now Tito?

Tito's hair was askew, and his tie, shirt, and jacket were disheveled. Had he walked through a windstorm to get here? I glanced out the rear window. There wasn't a hint of a breeze. He started toward Bailey. A twenty-something policeman blocked him.

"Bailey!" Tito waved.

Appleby signaled to the policeman to allow Tito to pass.

Tito hurried toward Bailey and slung an arm around her. "I was about to buy coffee and saw the police cars. The front door of the building was propped open. What is going on?" He caught sight of Kylie lying on the floor. "What happened? Did she have an accident?"

"No, she was . . . murdered," Bailey murmured.

"Mur—" Tito gagged. "But she was—" He stopped himself.

"Sir," Appleby said, "please continue. Miss Obendorfer was what?"

Tito broke apart from Bailey and faced the deputy. "Nothing."

"A witness spotted you on the premises earlier," Appleby went on, not glancing in Viveca's direction. "Did you see Miss Obendorfer at that time?"

"Yes, but she was alive when I left," Tito contended. "Alive. I did not do this."

Alexa hurried to him and hugged him. "Tito, I'm so glad you're here. I'm sorry I had to cancel our appointment. My car . . ." She smoothed the arms of his shirt and, clearly realizing she was being too demonstrative, stepped backward. "I can barely breathe. The gravity of all of this."

"Mr. Martinez," Appleby said, "did you have an appointment with Miss Tinsdale?"

"Yes."

Cinnamon joined the group. "Tell us about that, Mr. Martinez."

Tito's jaw ticked with tension. "I had a private pilates session scheduled. It's my regular appointment. I knocked. I waited. Alexa didn't show."

"As I said, I had a flat tire." Alexa shot a hand toward Tito. "I sent you a text."

Tito frowned. "I didn't get a text from you."

"I realize that now," Alexa said.

"Anyway, as I was leaving," Tito continued, "Kylie—Miss Obendorfer—appeared. She let herself in. She knew the code. She said Alexa texted her to meet her here."

Alexa shook her head. "No, I didn't."

Cinnamon called to the ponytailed technician. "Officer, bring me the deceased's cell phone."

The technician popped to her feet and brought the phone to her boss. Cinnamon scanned the log. "I don't see a text from Miss Tinsdale."

"Kylie lied," Alexa blurted. "Why would she lie about that?"

Cinnamon handed the phone back to the technician and eyed Tito.

"That's what she said." Tito pursed his lips.

"Chief Pritchett," Alexa said, "Kylie could be quite sly. For all I know, she caused my flat tire so she could come here and confront Tito at the studio, alone. She knew all of my clients' schedules. She was nosy to the point of being a fanatic about that."

"She didn't confront me," Tito exclaimed.

I studied the technician, who was scouring the crumpled and shredded paper. Had Kylie brought the paper? Had she hoped to confront and humiliate each and every one of her targets here? Had one of them killed her?

"I didn't stay," Tito added. "I wanted nothing to do with her."

"Didn't you like her, Mr. Martinez?" Cinnamon asked.

"That's not what I said. She . . . we . . ." Tito sputtered.

"Where did you go when you left?" Appleby asked.

"I'm doing a story on a local band." Tito hooked a thumb over his shoulder. "I went to the house that they're renting, except they weren't there. I was early. So I waited."

Cinnamon flipped a page in her notebook. "What was the address?"

Tito provided it. On Gardenia Avenue.

Cinnamon jotted the information. "Did anybody see you there? A mailman? A workman? Someone walking his or her dog?"

"No." Tito gazed worriedly at Bailey. "There might have been a gardener. I think I heard someone mowing. I'm not sure."

"Did the band members show up?" Cinnamon pressed.

"No. Turns out they got the day mixed up." Tito shifted feet. "They thought we were supposed to meet tomorrow."

"Tell us about your quarrel with Miss Obendorfer on Thursday, Mr. Martinez," Appleby said.

Oh, no. Had the technician seen that particular article and clued in the deputy? I gulped and gazed at Tito. Perspiration was beading above his lip and on his forehead.

"It was nothing," Tito said.

"Nothing," Bailey echoed.

"Kylie wanted to cover a story and asked me to back off," Tito said.

"Asked" was a stretch, I thought. Had the killer specifically brought the article about the fracas in order to frame Tito?

"Relax, Mr. Martinez," Cinnamon said. "We're simply trying to get all the facts. Tell me about waiting for the band in your car. What did you do? Send email? Reply to text messages? Did you call anybody?"

A small moan escaped Tito's lips. "I listened to a meditation tape."

"Do you do that often, or only after a confrontation?" Cinnamon's mouth twitched. She was baiting him.

"With a new baby, I" — Tito glanced at Bailey — "*we* need to find all the peace and calm we can. We grab it in minutes, not hours."

Cinnamon eyed my pal. "Do you listen to a meditation tape, Mrs. Martinez?"

"I exercise," Bailey snapped, unable to hide her annoyance.

Cinnamon narrowed her gaze. She couldn't possibly think Tito was guilty of murder, could she? After a long moment, she said, "Why didn't you let your wife know where you were, Mr. Martinez?"

"Why would I? We don't check in every hour." Tito's answer sounded as curt as Bailey's had. He lowered his chin in apology. "I was doing my job. I didn't have time for a chat."

"You said you were listening to a tape," Appleby countered.

Tito shot him an anxious look.

"Why are you mussed, sir?" Cinnamon asked.

"Mussed?" Tito assessed his attire and fiddled with his tie. "Because I saw the police cars and ran here. From my car. I'd parked it down the street."

"It's a loaner," Bailey added, as if that made a difference.

"I knew —" Tito hesitated.

"You knew what?" Cinnamon shifted feet.

"Bailey texted me," Tito answered. "I knew she was here. She didn't say what had happened. Seeing the police cars, I thought something had happened. To *her*. To my *wife*."

The technician handed one of the crumpled articles to Appleby, who then handed it to Cinnamon.

She scanned it and handed it back. "Sir, I'd like you to come to the station with us. We can talk further."

"Why?" Tito ran a hand down the back of his neck. "Am I a suspect? Do I need a lawyer?"

"We just want to talk."

Chapter 7

Bailey wasn't allowing Tito to go anywhere without her, and I wasn't letting her go alone. On the way to the precinct, I contacted Lola, and then I touched base with my aunt. I assured each that this was a misunderstanding and asked if they could take over for Tina with Brianna should Tito and Bailey be held up longer than necessary by the police. Both could and would. I breathed easier.

The precinct was teeming with activity when we entered—a fire at the north end of town; a pickpocket on the Pier; a car crash up the mountain—but I blocked all of the noise out as Bailey and I paced the beige hall outside Cinnamon Pritchett's office.

"Jenna," my pal whispered. "Who did this?"

"I don't know."

"We have to fix it. Tito—" Bailey pressed her lips together.

"He's going to be fine. We both know he didn't do this."

Who had killed Kylie? Who were her foes?

On my third pivot, I came up with a couple of suspects: Savannah Gregory and Midge Martin. Savannah blamed Kylie for her bad feet and her weight gain. I would imagine a future filled with pain and anger was enough reason to kill. Plus, she had been in love with Kylie. Had she told Kylie how she'd felt? Had Kylie rejected her? As for Midge, she believed Kylie had tried to smear her good name. Were there others who had hated Kylie? She certainly hadn't been the easiest person to get along with. I recalled Eugene Tinsdale arguing with his wife at the café earlier. The pronoun *she* had cropped up, after which Eugene revealed that they had been discussing Kylie. He'd said Kylie was leaving her post as a reviewer as soon as she got her affairs in order. He'd said she had another gig lined up. Was that a lie? Had something else forced her departure?

Bailey moaned.

"What's wrong?" I asked.

My pal was peering through the slatted louver blinds hanging in Cinnamon's office window, unable to tear her gaze from the activity within. Cinnamon had put her staff in charge of winding up the crime scene and had personally escorted Tito to the precinct.

"What's taking the chief so long?" Bailey knew Cinnamon nearly as well as I did, but she didn't dare show disrespect by referring to her by her first name.

"She's thorough."

"When will she be finished?"

Who knew? Interrogations could take minutes or hours.

I smiled supportively and said, "Hopefully soon."

"Tito looks awful. And scared." Bailey bit back a sob. "He's never scared."

"I bet he's not scared," I said. "I bet he's royally ticked off."

A nervous giggle burbled out of Bailey. "You're probably right."

"Relax." I slung an arm around her shoulders and gave a squeeze. "Questioning suspects is protocol."

Bailey shimmied out of my grasp. "Will they question Alexa? Or Viveca? Who else would have access to the studio? Not Tito. He—" She punched a fist against her palm. "My husband needs an alibi. A witness."

"On the way here, I reached out to Flora Fairchild and asked her to start a phone tree to find a witness. You know how much she loves to glean gossip. I'm sure there was someone who saw Tito sitting in his car." I rested a hand on my pal's shoulder. "Do you want a cup of coffee?"

"I couldn't possibly. The acid . . ." She wrapped her arms around her torso.

"Water?"

"No." Bailey glanced toward the window. "What are they doing?"

I peered past her. "Asking Tito to empty his pockets."

"I can see that," she hissed. "Why?"

"They probably want to take a peek at his cell phone, you know, to scan texts, email messages, and such."

Tito removed his wallet and cell phone, as well as a notepad and the pen Bailey had given him for his fortieth birthday. He tossed some spare change on the table, too, and a tube of something.

Appleby donned cotton gloves and viewed the cell phone, his forefinger scrolling through what had to be Tito's text messages. He shook his head at Cinnamon, who said something to Tito, who mouthed: *I told you so,* which I determined meant he hadn't received a message from Alexa.

That didn't surprise me. As snazzy as all the digital gadgets were nowadays, sent messages still fell through the cracks. How often had Rhett told me he'd missed a text or email from me? My boss at Taylor & Squibb often said that it was a wonder the Internet worked at all.

"What's the deputy doing now?" Bailey asked, her voice skating upward.

Appleby had picked up the tube.

"Is that lipstick?" Bailey peered worriedly at me.

"No, it looks like—" My mouth went dry.

"What?" Bailey asked.

Even from a distance, I could tell the tube was a distinctive yellow color, typical of a popular lip balm brand. Its cap was pink, meaning the balm itself was pink in color. The killer had used something similar to write *You should have reformed* on the mirror at the studio.

Appleby held the tube out to Tito, who shrugged and gestured toward the exit.

Cinnamon swung around and beckoned Bailey and me to enter.

Trembling, Bailey stepped into the office first. I followed and closed the door. The windows and louver blinds rattled.

"Does this belong to you, Mrs. Martinez?" Cinnamon asked, indicating the lip balm Appleby was holding.

Bailey drew near and examined the tube. "I have some like that. Sure. At home. And in a purse or two. Don't you?"

Cinnamon glowered at my pal, and my gut tightened further. If Bailey's DNA matched any found on the tip of the lip balm, and if the lip balm matched the goo on the mirror at the crime scene, Tito was in big trouble.

Cinnamon asked Bailey and me to leave and resumed her interrogation.

An hour later, the tube of lip balm and the article about Tito's argument with Kylie notwithstanding, Tito was released on his own recognizance. Until the police lab could come up with definitive DNA matches, any other evidence against him was circumstantial. His clothing, other than being mussed, hadn't shown any signs of him struggling with Kylie. She hadn't scratched him in any way. None of her hair was found on his person. In fact, I'd heard the technician at the crime scene say that none of Kylie's hair was anywhere on the premises, plus fingerprints had been wiped from the reformer. The killer, other than leaving the mess of paper and the writing on the mirror, had cleaned up after the crime.

Bailey gazed over her shoulder at me as she guided her husband out of the precinct. *Call me,* she mouthed.

I caught sight of Cinnamon through her office window, sinking into the chair behind her desk. Appleby set a glass of water in front of her, said something, and left.

Feeling the need to learn more of the chief's thoughts on the case, I tiptoed past her assistant's desk — the assistant had taken a break — and rapped on the doorframe. "May I come in?"

Cinnamon greeted me with a nod. "Sure."

"Are you feeling okay?" I asked.

"Morning sickness."

"Even in the afternoon?"

Cinnamon threw me a saucy smirk. "All day, every day. They call it morning sickness because most often it starts in the morning. My hormones are going whacko." She motioned to the chair opposite her desk. "Sit."

I did.

There were no plants in her office. A few plaques of commendation hung on the wall as well as photos of her with city leaders. Her desk was neat. Every writing implement was stored in a pencil holder. Files were stacked and marked with color-coded tabs. One silver-framed photo of Cinnamon and her husband, Bucky, at their wedding stood on the corner of the desk.

"You don't honestly think Tito Martinez is guilty, do you?" I asked. "He's salt of the earth."

Cinnamon glowered. "Really? You're going to hit me while I'm down?"

"He had no reason to want Kylie O dead."

"They argued. Publicly."

"He didn't care about her turf at the newspaper," I said.

"That's not what witnesses say." She raised an eyebrow. "Yes, a few have already come forward."

I sat taller. "Okay, sure, Tito wanted to do a few stories about what's cooking this week, seeing as the week's news is all about food, but he wouldn't kill for a story."

Cinnamon propped her elbows on the desk and tented her hands. "Tito has a temper."

"Which has been, forgive the pun, *tempered* since marrying Bailey. He's happy. He wouldn't think of upsetting the apple cart." I grimaced. "Sorry. Food Bowl terms are cluttering my brain."

My cell phone chirped in my pocket.

"Need to answer that?" Cinnamon asked.

"No." If it was Rhett, I'd deal with him later. "Would you like to consider other suspects?"

"I'm always open to ideas."

I tilted my head. "No, you're not. At least not from me."

"Because you're not a cop."

I folded my hands in my lap. "Does being a cop automatically make you privy to the nuances of relationships?"

"Not necessarily."

"Or bring you up to date on the town gossip?"

Cinnamon ran her tongue along her upper teeth. I could tell she was doing her best to tamp down a snappy comeback.

"Look," I said, "I don't like throwing anyone under the bus, but you do realize how much Kylie O made people's blood boil, right? Like all the restaurateurs who received bad reviews from her?"

"I'll admit she was not winning Miss Personality awards."

"You read the articles at the murder site, didn't you?" I mimed crumpling paper. "In addition to the article having to do with Tito, there were others about Savannah Gregory, Midge Martin, and Eugene Tinsdale. Each involved Kylie. Each had an edge to it. Those three should be considered suspects, don't you think?"

"The article with Mr. Tinsdale wasn't edgy. In fact, it was sweet. On the way to the precinct, I called him. He said he was with Miss Obendorfer in Las Vegas when she won an award."

"Why was that one included in the mix, huh?" I asked. "Did Kylie bring the articles? Did the killer?"

Cinnamon righted the lower edge of the stack of folders on her desk.

"What did the shredded paper reveal?" I asked. "Do you know?"

"Not yet."

I worked my tongue inside my cheek, waiting for more.

"The lip balm is damning," Cinnamon said.

"If the DNA matches Bailey's."

"Or Tito's."

"He wouldn't use a colored lip balm."

"There's often contamination arising from the sharing of a lipstick, and in fact, male cellular material can be found on a lipstick following kissing."

"Ew." I wrinkled my nose.

"Yeah, it's sort of gross to think about. Look, Jenna, thanks for your offer of help, but" — Cinnamon placed her hands flat on the desk and pushed to a stand — "we're done."

I rose, too. "I hear chamomile tea is good for morning sickness."

"Who told you that?"

"I saw a pop-up ad on Facebook."

Cinnamon grinned. "Usually, you get pop-up ads because you've been researching something online. Have you been checking out morning sickness for any particular reason?"

I smirked. "I'm not pregnant."

"The lady doth protest too much, methinks."

I thumped her desk. "Tito is innocent. Trust me."

Cinnamon nodded somberly. "I sure hope I don't have to arrest him."

Chapter 8

Friday traffic at the Cookbook Nook was hopping when I returned. The line at the register was long. Aunt Vera was ringing up each sale while Gran packed the books and gift items into bags and tied the handles with raffia. The crafts table in the far corner, which was covered with a plastic cloth, was filled with children under the age of ten waiting for a class to start.

Aunt Vera abandoned her post and hurried to me. She drew me into a warm embrace. Stroking my hair as she had when I was a child, she murmured, "You poor darling."

I wriggled free. "Aunt Vera, I'm fine. Sad for Kylie. Worried for Tito and Bailey. But I'm fine."

She pushed me away and held me firmly by the shoulders. Studying my face, she said, "You're jaded."

"No. I'm still shocked by murder. By the reality and finality of it. Trust me." How I wished I could control life with the wave of a wand. "Where's Tigger?"

"Up there."

I was surprised to see him crouching at the top of his cat condo. Usually, he loved toying with anyone who did crafts. He bolted from his perch and leaped into my arms. He yowled and butted my chest with his head. Had he sensed something was amiss and waited for my return? I assured him I was all right and Bailey was, too. The text message I'd received when in Cinnamon's office had been from Bailey, not Rhett. She and Tito had arrived home safely. He was sitting in a rocking chair, singing to Brianna.

Pepper strode into the store and clapped her hands. "I'm ready."

Gran and Pepper were leading the crafts class. Gran was quite the crafts lover. She had to be, with three granddaughters. Pepper, who had been a crafts person since birth, was joining in because she believed that helping out at my store would help grow her business.

"Ready, children?" Gran asked as she and Pepper weaved through the customers to the table. "What are we making?" she asked as she drew near.

"Papier mâché ice cream cones," a towheaded girl chimed.

"And what is the prize for the very best one?" Pepper asked.

She'd dressed for the occasion by donning a T-shirt that read *Everything in moderation except craft supplies.*

"An ice cream cone from Taste of Heaven!" a boy cried.

"Right. So let's get started." Gran brought out paper cups, tape, felt pens, sheets of paper, newspaper, a tub of papier mâché solution, and small aluminum baking dishes.

As Pepper handed out the cups and Gran launched into the instructions about forming the base of the cone and filling it with wads of paper, my thoughts shot to the crime scene. The articles. The possible suspects.

What had been on the shredded paper? The act of shredding something suggested a lot of anger. Had Kylie shredded it or had the killer? I recalled the few pieces I'd touched. Some had felt like glossy paper, some like heavy bond paper. Had there been words on it? A photo? Another newspaper article? If only I could conjure up an image.

. . .

An hour before closing, I telephoned Bailey. She answered after one ring. Tito was doing fine. He was already pursuing a new story about a man who was opening up a day spa in the mountains. She asked if I'd pried anything out of Cinnamon to give Tito and her hope. I didn't tell her that Cinnamon had dismissed me. I didn't have the heart. Instead, I said that I'd given Cinnamon a few suspects to consider. Bailey didn't ask who. Knowing I'd offered up other names seemed to calm her. I asked Bailey if she still wanted to meet me for our jaunt along Buena Vista to dine on snacks provided by the food vendors. She begged off. She wasn't up to it. Before ending the call, she promised she would not worry through the night. I knew she would.

With Bailey out of commission, I texted Rhett and asked if he could join me to explore the food vendors on the boulevard. I added that his main event at the bistro was over, and his staff should be able to handle a normal crowd for a short while. He replied that he could give me an hour.

Taking what I could get, I rode Tigger home on the Schwinn, quickly changed into jeans, ecru sweater, a light puffy jacket, and walking shoes, and then drove my VW back to town and parked at Fishmerman's Village. I walked the rest of the way drinking in the wonderful aromas of food, food, food.

A breeze had kicked up and banners were flapping, but no one strolling along the boulevard looked in the least put out. The foot traffic was not deterring folks from entering their favorite restaurants, either.

Rhett met me in front of Intime, looking a little harried. He wasn't wearing his chef's coat, but his shirtsleeves were rolled up and his collar was stained with some kind of white sauce. He kissed me on the cheek.

"Are you okay with time?" I asked. "You seem—"

"I'm making time." He gently rubbed my lower back, a gesture of affection that I adored. "Your aunt told me about you finding Kylie O. This has to have been quite a shock, sweetheart. How are you?"

"Hanging in."

Since I'd moved back to Crystal Cove, there had been a number of murders. In the fifteen years prior to my return, there had been zero. Zilch. None. I didn't believe I had bad juju, but at times I wondered whether I was the lure for such evil. Rhett and my family assured me I wasn't the cause. Crime was on the rise everywhere.

"I'm fine," I said, "but Bailey, not so much. Tito is a suspect."

"No way."

"Way." Lowering my voice, I briefly filled him in on the investigation: Kylie strangled in the tower-style reformer; the crumpled and shredded paper; the writing on the mirror. "I can't imagine how Alexa is doing. It was her best friend. Her studio. I'm sure the incident will hurt business." Murder on the premises was never good for building clientele. "Of course, Cinnamon wants no help from me."

"You've spoken with her?"

"I went with Bailey and Tito to the precinct."

Rhett bumped my shoulder with his. "But if you have solid information, you'll share it with her."

"If relevant."

I looped my arm through his, and we strolled north on Buena Vista in the direction of the lighthouse. We stopped at the first cart vendor we came to—Tacos Terrifico. Each taco was made with shredded everything: lettuce, chicken, and cheese. Even the tomatoes and peppers were julienned.

"Love the sauce," Rhett murmured.

"Me, too," I said. "Just the right amount of cayenne."

We moved on to another vendor selling pulled pork sandwiches. The aroma was divine.

As we waited for our mini meal, Rhett said, "Listen, about me missing this morning's wedding planner meeting . . ."

"Forget it," I said. "I know you're busy. Harmony Bold and I accomplished a lot."

"Whatever you decide will be fine with me. You know that."

I turned to him. "Yes, but I want you to take part at some point."

"I will. Going forward. I got bogged down this morning. I've asked the investors if we can afford a third manager."

The investors, who years ago had financed Rhett's parents' restaurant in Napa Valley, had lured Rhett back into the restaurant business—he still owned but didn't manage Bait and Switch Sport Supply, located on the Pier. The investors had promised that Rhett wouldn't be the sole executive chef or manager. True to their word, they had hired a second executive chef and a second manager, but that hadn't been enough extra manpower to cover the intense experience of what the bistro planned to offer.

I rubbed his arm. "I'm cool with your schedule. For now."

"I'm not." Rhett paid the vendor for our sandwich and offered me the first bite.

Happy to oblige, I bit into it and hummed my appreciation. "Delicious. Cayenne is the flavor of the day."

Rhett took a bite and said, "I will work this out. Trust me."

As we polished off our sandwich and headed for a dessert vendor offering vanilla and chocolate coconut haystack cookies, I caught sight of Eugene and Audrey strolling in our direction. Eugene was dressed casually in tan trousers, a blue button-down shirt, and a tweed jacket. Audrey wore an atypical black sheath and black wool coat and scarf, as if she'd dressed for a funeral. She appeared to have been crying.

Eugene caught sight of me and tapped Audrey's arm. Quickly, she pinched her cheeks. Why? Did she think Rhett or I would judge her for mourning Kylie? Or for worrying about her daughter's emotional well-being?

"Rhett," Eugene said, extending his arm. "Great meal at your restaurant."

Rhett shook hands with him. "Thank you, sir."

"Don't *sir* me." Eugene smiled, but his eyes glinted with tension. "That won't get you better reviews in the food —" He coughed hard, as if he were choking on a clam shell.

"Are you all right?" Rhett laid a hand on Eugene's shoulder.

"What was I thinking?" Eugene sputtered. "That last comment was in bad taste, seeing as Kylie . . ." He hitched his chin toward me. "I'm sure you've heard from Jenna what happened to our food reviewer, Kylie Obendorfer."

"I'm sorry for your loss." My gaze swung from Eugene to Audrey. "I know you were both close to her."

"Thank you," Eugene said. "She was like a second daughter."

Audrey sniffed. "Who would want to kill Kylie? Like *that*?"

Or at all, I thought, but kept the words to myself.

"Don't you have any suspicions?" I asked.

"Not a one." Eugene heaved a sigh.

"Alexa said it was gruesome." Audrey fiddled with the tails of her scarf. "Using the equipment at the studio as a weapon. Unheard of."

"Macabre," Eugene muttered.

I'd worked hard all day to erase the gallowslike image from my mind. Rhett had grown a little pale when I'd described it to him.

"How is Alexa doing?" I asked. When Bailey and I'd left the fitness studio, Alexa had been sitting in her small office, staring blankly through the glass window as the police continued to collect evidence. I wouldn't have called her catatonic, but she had definitely drawn into herself.

Audrey said, "She's home now. Sleeping."

"I hope she'll see a therapist," I said. "Stumbling upon a dead body, especially that of a friend, can rock your world."

"I'm sure she will," Audrey said. "Our family therapist is an amazing person."

Eugene gazed at his wife, his expression distant, as if he were working hard to process each word.

Audrey worried her hands together. "Who would write such a horrible message on a mirror? Why on earth would Kylie need to reform?"

Perhaps because of her abusive behavior toward others, I mused, and instantly chided myself for the callous notion. Kylie was dead. No matter how she'd treated colleagues, clients, or enemies, she hadn't deserved to be murdered.

"Eugene, were you able to talk to Kylie about, you know"— I rotated a hand—"getting her affairs in order?"

Audrey shot her husband an irritable look. Was she upset that I'd overheard them arguing, or upset that he'd chatted with me afterward? With Kylie's death, the topic of her leaving the newspaper was moot.

"No, sadly," Eugene said. "By the way, after running into you, I got to thinking about how I could avoid downsizing and stay afloat."

"That's good to hear, Eugene," Rhett said. "Nothing is smooth sailing in this economy."

I said, "Are you going to ask my aunt to help you?"

Eugene shook his head vehemently. "Not a chance. I wouldn't put Vera through that torture again. One should never borrow from a friend. It creates wedges. Because your aunt is a saint our friendship weathered that storm." He inhaled sharply and let it out. "No, I've reached out to an investor who is quite familiar with the newspaper business and knows exactly what I need to do to survive."

I tensed. Was it the same investor Alexa had alluded to, the one Kylie had contacted? Could there have been some kind of conflict of interest? Might that have factored into who had killed her?

"As it turns out," Eugene went on, "he's a trust fund baby and one of Audrey's students. He's quite an artist, thanks to her."

Audrey blushed.

"He lives and breathes the news, and he can't imagine not having a physical daily paper to read. Digital, he says, is for the birds. That's where we were earlier today," Eugene went on. "At the exact time Kylie . . ." He suppressed a sob.

"That Kylie was found," Audrey finished.

When Eugene wrapped an arm around his wife's back, a shiver

ran down my spine. Why? Because it felt as if Eugene were thanking Audrey for providing him with an alibi.

Did he need one?

Chapter 9

Rhett and I walked on and dined at three dessert vendors. Before parting ways, he whispered, "Listen, about tomorrow night and the Pier and going to the barbecue afterward —"

I put a finger to his lips. "I'll manage. Don't worry about canceling."

"I love you," he whispered.

"I love you, too."

His good-night kiss was as sweet as sugar. I relished it.

Tigger attacked me the moment I walked in the door of my new house. Attacked, in a good way. He butted my ankle and mewed for me to pick him up. Was he upset by the aroma of fresh paint, or was he acting needy because he'd had to stay home while I gallivanted? Whatever the reason, I nuzzled him, promised him he was fine, and carried him to the couch. We snuggled for a half hour before I called it quits and sank into bed.

At sunrise on Saturday, I awoke feeling groggy and forlorn. Not about me or my future with Rhett, but about Bailey and Tito and, yes, Kylie. Tito wasn't guilty of murder. I was certain of it. Who was?

As I ran on the beach, took a brisk shower, and downed a protein-rich breakfast, I thought again about Eugene Tinsdale. Had he spit out his alibi last night on purpose? Did he think I would vouch for him if Chief Pritchett questioned me? Was Eugene even on Cinnamon's radar?

Getting dressed, I decided I couldn't and wouldn't vouch for Eugene. My aunt might know him well, but I didn't.

The doorbell chimed. I hurried to it and let Keller inside. He was a rangy guy with an easy demeanor. The white bib overalls he was wearing over a white long-sleeved shirt made him look that much leaner.

One-handed, he whipped off his cap and swooped a thatch of brown hair off his face. "Hey-hey, Jenna. Too early?"

"Right on time."

"My mother said being on time shows respect."

"I would agree."

"She's watching Min-yi today."

"Lucky her." I smiled.

"What's on the agenda this morning?" Keller asked.

"Painting the three walls in the master bedroom. The paint is in the corner of the room. Leave the wall behind the master bed blank."

"Aren't you going to paint a mural there?" Keller set his toolkit on the floor and pulled gloves from the back pocket of his overalls.

"Yes."

"Then I ought to get rid of the blue paint and paint it neutral. No extra charge." As Keller donned the gloves, he added, "Don't worry. I won't leave a mess. You won't even know I've been here."

The words *leave a mess* caught me off guard. How had the killer left no trace of himself or herself at the crime scene? Had he or she worn a hat? Mask? Gloves?

Tigger meowed.

"Yes, cat, we're on the move. We don't want to be late." I scooped him into my arms and said goodbye to Keller.

By the time I arrived at the shop, Gran had set up the register, organized all the shelves, and straightened the aprons hanging on hooks.

"My, you've been busy," I said as I set Tigger on the floor and stowed my purse in the stockroom.

"Busy hands. You know me."

"Nice dress," I said.

Gran swiveled while pulling the seams of the flared skirt. "Isn't it cute?"

"Very flattering." I liked everything Gran wore. She had exquisite taste, and the budget to afford it.

"I thought it would be fun to dress up for today's demonstration," Gran said. "Midge is one of my favorite restaurateurs. I adore her chopped club salad. She throws in amazing croutons. Do you think she'll sign her cookbook? I picked up a copy."

"I'm sure she will."

"How about a little music?"

Without waiting for a reply, Gran ducked into the stockroom and switched on a CD mix I'd made for this week's festivities. I liked to have music playing through the speakers while people browsed; music lightened moods. Today of all days, music would help me slog through. Migos' upbeat "Stir Fry" was first in the queue.

"Here you go." Gran returned with a mug of coffee featuring the words *You never have enough cookbooks to look at.* "You look like you could use a cup." She handed it to me. "By the way, the independent publisher was true to her word. Her representative showed up minutes after I arrived with twenty extra copies of Midge's cookbook."

"Terrific."

Gran took a sip of her coffee and set it aside. "Do you want to talk about yesterday?"

I shook my head. "No. Let's keep my head in the game. Demo. Satisfied customers. Sales."

Gran returned to fussing about the displays.

Minutes later, Midge sailed into the shop. "Morning! I'm off to collaborate with Katie." Her frizzy hair was sticking out at odd angles and her plaid shirt was half tucked into white skinny jeans. "Jenna, is there anything you need from me before I zip away?"

"No, I'm good, but don't rush. You have plenty of time."

"In the restaurant business, there is never *plenty of time.*" Midge shook a finger. "You should know that better than most. If you don't, have Rhett clue you in." She blew me a kiss and rushed down the breezeway toward the café.

Gran chuckled. "What a whirlwind. I suppose one has to be in order to become so successful."

"Too-ra-loo," my aunt chimed as she strolled into the shop, the folds of her emerald green caftan swishing to and fro. Suddenly, she pulled to a halt and clapped her hand over her heart. "Oh, goodness. What am I thinking? No cheery hello today, not with another murder in town." She set her matching turban on the vintage kitchen table. "Z.Z. contacted me this morning. She is distraught and has declared an all-out war on crime. She wants to install security cameras on every streetlamp and building."

"Like closed-circuit TV?" I asked.

"Mm-hm."

Gran said, "No one will appreciate Big Brother watching."

"If it means we're safer," my aunt countered, "then what could be the harm?"

"The loss of personal freedom," Gran quipped. "Don't get me started."

"Tosh." Aunt Vera scanned the shop. "Enough chatter about what we can't control. Let's get this place set up for Midge and Katie."

"Yes, boss." Gran saluted.

For the next hour, the three of us rearranged the shop, moving the mobile bookcases and setting out folding chairs. Around eleven, I telephoned Bailey, wondering if Tito had consulted an attorney yet. She didn't answer her cell phone, so I left a message and dialed Lola. She answered, but she didn't know much more about her daughter than I did. She promised she would do her best to get an update before arriving for the demonstration.

At a quarter past eleven, Bailey called me back and asked if she could skip coming in. Tito and she were, indeed, meeting with a defense attorney. Tito had written an article on the woman a couple of years back, when she'd defended a murderer in Santa Cruz. I told Bailey that, of course, she could skip work, asked her to touch base after she met with the attorney, and then invited Tito and her to join me at the Pier for dinner. Bailey leaped at the opportunity and added that she'd already hired a friend of Tina's to watch Brianna for the evening.

Minutes later, as customers swarmed in and began purchasing Midge's newly delivered cookbooks, Flora Fairchild hurried into the shop, her face as flushed as the pink dress she was wearing. She weaved through the crowd toward me, nabbed my elbow, and dragged me toward the stockroom, out of earshot of the others. Lowering her voice, she said, "Per your request, I've started a phone tree. However, so far no one claims to have seen Tito Martinez on Gardenia Avenue or anywhere near there. I'm sorry."

"Not as sorry as I am."

"We'll keep trying." Flora petted my arm. "Lots of people leave town before the holiday and refuse to answer their cell phones. Tell Bailey and Tito to keep their chins up."

"Will do."

"Hello, everyone!" Katie yodeled as she and Midge entered through the breezeway, Katie pushing her mobile cooking cart and looking primed for action in a checkered dress and crisp chef's coat. Midge had donned a chef's coat as well.

"Let's get started," Katie said. "Take your seats and say hello to our guest of honor, Midge Martin."

The audience obeyed, many without finalizing their purchases. I wasn't worried. We'd never had an audience member walk out without paying.

"Hi, all!" Midge raised her hand in greeting.

"Midge and I are going to show you how to shred with confidence," Katie declared. "Are you excited?"

The audience responded in the affirmative.

After describing her cart and its overhead mirror, Katie said, "Afraid of this flat-faced sassy girl, also know as a mandoline?" She held one up, displaying it right and left. "Don't be." Next, she raised a cheese shredder. "Scared of scraping your knuckles? Forget about it." She uttered *The Sopranos* catchphrase with a New York Italian accent.

A few in the audience caught the reference and laughed.

Midge said, "Today, we'll be making a variety of salads, appetizers, and vegetarian pizza."

"Are we expected to be here for the entire afternoon?" Flora tapped her watch.

Midge grinned. "Very funny, Flora. We'll do this all in a matter of two hours. Are you game?"

The audience applauded.

"Let's get shredding." Midge wielded a large chopping knife and cackled.

Midge's maniacal display caught me off guard. I pictured Kylie, strangled in the reformer, the shredded papers and articles scattered helter-skelter. Was everyone who'd been mentioned in an article a suspect? If Midge were the killer, why would she have deliberately implicated herself by including an article about Kylie and her? Was throwing in that article a ploy to confuse the police?

"Prep always comes first," Midge said, "as you'll notice in my cookbook." Like an accomplished sous chef, she sliced and diced onions, carrots, cucumbers, and zucchini with ease while providing tips about how to keep one's knuckles and fingertips out of the way of danger. "First and foremost, choose the right-sized grater. If the hole is too small, food, like a semi-hard cheese or potatoes for hash browns, will get caught and cause you to snag your knuckles. Ouch! You can use the finer grate for harder cheeses, like parmesan, and for zesting lemons and the like." The overhead mirror allowed the audience to view each stroke. "If you have all the prep work done ahead of time, assembling is a snap."

Holding the mandoline at an angle on the cutting board, Katie scalloped pre-peeled potatoes.

Gran raised her hand. "Do you do all the prep yourself at your restaurant, Midge?"

"No. Like Katie, I have a number of helpers."

"I don't have any helpers at home," a redhead in the audience said.

"Neither do I," Midge declared. "And I wouldn't want any in my personal kitchen. That way, I can make something in my own time, my own way. Don't you agree, Katie?"

"I sure do. One more thing . . ." Katie stopped slicing. "I like to set out an array of spices ahead of time. I place the jars on the counter so the flavors are readily available." She fetched containers of cinnamon, thyme, basil, and rosemary from the cabinet at the back of the mobile cart and placed them by the cut vegetables. "Seasonings are the spice of life," she crooned, and laughed at her own joke.

As Katie and Midge continued to banter, a feeling of dread washed over me. Katie was such a natural in front of a crowd that I feared, if I weren't careful, Midge might ask her to join her on her cooking show. If she did, would Katie quit the Nook Café? No way. Katie made a lot of money as the Nook's chef, and the minor partnership in the shop had to count for something, didn't it? On the other hand, fame could go to one's head. I hoped having a ten-month-old girl would ground her.

"Time for pizza!" Midge shouted halfway through the presentation. "We all love cheese, right? The more the merrier."

Katie said, "As long as you can eat dairy."

"They make some wonderful lactose-free cheeses now," Midge countered. "There is a provolone to die for," she said, and then balked. She shot a look at me and mouthed, *Sorry.*

I offered a supportive smile. Certain indelicate phrases were bound to spill from a person's lips following a murder. It couldn't be helped.

When the duo finished the demonstration, showing off the minced onion appetizers, shredded chicken and vegetable salad, and the thin-crust pizza with grilled julienned zucchini, Gran bounded to her feet and applauded like a true fan. The rest of the audience followed suit.

Katie motioned to Midge, who bowed. "Thank you, Midge, for making this so easy."

"My pleasure."

"And don't forget to buy one of Midge's cookbooks," Katie said.

A few audience members raised their purchases.

"Also, Katie has been a doll," Midge said. "She made recipe cards for the shredded chicken salad, plus she created cellophane packets of the exact spices she used in it. You can't mess up." Midge held up a card and packet. "You'll find them on the tasting table in the breezeway, where we've set samples of what we've cooked today. So don't be shy. Have a taste and take a card."

More applause.

Aunt Vera said, "Midge will be signing her cookbook over there" — she indicated the vintage table — "if you'd form a line."

Before Midge moved to the table, she took a sip of water from a glass Gran provided and then pulled a lipstick from her jeans' pocket. As she started to apply it, I realized it wasn't a lipstick. It was a lip balm, exactly like the one found in Tito's jacket — yellow tube, pink top.

My heart did a hiccup.

• • •

Late in the afternoon, after the hubbub of the day's event had waned, I was in dire need of fresh air, a double-shot espresso, and a nutmeg cookie, not necessarily in that order. My energy was flagging, and worry was gnawing my insides to a pulp. Bailey hadn't touched base to tell me how the appointment with the attorney had gone.

I advised my aunt of my plan and headed out. A few street vendors were selling their wares along Buena Vista Boulevard. I had no doubt more would show by the time the evening diners were strolling the street.

Latte Luck Café was bustling as I entered. All of the wooden tables were filled. The brown leather booths were, too. The enticing aroma of sugar and spice hung in the air. Many of the people standing in line were pointing at the sepia pictures of Crystal Cove in the early nineteenth century that hung on the walls. I took up the rear and peered over shoulders, hoping to spy Savannah beyond the counter. She was the one who made my beloved nutmeg cookies. I didn't see her.

When I arrived at the order area, I asked the freckle-faced young man if Savannah was in.

"Nope," he said. "Not today or yesterday."

"Is she sick?" I asked.

"Yep. Migraine, I think. You want to talk to her mom?" He hitched his chin at Shari, who was icing a cake. Clad in her pink-striped apron, her hair tucked beneath a pink-striped cap, she reminded me of a peppermint stick.

Shari nodded a *hello*. "Something wrong, Jenna?" She always had a warm smile.

"I was hoping to buy a nutmeg cookie."

"We're out. Savannah's been a bit under the weather. Order a cinnamon roll." Shari hoisted her piping bag. "I know you love those. I made the last batch of the day minutes ago. I'll add extra icing."

"That's okay. I'll settle for a double-espresso and some coconut macaroons for tonight's dessert."

"Suit yourself."

As I waited for the young man to fill my order, I considered Savannah's absence. Had her headache started Thursday night after her peeve with Kylie? Had she lurked outside Kylie's house all night and followed her yesterday morning to Your Wellness? Given the women's past friendship, Savannah might have learned the entry code to the fitness studio from Kylie. Maybe after Kylie sneaked inside, Savannah—

"Jenna," a woman called.

I spied Harmony Bold sitting at one of the booths, dressed more casually than when we'd met yesterday, her long hair knotted in a messy bun. She hailed me and set her cell phone aside.

I paid for my order, took my coffee and goodie bag from the clerk, and settled opposite my wedding planner in the booth. "I didn't know you frequented this place."

"I had to check on the family businesses seeing as . . ." Harmony frowned and glanced out the big bay window. "Seeing as a murder happened on the second floor."

I followed her gaze. "I thought the Boldines owned the building."

"They do. I'm a Boldine. I shortened my last name to Bold for business purposes. After all, a wedding planner must be bold, don't you think?" She winked at me.

"Why are all the shops closed?" I put the bag with the treats on the seat beside me.

"Since Mom and Dad went on a long-awaited cruise, my sister and brother decided it was time to hightail it out of town, too. Neither of them are foodies. Both suffer from severe allergies. I seemed to have dodged that bullet."

"You didn't want to join them in a retail business venture?"

"Ack. Me and steady hours?" Harmony swiped the air. "Like oil and water. But I sure do appreciate utilizing their expertise when it comes to my business. What wedding planner can't avail herself of a jeweler, a florist, and a crystal and china shop?" She laughed. "By the way, my sister, the florist, knows everyone in the flower business. One of her best friends operates out of Napa. It's going to be a cinch for your wedding."

"Small world."

"Indeed." Harmony sipped from her to-go cup. "Best latte in the world. I get two every day, much to the chagrin of my pocketbook. One at ten and another in the late afternoon. I can't make coffee to save my life." She popped the lid on her latte, added a packet of sugar, swirled it in using a wooden coffee stirrer, and reapplied the lid. "Geez, I'm sorry. Listen to me prattling, being totally insensitive." She set the stir stick on a napkin. "How are you? I heard that you found . . . Kylie O."

"Yes. Actually, Alexa, Bailey, and I did." I took a sip of my espresso.

"I can't imagine seeing a dead body. Was it horrible?"

I nodded, the image flicking at the back of my mind.

"The police contacted my parents right away," Harmony said. "They needed to know my family's whereabouts."

"My best friend's husband is the main suspect."

"Tito Martinez?" Harmony asked. "He's a good guy."

"I agree."

Harmony nudged her coffee to the side and folded her arms on the table. "I was here yesterday morning. I didn't see Tito, and I didn't see Kylie. I'm not sure what I would've done had I seen either of them. I didn't know they had a feud going."

"They don't. *Didn't,*" I corrected. "Kylie wasn't upset with Tito, and he wasn't mad at her, either. He didn't kill her." I glanced across the street and, due to the conversation with my aunt and Gran earlier, noticed something I hadn't on Friday. "I see spotlights to illuminate your family's building, but I don't see any security cameras."

"That's right. My mother doesn't believe in them. Dad wanted to install them, but Mom wouldn't let him. She believes in the kindness of humanity." Harmony winced. "With the murder, of course, that's going to change. They've already ordered an installation for Monday. You know" — she tapped the table — "maybe Midge Martin saw something."

"Midge?"

"When I was having my first coffee, I saw her peering through the windows. She might have had business with my mother. She buys a lot of jewelry at the shop."

I sat taller and peered again at the Boldine Building. Kylie had accused Midge Martin of forging a recipe. Midge had been lurking around the exact location where Kylie had met her doom. And Midge had an exact replica of the lip balm used at the crime scene.

What were the odds?

Chapter 10

I returned to the shop, wondering whether Cinnamon would welcome my theories about Midge. There were two customers. Gran was seeing to them. As I strode toward the stockroom to call the precinct, Deputy Appleby and his daughter, Sasha, nearly ran me over as they passed through the arch from the breezeway. My aunt trailed them, worrying her phoenix amulet.

"Honestly, Dad?" Sasha dodged me without offering an apology. Like the deputy, she was a big woman with a prominent moose-like jaw. That didn't sound like much of a compliment for a lady, but she was handsome in a wholesome way and usually glowing. Not today, however. She was scowling at her father. "You know Steven and I don't begrudge you and Vera having a relationship." Sasha didn't appear to have an inside voice. "I never—"

"Begrudge?" Appleby said sharply. He set a doggie bag from the café on the vintage table and folded his arms across his massive chest. "You and your brother don't get to *begrudge* me anything."

Sasha sighed. "You know that's not what I—"

"I make my choices," Appleby retorted.

"Okay, fine, but"—Sasha shot a hand between my aunt and the deputy—"why do you have to get engaged? It's not like you're going to have children."

Engaged? I gulped. News to me. Gran threw me a questioning look. I shrugged: *Got me.*

"Vera and I want to be in a committed relationship," Appleby stated. "We're old-fashioned that way."

"Antediluvian," Sasha muttered.

"Mind your manners," Appleby warned.

"It was Steven's word," Sasha said. "Will you sell your house? Will you pool finances? It's not like you bring anything to the marriage cash-wise, Dad."

Appleby blanched. "Do not get cheeky with me, young lady. We will not discuss finances here. Besides, Vera knows exactly what I'm worth."

"All the tea in China," Aunt Vera joked. "Yin to my yang. I'm blessed that he's in my life." She blew a kiss to Appleby and then addressed Sasha. "Dear"—she clutched Sasha's forearm—"up until today's announcement . . ." My aunt paused. Given the way she was gazing at Sasha, I wondered whether she was trying to telepathically influence her. Perhaps she hoped heaping spiritual blessings on Sasha would erase Sasha's negativity and open her heart. "Up until now" — Aunt Vera began again — "you and I have gotten along very well."

Except for when Sasha hadn't allowed my aunt to hold her baby the other day, I mused. *Harrumph and hogwash,* as my grandfather used to say.

"Let's sit for a moment," Aunt Vera suggested. "Maybe I could give you a tarot reading. I know you appreciate a good reading."

"Who told you that?" Sasha shot her father a scathing look. "That was a secret, Dad."

Appleby held up both hands. "I didn't say a thing. Vera is intuitive."

Vera chuckled warm and low. "Sasha, dear, a fellow tarot reader let the cat out of the bag, not your father. Please, let me do it this once. Perhaps the reading will ease your mind about your father and me. We're in love. We're planning a long future. I'd like you to be happy for us."

My aunt reached for Sasha's hand. As if in a trance, Sasha raised her arm. Submissively, she allowed my aunt to guide her into a chair. Then Aunt Vera pulled a packet of tarot from the pocket of her caftan and handed it to Sasha.

"Shuffle the cards, dear. Feel their power." Aunt Vera hitched her chin at Appleby, shooing him away.

He strode to me, looking sheepish. "Sorry you had to witness that."

"Emotions run deep," I said in commiseration, and then shook his hand. "Congratulations." Even though I didn't wholeheartedly agree that they needed to get married. Why do it? Everyone knew my aunt and Appleby were devoted to one another for life. A ceremony wasn't going to change that. Maybe I was underrating the value of whatever memories came with the tradition. I added, "I hope your son will come on board."

"He's fine with everything," Appleby said, but his face belied his calm.

"I heard Sasha. Steven is definitely not on board."

"I'll convince him."

Ha! I imagined arm wrestling might be in their future.

I turned my attention to the tarot reading. The card that my aunt had already placed on the table was the Fool. It represented new beginnings and having faith in the future and was considered a positive card. I presumed the card signified my aunt and the deputy and their future together, but then she revealed the second card — the Empress, a beautiful card with a full-figured blonde who possessed a peaceful aura. It was reversed, meaning it was turned upside down. Though traditionally the Empress would represent abundance and power and the creation of life or the start of a new family, when reversed the card held a different meaning. It still indicated feminine power, but it also suggested that the person receiving the reading needed to get in touch with the love that flowed within. Not my aunt. Not Appleby.

My aunt gazed at Sasha. Although she spoke softly, I heard the question she asked. "Are you pregnant with another child, dear?"

Sasha nodded ever so slightly.

"That would explain why you're so protective of your little one as well as your father." Aunt Vera squeezed Sasha's hand. "I promise you that I will not come between you and him or the children. He will be here to give you and them all the support you need. Do not worry."

Aunt Vera ran her index finger across Sasha's tight forehead. Sasha didn't recoil. She leaned into my aunt's touch, and I felt relieved. The two were bonding yet again.

Appleby looked pleased.

"Jenna!" Keller raced into the shop and made a beeline for me. His white overalls were splattered with eggshell-white paint as well as dirt. A few leaves stuck to the seams. "So glad I found you."

Where else would I be? I thought, and then realized that, indeed, I had been out and about over the past few days. I didn't maintain an eight a.m. to six p.m. regimen in the shop, thanks to having terrific assistants.

"What's up?" I asked.

"The skylight in the master might leak with the next rain."

"Oh, not good."

"Nope, not good at all. I found a discolored patch on the hardwood floor as I was setting out my tarp."

"I've never seen a discolored patch," I said.

"It was under the area rug."

The blue-themed area rug had belonged to the previous owner. We hadn't replaced the flooring in the master yet. It was on the to-do list.

Keller jutted a hip. "You had a house inspection before you took occupancy, didn't you?"

I shook my head. My aunt, who had known the previous owner quite well, had paid all cash. Having seen regular work done on the house, Aunt Vera had trusted that everything was in tiptop shape. Oops. Trust. What an iffy and intangible thing.

"Well, I took a peek at the skylight," Keller said.

"How did you get up there? I don't have a ladder."

"I've got one on the truck, but I didn't need one. I climbed the tree in the backyard to access the roof. I love to climb. Climbing lets you reach for the sky. Expand your horizons. Think of possibilities."

I smiled. Keller could wander during any conversation.

"The skylight," I said, redirecting him.

"Right. You'd be wise to get a whole house inspection. You can purchase a home warranty, too, for all the new as well as the old appliances, the water heater, yada-yada." He placed his hands on his hips. "It's worth it, if you ask me. Houses are big investments. Costs can come out of the woodwork." He squinted toward the breezeway. "Okay, that's it. Think I'll say hello to my bride before heading back to work."

With no hesitation, he strode toward the café.

My aunt joined me. "I heard all that. I'm sorry. I should have—"

I stroked her forearm. "It's fine. Rhett and I need to pay more attention and plan for any unexpected events." I kissed her cheek. "I'm glad you and Sasha got things resolved."

"Me, too, however, for some reason . . ." Aunt Vera frowned. "I can't put my finger on it, but I still feel like a storm is brewing."

• • •

Late in the afternoon, I finally found time to call Cinnamon. I reached her voice mail, so I left her a message outlining my concerns about Midge Martin. If she was considering Midge a suspect, then a witness seeing Midge outside the Boldine Building on the morning Kylie was murdered had merit.

After closing the shop, I took Tigger home and dressed for my outing on the Pier.

Cart vendors as well as the two restaurants on the Pier had agreed that appetizers would be the Pier's focus for Food Bowl. I met up with Bailey and Tito at seven outside Mum's the Word diner. The place was overrun with customers. A line weaved out the door and along the boardwalk. One of the nearby vendors had been granted a liquor license with the caveat that the beverages could not leave the Pier. I purchased three glasses of wine and handed one to each of my friends.

Standing beside the Pier's railing, looking north toward the lighthouse, we toasted Tito's innocence.

"Here's hoping," Tito muttered.

"You are innocent, *mi amor*," Bailey whispered. "We all know it."

If only we could prove it, I thought.

"There sure are a lot of artists on the beach for this time of night," Bailey said. "Is that Audrey Tinsdale? I think she's teaching a class." She pointed. "See the three easels?"

I followed her finger and nodded. "It sure is."

Audrey, distinctive in her colorful smock and leggings, was guiding three students, each painting the view of the northern coastline.

"I wonder how she's doing," Bailey said. "She was close to Kylie."

"The whole family was."

I recalled the meeting with Audrey and Eugene last night on the boulevard. Both had seemed distraught about Kylie's death, yet I was still puzzled as to why Eugene felt the need to tell me his alibi. Was it because I'd observed Audrey and him arguing about Kylie? Had he been protecting his wife?

After we sipped our wine, Tito went in search of food, and Bailey said, "Jenna, we're going to take in the movie at the end of the boardwalk later. It starts at nine. Do you want to join us?"

"What's playing?"

"Who Is Killing the Great Chefs of Europe? With George Segal and Jacqueline Bisset."

"Sure." Seeing as I wasn't going to the All Star Barbecue event with Rhett, I had time on my hands. "So, c'mon, don't keep me on tenterhooks. What did the attorney tell you?"

"She's on the case." Bailey led the way to a small café table and perched on one of the backless stools.

"On the case." Tito snorted as he set three shrimp kebabs served on a bed of spicy cole slaw on the table. After taking a bite of his appetizer, he said, "What does *on the case* honestly mean?"

"She's putting out feelers."

"Feelers."

"Making calls."

"Calls." Tito grumbled and took a sip of wine. "Has she found someone who saw me on Gardenia Avenue? No, she has not."

"Neither has Flora Fairchild," I said glumly. "But she's not giving up. You know how much Flora likes you, Tito."

"Because I gave Home Sweet Home a great write-up when it opened."

Home Sweet Home sold beautiful gift items as well as home décor. Invariably, Flora updated her stock. I rarely visited the shop without finding something new.

We sat in silence, each of us nibbling on the shrimp.

After a long moment, Tito set his wine on the table and eyed his wife. "Gossipmongers are telling everyone I had it in for Kylie. I didn't."

"We know, sweetheart. We know." Bailey gazed at me. "Jenna, you've got suspicions. You told me so. Who do you suspect?" She curled her fingers, begging me to reveal something . . . anything. "C'mon, tell us your theories. You're a natural amateur sleuth."

I moaned softly. That was not the reputation I'd sought following college. I'd been hoping for go-getter, freethinker, and creative wizard. When I'd worked at Taylor & Squibb, I'd relished whenever my boss said I'd come up with a brilliant idea or he'd praised me because I'd thought outside the box. Was now the time to do that?

"Spill," Bailey demanded.

"Let's get a little more to eat." I gathered our empty plates, tossed them in a garbage can, and led my friends to another vendor, where I purchased a trio of mahi-mahi bites — each grilled in a lime marinade and tucked into a cupcake liner.

After we sat at a new café table, I told them about the two main suspects I was considering: Savannah Gregory and Midge Martin.

"Understand, I really like both of these women," I said, "but we know Tito isn't the killer, and someone else is. I don't want to rule anyone out."

"I can't imagine Midge killing anyone," Bailey said. "She's so easygoing and confident."

Tito said, "I am certain that an easygoing, confident person has murdered someone at some time in history."

"Yes, true, but" — Bailey screwed up her mouth — "a personal attack by Kylie couldn't have meant much to Midge."

"Reputation is everything to a celebrity," Tito said.

"True, but Midge is fair game now that she's a TV personality," Bailey countered. "Lots of people will be taking potshots at her. She had better grow a thick skin."

"I suppose so," Tito murmured.

I nibbled the mahi-mahi. It was moist and savory.

"Go on, Jenna," Bailey said. "Why do you suspect Midge?"

"My wedding planner, Harmony Bold, saw Midge outside the Boldine Building yesterday morning. I don't know if it was before Viveca saw Tito or before Tito saw Kylie or . . ." I polished off my snack. "According to Harmony, Midge regularly did business with Harmony's mother, who owns the jewelry store."

"Maybe Midge entered the building and hid in Your Wellness until Kylie arrived," Bailey said.

"How would Midge have gotten the code?" Tito asked.

Bailey thwacked his arm. "Didn't you hear Jenna? She frequents the jewelry store."

"That would get her into the building's foyer, not into the studio," Tito argued.

I sighed. "There are lots of unknowns."

Tito nudged his fish appetizer out of reach. "I have to admit Viveca's account of having seen me is bothersome. I was standing by the front entrance for a brief two minutes. Was she looking out the café window at the exact right moment, or was she lying in wait?"

"To what end?" I asked.

"Maybe she had reason to kill Kylie."

Bailey shook her head. "I heard her answering the police

questions. Viveca has worked for Alexa for one month, and she said she hasn't—*hadn't*—had any interactions with Kylie. Ever."

"Hold on," I said. "That pilates class where Kylie took on Alexa. When was that?"

"Two months ago," Bailey said. "Viveca hadn't been hired yet."

"Does that prove she's innocent?" Tito asked.

Bailey rubbed Tito's arm. "Most likely."

"But not Midge," he said, grasping at straws.

"Like Jenna's wedding planner said, my love, Midge being in the vicinity could have been a coincidence. I suppose Jenna could ask her outright." Bailey looked pleadingly at me. "Would you?"

"Uh-uh. I'll leave that to Cinnamon."

Bailey set her appetizer aside and leaned forward, elbows on the table. "Have you at least mentioned the Midge sighting to her?"

"I left a voice mail, but I'm afraid she'll think I'm overstepping."

"Why? You weren't investigating," Bailey said. "You were having a conversation with your wedding planner, and Harmony mentioned seeing Midge because of her family connection to the building."

"Tell us why you suspect Savannah Gregory," Tito said between bites.

I told them about seeing Savannah on Thursday night, lingering outside Intime, tears in her eyes. "Savannah confided that Kylie had introduced her to running but shared that running had ruined her feet, which had made her pack on weight. I deduced that she had feelings for Kylie, but Kylie didn't share them. Savannah was angry. Hurt."

"Is any of that motive to want her dead?" Bailey asked.

"People have killed for less." I added that Savannah went home with a migraine yesterday.

"If Savannah was faking the migraine," Tito said, "she might have been able to slip out of her house and sneak into the fitness studio."

"Unnoticed?" Bailey sat back and folded her arms. "She's a big girl. It would be hard for her to sneak in anywhere, and no one has mentioned seeing her so far."

If only the Boldine Building had had security cameras in place.

"Would Savannah's mother cover for her?" Bailey asked.

"For murder?" I shook my head. "I don't think so."

"I would protect Brianna at all costs."

I petted her shoulder.

"Is there a rear entrance to the building?" Tito asked.

"No. There are side entrances at either end of the complex," I said, "and those are visible from Buena Vista Boulevard, too." I rose to my feet. "Dessert, anyone?"

"Isn't everything an appetizer?" Bailey asked.

"I don't think so, merely appetizer-sized portions." I hooked a thumb. "I noticed cheesecake bites at the Seaside Bakery."

"I could use a coffee." Tito offered his hand to Bailey and pulled her to her feet.

"You know, Jenna," Tito said as we waited inside the bakery for our desserts, "Eugene Tinsdale was close to Kylie. Almost like a father or a mentor to her. He might know more about her acquaintances and who might have wished her—"

"He doesn't," I said. "Rhett and I ran into Eugene and Audrey last night while tasting food along the boulevard. The Tinsdales are mourning Kylie, but they don't have a clue who might have killed her."

I paid for the desserts and doled them out. We slipped outside into the cool night air.

"By the way," I said, "did you know Eugene might have an investor who could bail him out of losing the newspaper?"

"You're kidding," Tito said. "That's great."

"Speaking of investors," I went on, "Alexa believed Kylie had found an investor, for the same reason, to either buy out or help Eugene."

"Eugene's a good guy," Tito said. "He doesn't deserve to lose everything solely because circulation has waned. The darned digital phenomena—" He screwed up his mouth. "I wish I could afford to buy the paper."

Bailey squeezed his bicep. "Maybe Kylie's investor would be willing to—" She released Tito as if he were a hot potato. "I didn't mean . . . Jenna, please don't think that Tito or I would have, you know, iced Kylie so we could approach the investor."

I gawked at her. "Are you nuts? I didn't think that at all. You were proposing a solution, not plotting a murder." I offered a supportive smile. "Look, I know we're all on edge because another murder happened in our town—"

"And because I'm the main suspect," Tito cut in.

"But we will figure this out," I assured them. "We'll make sure the police find the real killer. Promise."

Chapter 11

Sunday morning, after a long run to clear my head, a brisk shower to brighten my mood, and a quickie egg-in-the-microwave breakfast that I enjoyed on the patio, I left another message for Cinnamon and asked her to call, despite misgivings that she might jump all over me for interference in her investigation.

A half hour later, I arrived at the shop feeling hopeful for Bailey and Tito. I couldn't explain why. I hadn't dreamed anything unusual. The weather was the same as the day before, pleasant but not overly sunny. Maybe the lingering paint fumes in the house had influenced me, or the sound of church bells had filled me with hope, or perhaps my spirits had lifted thanks to the enticing aroma of vanilla that I'd inhaled the moment I'd stepped into the shop. Whatever the reason, I appreciated it.

"Morning, Gran," I trilled.

She had beaten me to work yet again. "Morning, Jenna. Don't you look ready for autumn? Very attractive."

"Thanks." I'd donned a burnt orange lace-up sweater over jeans. "Did Katie bring a snack for us already?"

"Nope. I added vanilla to the coffee." Dressed in a tangerine-colored sweater and matching trousers, Gran seemed ready for spring.

I set Tigger on the floor. He bolted to the top of the kitty condo and hurtled down each flight.

"What's gotten into him?" Gran asked.

"Who knows?" Sometimes Tigger acted like a kitten and, at other times, a sage old cat. Today was a kitten day. "What's with the mess?"

Gran was sitting on a stool at the children's table, facing a pile of brightly colored shredded paper as well as an assortment of sticks, wires, bells, popsickle sticks, teeny plastic balls, and interwoven tubes that reminded me of the infuriating Chinese finger traps.

"I'm getting ready to teach a class on making a Bonka-style bird toy," she said.

"A what?" I sat on a stool and fingered through the array. I lifted a length of gold chain.

"A Bonka-style bird toy." Gran swished her hand above the

items. "With all these goodies, we'll fashion a toy that birds go gaga for. They peck and chew to their hearts' delight."

"How do you know so much about them?" I asked.

"My granddaughters adore their parrots and parakeets."

"They have both?"

"Indeed. Their mother is a saint." Gran chuckled. "The girls and I have made dozens of these. Today, I'm providing all the crafts, but I thought the shop could sell a few books to go along with them, so I preordered those. Hope you don't mind." She motioned to a stack of books at the far side of the table. "One is a cookbook for a bird's diet. We have a few in the shop for cats and dogs, so why not birds?"

I lifted *The Healthy Bird Cookbook: A Lifesaving Nutritional Guide and Recipe Collection* and browsed through it. "And the other books you've assembled?" I saw titles that included *The Parrot Problem Solver* and *Good Bird! A Guide to Solving Behavioral Problems in Companion Parrots*.

"They're helpful and should sell well."

I set the cookbook on the stack. "Who knew people cooked for birds? I assumed everyone bought bird food at a pet store."

"Birds can be finicky. They need proper food to keep their beaks and feathers up to snuff." Gran held up a bird toy she'd already made, which consisted of three tiers of finger traps plus a basket stuffed with shredded yellow paper. She shook it. The bell hanging from the bottom of the basket jingled. "Isn't it charming?"

Tigger meowed.

I searched for and found him beneath the table, pawing through scraps of newspaper. My insides jolted. The vision reminded me of the messy floor at Your Wellness when we'd found Kylie.

"Are you all right, dear?" Gran asked. "You yelped."

"Did I? Sorry. I didn't see newspaper on the table. But it's there. On the floor."

"I'd set a stack on one of the stools. It must have fallen off. I thought the children might use the newspaper to fill the baskets. Is that an issue?"

"No, it's . . ." My mind flooded with the same thoughts that I'd mulled over when Gran had led the papier mâché crafts session — the shredded paper at the crime scene. It hadn't been newspaper, more like bond paper. Some had red and black ink on it. Was that significant?

"Do you want me to throw it out?" Gran asked.

"No, of course not."

"Good morning." Katie appeared from the breezeway carrying a plate of treats. "Gran texted me with her plan for today, so I came in early. I'll be setting out a variety of coconut-based, kid-friendly cookies. You know, coconut dreams, my famous protein-rich cocoa bliss balls, and the like." She thrust a plate in my direction. "Hungry? I'll make some butterscotch pretzel haystacks, too. Those are always a kid favorite."

On the plate sat five yummy-looking cookies. I adored coconut. "Don't mind if I do. With a cup of vanilla coffee." Casting off the jumpiness from seeing the newspaper, I bounded to my feet and fetched myself a cup of coffee from the stockroom.

"Also"—Katie raised her voice so I wouldn't miss a word—"at the café, I'll be serving my version of bird's nest kale salad, made with soft-boiled eggs, chopped kale, julienned carrots, and wonton strips. It's going to be so good, if I do say so myself."

I pushed through the break in the drapes. "I can't wait to taste test it."

"If you approve, I'll serve it tomorrow as one of our daylong lunch choices," Katie added. "By the way, Min-yi will be visiting her mama in the kitchen today, if you want to see her, Jenna."

"You bet I do."

At noon, I went to the café for a baby fix. Min-yi, an adorable girl with jet-black hair and alert saucer eyes, loved sitting in a high chair and playing knock the blocks off the food tray. I was happy to oblige. Bend, pick up, and replace was good for my core muscles. When Min-yi went down for a nap, Katie made me two test items: the bird's nest kale salad and a grilled cheese sandwich with shredded parmesan grilled into the crust. Both were incredible.

Midafternoon, Cinnamon finally touched base. I took the call in the stockroom.

"Bucky and I missed you guys at the All Star Barbecue last night," she said.

"Rhett had to cancel, so Bailey, Tito, and I went to the Pier instead and caught the outdoor movie."

"You missed a great meal. I had my fill of ribs for a year."

"I'm envious."

"So, tell me about Midge Martin," she said, "although you realize we've got Midge on our radar because of the article found at the crime scene, don't you?"

"Yes, of course." I shared that Harmony had seen Midge near the Boldine Building on the morning of the murder and that I'd noticed Midge using a lip balm like the one found in Tito's pocket.

"Anything else?" Cinnamon asked.

I mentioned Savannah and outlined her motive. "She missed work Friday morning. Supposedly, she had a migraine."

"Okay. Thanks."

"I want you to know that I like both of these women, and I doubt either had anything to do with Kylie's murder, but with Tito—"

"Jenna, leave the rest to us." Cinnamon ended the call.

I couldn't tell by her solicitous tone if she'd been peeved or not. Honestly, I didn't care. I owed it to Tito and Bailey to be proactive.

At six p.m., after a raucous afternoon of dozens of tourists buying nearly every local restaurant cookbook we'd stocked and twenty-plus children making Bonka-style bird toys—Gran gave me a bird toy for Tigger—I closed up shop, drove my sweet cat home, and dressed for the family dinner.

• • •

Ever since I'd moved back to Crystal Cove, my family met for dinner on Sunday evenings, at my father's house or my aunt's house. Tonight, we were sharing our meal in Aunt Vera's dining room. The weather had cooled, making it too chilly to sit on the verandah facing the ocean. Sometimes, only the immediate family attended our dinners. At other times, the group included friends or significant others. Tonight's meal was a mix-and-match affair.

My father had arrived solo because Lola had to prepare for Tuesday's bash at the Pelican Brief Diner. Deputy Appleby was a no-show because he was canvassing people who had dined at Latte Luck Café on Friday morning in the hope that someone had seen more than Viveca or Harmony had. Jake Chapman, one of my father's dearest friends and the man who had saved my father from drowning over fifty years ago, had joined us; however, he was alone, as well. Although he was dating our mayor, Z.Z. couldn't take a moment to enjoy a soiree because she felt it was her duty to make the rounds of all the foodie venues. Bailey had shown up, but Tito had opted to stay home with the baby. Sadly, he wasn't in the mood to be hospitable.

I'd hoped Rhett, now that Intime's big night was over, would have been able to break free, but he hadn't. As I was heading out my door to walk to my aunt's house, he'd sent me a text apologizing. When I'd read it, my heart had wrenched, but I'd texted him that I understood. And I did. Soon, the investors would increase the staff, and all would be right with the world . . . and us.

"You're looking glum, Jenna." My father, who'd sneaked up behind me in my aunt's kitchen, poked me in the rib cage.

"Hey." I whipped around, potholders on both hands. "Dad, you're lucky I wasn't gripping the platter of spaghetti yet, or you could have ended up with spicy meat sauce down the front of your nice shirt and trousers."

My father held up his hands, palms forward. "Sorry. Never scare the chef. Lola warns me all the time."

"I'm not the chef. I'm the chef's helper." I nodded to my aunt, who was tossing a green salad. "I spooned the sauce onto the spaghetti. That's all."

He appraised the platter. "You did a masterful job." He kissed my cheek, then said, "Hi, Sis. You look pretty in pink."

"This caftan is maroon," my aunt said.

"Making sure you're not colorblind," Dad joked.

Aunt Vera chortled. "Grab the basket of bread, you goon, and take it to the table. And ask Jake to pour the wine. It's over there." She pointed to a bottle of chianti on the counter.

"On it." My father glanced at me over his shoulder as he neared the door. "Sweetheart, are you sure you're okay? Your forehead . . ." He twirled a finger.

"I'm worried about Tito. The police haven't arrested anyone. If he's their sole viable suspect—"

"Let's get seated," my father said, "and we'll discuss."

Most of my aunt's house was decorated with beach-friendly décor—rattans and florals and glass tabletops—but the dining room was upscale. Aunt Vera was never eager to show off her wealth, but when dining, she believed that her guests should be treated like royalty. On the far wall was a built-in hutch with an enviable amount of storage tucked into cased millwork with clever pop-latch doors. The oval mahogany table and oval-backed, white-padded chairs gave the room a subtle but elegant vibe. The white and silver-scrolled chandelier was sheer class, and the Persian silk and wool area rug was top-of-the-line.

After the five of us settled at the table and filled our plates, my father raised his wineglass in a toast. "To Vera, for an exceptional meal."

I said, "Hear, hear."

Jake, a lean, wiry man who reminded me of an aging cowboy, said, "Vera, if I weren't crazy for Z.Z., I'd be pursuing you. A woman who cooks with oregano always wins my heart."

My aunt flapped her hand. "Jake, you're a flirt and a liar. Until you fell for Z.Z., your heart always belonged to your beautiful departed wife."

And one other woman, we'd discovered about a year ago — Jake's first love.

"Well, you'd be next on my list," Jake said, his green eyes glinting with charm. He shrugged out of his leather jacket and hung it on the back of his chair.

"Now," my father said, "let's talk about — "

The doorbell chimed.

"Expecting anyone?" my father asked.

"No," my aunt said. "Jenna, would you answer, please? We can make room for one more."

When I opened the door, I was surprised to see Tina Gump, as leggy as ever in a miniskirt that was barely long enough to be called a skirt. She hoisted a to-go bag from Intime. "This is from Rhett. He wanted me to tell you how sorry he was."

My heart warmed. "When did you see him?"

"I deliver for the restaurant on Sundays."

I took the bag from her and smiled. "I knew you were industrious, carrying a full load of classes as well as serving as Brianna's nanny, but you deliver food, too?"

"I can't afford new duds unless I have extra cash," Tina said.

"My father is only covering tuition and books." For years, Tina had been estranged from her father and had turned to her uncle for advice and support. Now, however, she had returned to her roots, and she and her father were forging a new bond. I was happy for her.

"Well, good for you for following your dream," I said. "I can see school is boosting your confidence."

Tina grinned, no longer the fearful young woman I'd first met.

"Can you come in for a minute?" I asked.

"A few. Sure. I'd love to see everyone, but then I have to get back to work." Tina stepped inside.

I ushered her to the dining room.

My aunt hurried from her chair to envelope Tina in a hug. "Don't you look fabulous?" Aunt Vera tenderly toyed with a tendril of Tina's wavy hair, which Tina had swooped into a messy updo. "How's culinary school?"

"Cooking." Tina winked at my aunt. "Hi, Bailey. Jake. Cary."

It had taken six months of encouragement until Tina felt comfortable using everyone's first names. She'd been raised to address people formally, using Miss, Mister, or Missus.

I unpacked the bag Rhett had sent over and removed the aluminum carryout container. "Score!" I shouted. "Rhett sent us onion appetizers. By my count, at least two apiece. Dig in." I passed the container around the table. Who needed decorum when tasty food was piping hot?

Tina perched on the chair beside Bailey. "How's Tito doing?"

"That's what we were going to discuss," my father said.

Bailey frowned. "He thinks everyone believes he's guilty."

"I don't," Tina rushed to say. "No way."

Each person at the table echoed Tina's sentiment.

Bailey lifted her wineglass but didn't take a sip. "Have you heard anything from Flora?" she asked me.

"Not a peep."

"What's Flora doing?" My father passed the breadbasket around the table.

"I asked her to set up a phone tree to see if anyone . . . *anyone*," I stressed, "might have seen Tito on Gardenia Avenue on Friday morning."

Jake said, "I was on Gardenia on Friday, but I'm sorry to say I didn't see Tito's Prius."

"He wasn't driving his Prius," Bailey said. "It was in the shop. He was driving a loaner. A Celica."

"What color?" Jake asked.

"Dark blue."

"Broken front headlight?"

Bailey gasped. "Yes. Did you see it? Oh, Jake, please say yes."

Jake grinned. "Yes." He crossed his heart.

"Where?" she begged.

"Parked in front of that two-story Mediterranean with the giant red door." Jake widened his hands as he mentioned the door. "You know the one I mean. It's three times the size of a regular door. The owners rent out the house."

"That's where the band is staying," Bailey exclaimed.

"Why were you in the area, Jake?" my father asked.

"I was playing chess with a buddy."

"Oho, Jake," my father said. "A new secret revealed. I didn't know you played chess." He leaned forward on his arms. "How did I not know that?"

"I took it up recently."

Jake was extremely smart. He hadn't gone to college, for a number of sad personal reasons, but when he learned something, he excelled at it.

"Drop by the shop," my father said. "We'll play a game or two." Dad loathed boredom. He needed to keep busy. Chess was one of his passions. I'd never won a match against him. Neither had either of my siblings.

Bailey tapped the dining table. "Enough talking about chess. Jake, when did you see Tito in the Celica?"

"Let's see." Jake gazed upward. "I arrived around ten. The Celica wasn't there then. But when I went outside for a stretch at eleven—I needed some fresh air after getting my clocks cleaned—I saw it." Jake focused on Bailey and tented his fingers. "It was still there about an hour later when I left."

Bailey whooped. "That means Tito's alibi will hold up. He couldn't have killed Kylie. Oh, Jenna, we have a witness."

I blew her a celebratory kiss.

"Hold on," my father said. "Jake, you saw the car, but did you see Tito?"

Bailey said, "He was sitting in the car, listening to a meditation tape."

Jake pursed his lips. "I saw someone. I can't specifically say it was Tito."

"Who else would it have been?" I rasped.

"It was Tito." Bailey spanked the table. "My Tito. You have to tell the police, Jake."

"Will do." Jake saluted, knowing full well how important an alibi was, given his run-in with the law last year.

My father folded his arms. "If that's the case, if Tito is no longer a suspect, then who else would have wanted Kylie Obendorfer dead?"

"Midge Martin," Bailey stated.

"I agree." Tina bobbed her head.

I gaped at her. "How do you know Midge?"

"I deliver food for her restaurant, too. On Saturdays."

"Why would Midge want Kylie dead?" I asked, hoping to hear a stronger motive than Kylie claiming Midge had filched a recipe and had dubbed it her own.

"Her daughter," Tina said, and quickly paled. "Oh, my, what have I done? No, no, no. I shouldn't have . . ." She swatted the air. "I shouldn't have talked out of school."

I put a calming hand on her arm. "Whatever you know and, if it's a fact and not gossip, then you can tell us."

Tina squirmed in her chair. "Okay, last week" — she whispered, as if speaking louder might make whatever she had to say untrue — "I heard Midge and Kylie quarrelling. Kylie had slipped into the kitchen when I was packing the delivery warming bag. Intime likes me to transport items one at a time. Midge thinks it's okay for me to do three or four deliveries on my route."

"Go on," I encouraged.

"Anyway, Midge and Kylie were arguing about Midge's daughter, Marigold," Tina said. "Midge was blaming Kylie for ruining Marigold's self-esteem. From what I could gather, Kylie had butted in on Marigold's home economics class a while back. That's it. That's all I know. I couldn't stick around to hear anything else because I had to get going on the deliveries." Tina rose from her chair. "Like I should now. Bye."

The Roadrunner couldn't have fled the house faster.

Chapter 12

Monday morning, Bailey rang me as I was running on the beach. She hadn't been able to sleep. She'd worried all night about whether the police would believe Jake Chapman's sighting of Tito. Seeing as she was on pins and needles waiting for the answer and because she wasn't one hundred percent certain that Jake's testimony would exonerate her husband, she'd decided to go to Crystal Cove High School and meet with the principal. She wanted to follow up on Tina's account regarding Midge's daughter. She believed if she could provide a better motive for Midge, then Cinnamon might haul Midge into the precinct and grill her.

"Will you go with me?" Bailey begged. "Please?"

After eleven a.m., I expected a steady stream of customers at the shop, seeing as that was when the Nook's six-hours-of-lunch event would commence, but the first couple of hours would be quiet.

"Sure," I said. How could I refuse?

I ate a quick breakfast, dressed sedately in a white silk blouse, tweed blazer, and beige trousers, and took Tigger to the shop. Gran arrived minutes after I did. Quickly, I explained my mission with Bailey and asked Gran to watch over things. I added that Aunt Vera had texted me; she was already on her way in. She had scheduled an early-morning tarot reading. Gran assured me that the two of them could manage the shop.

Crystal Cove High School was located near Azure Park. Its architecture matched the rest of the town, with its white buildings and red-tiled roofs, but it wasn't a large campus, serving less than a thousand students. I had wonderful memories from my years there — art classes, acting in a play or two, rooting for the Toreadors, and, yes, attending a few parties.

Principal Baker was the same woman who had overseen my years at high school. She was also the home economics teacher who had guided Katie to her glorious future as a chef. If only I'd have taken a class or two back then.

"You're here!" Bailey cried as she hopped out of an Uber near the administration office. She grabbed me in a bear hug and released me. "I see you got the outfit memo." She flourished a hand in front of her clothes: white blouse, beige slacks, tweed jacket. "Have we dressed to impress?"

I smiled. "I decided to up my game to show respect."

"Me, too. Great minds think alike." Bailey linked her hand around my elbow and ushered me into the building.

The receptionist, Mrs. Garofalo, the same cherry-cheeked woman who'd sat at the L-shaped oak desk for nearly two decades, greeted us. "Ladies, you look like the Bobsey twins."

Bailey giggled. "Not on purpose."

"I used to dress like my best friend, too," Mrs. Garofalo said. "It was like we had ESP. She still calls me, out of the blue, exactly when I'm thinking of her. It's nice to have that kind of friend." She depressed the intercom button on the telephone and announced that we were here.

Principal Baker replied through the speaker, "Send them in."

After speaking with Bailey, I'd called the school and requested an appointment.

Mrs. Garofalo gestured to the closed door. "Enter at your own risk." It was her typical quip, one I'd heard her say numerous times. Not to worry. Principal Baker was a pussycat.

"Thank you," I said, and led the way.

Principal Baker rose from her boxy desk as Bailey and I entered. She'd aged a lot in thirteen years. I figured she was close to my aunt's age, mid-sixties. Smile lines feathered around her gentle eyes and full mouth. She hadn't dyed her hair, which was shockingly white. Once thin, she'd grown thicker at the waist.

Photographs of Principal Baker and many prominent people from Crystal Cove hung on the wall behind her desk.

"Welcome, ladies." She gestured toward slatted chairs opposite the desk. "Come in. Please sit."

A photograph on the desk caught my eye—Principal Baker beaming with six little girls wearing aprons and holding spatulas in front of an array of cookies.

"Are they your granddaughters?" I asked.

"My pride and joy. They keep me young. How are you both?"

I replied, "Fine."

Bailey said, "Not so fine. You might not know this, but I got married, and now my husband—"

"I heard," Principal Baker said. "He's a suspect in a murder. I'm so sorry."

"He's innocent," Bailey said. "Someone can verify his alibi."

"The person who can," I said, "should be talking with the police this morning."

Bailey twirled a hand. "In the meantime, we were wondering if you'd tell us about—" Her voice cracked.

"If you'd tell us about Midge Martin's daughter, Marigold," I finished.

"What about her?" Principal Baker folded her hands on her desk.

"A friend of ours," I began, "overheard Midge Martin arguing with Kylie O—"

"Kylie Obendorfer," Bailey cut in. "The victim."

"I knew Kylie tangentially," Principal Baker said. "Go on."

"Our friend heard the two women arguing," I continued. "Midge accused Kylie of ruining her daughter's self-esteem. Would you happen to know what that was about? Apparently, Kylie had butted in on Marigold's home economics class. *Your* class."

Principal Baker pursed her lips and unfolded her hands. She squared a few items on her desk and then gazed out the window with the view of the schoolyard. When she returned her focus to us, she said, "This is a delicate matter and should not be made public."

"Of course." I glanced at Bailey. She agreed, albeit reluctantly.

"First of all, Kylie didn't butt in on a class," Principal Baker said. "In September, she was writing an article about a cookie bake-off we were sponsoring. Ten regional teams were competing. Marigold was one of our prized bakers. Something went amiss, and Marigold's double chocolate chunk cookies exploded in the oven. No one knows what happened. Did one of the other teams sabotage the recipe? Possibly. Nothing could be proven."

"Kids can be cruel," I said.

"As for Kylie," Principal Baker went on, "she didn't just make fun of Marigold; she taunted her mercilessly in article after article. In addition, Kylie fat-shamed the girl, which made no sense. You see, Marigold was as thin as a rail."

I didn't read the foodie section with regularity; I'd missed the tirade. "And the newspaper's owner allowed this harassment?" I asked.

"I'm not sure Eugene—" Principal Baker peered at a picture hanging on the wall of Eugene, Audrey, and herself at a ribbon-cutting ceremony. "Eugene and I go way back. We attended grammar school together. Anyway"—she flicked the air—"to be truthful, I'm not sure Eugene was paying attention to what he was publishing at the time. He's had a lot on his mind, what with finances floundering." She folded her hands again. "As for Kylie's mean-spiritedness, I'm not sure where that derived from."

I said, "I suspect Kylie and Midge have had an ongoing feud."

Principal Baker tapped the edge of her desk. "Here's the tragedy, however. Marigold took a steep dive after that. She started binge eating and purging. She gave up baking and began to blame her mother for all her problems."

"And Midge blamed Kylie for the rift," Bailey whispered.

"I imagine so." Principal Baker studied her fingernails. "Marigold has grown quite somber. I've asked her to meet with our guidance counselor, but she has refused."

"Does she have any friends?" I asked. "Does she socialize?"

"She has a boyfriend," Principal Baker said. "He's an artist. You'd appreciate his style, Jenna, although his work is filled with despair."

• • •

When we left the principal's office, I said to Bailey, "Let's check in with Cinnamon."

"No, first I want to go to Shredding." She looked about ready to burst.

"Bailey . . ." My tone was cautious. "We're going there tonight for dinner, remember? We can—"

"I want to talk to Midge now. Please. Let's clear the air. Let's find out what happened. It's not time for the restaurant to open yet."

"Bailey, I'm going to sound like our chief of police for a moment. This is scary stuff. A killer is on the loose, and it's no laughing matter. You can't storm in on—"

"Stop!" Bailey held up her palm. "Over the past couple of years, you have stormed. You have charged. You have done what every woman in your situation would do, taken the lead. Alexa would tell me to be brave; be bold. Well, that's what I'm going to do. I'm going to boldly protect my husband. If you're not going with me, I'll go alone. Midge will be there. She'll be in prep mode." Bailey marched toward Buena Vista Boulevard.

I chugged after her. "You are so like your mother."

"Tell me about it."

The main drag was once again open. Cars were streaming along. Foot traffic was at a minimum. As we were passing Nuts and Bolts, I peeked inside. My father was standing at the counter, playing chess with Jake, who was sitting on a stool.

"Bailey." I tapped her shoulder. "Let's ask Jake what happened with the police. If Tito is cleared—"

I gripped her elbow. She resisted, but then gave in.

I opened the door to my father's shop. A bell chimed overhead. The place was deep but narrow. Streamlined shelves, each categorized with labels made from a label machine, held multiple boxes of screws, nails, and whatnot. Dozens of pictures commemorating family adventures lined the wall behind my father. I especially loved the one of my sister, brother, and me, twenty-some years ago, rock climbing. My sister had broken every fingernail and had bemoaned her fate for days.

My father grinned. "Well, well, look what the cat dragged in. Shouldn't you be at work?" he asked.

"Bailey and I had an errand to run." I strode to the counter and patted Jake on the back. "So, did you talk to the police?"

"Not yet. I left a message."

Bailey huffed. "Jake, you promised. You crossed your heart."

He nodded sheepishly. "You're right. Time is of the essence. Mind you, Chief Pritchett probably thinks I'm an old crank with nothing to offer, but I'll go to the precinct right now." He tapped the chessboard. "Don't move anything, Cary," he warned. "I've got a photographic memory. I know where every man is. And it's my turn."

As Jake strode out the door, my father snickered. "Bailey, you sure know how to get your way. Just like your mother."

"That's what I said." I jutted a hand at my pal.

Bailey winked at him. "She's my idol. She taught me every trick in the book. Now, Jenna" — she gripped my arm — "let's go."

I didn't fight her. I knew she would hound me until she'd accomplished her mission.

Midge's restaurant, Shredding, was located on Buena Vista Boulevard between Say Cheese, a gourmet cheese shop, and the bank. Like my father's shop, the restaurant was narrow but it was airy with an appealing green-and-white décor, floor-to-ceiling windows facing the boulevard, and lots of potted plants, giving the place the feel of a botanical garden.

The waitstaff was setting tables with white tablecloths as we entered. The enticing aroma of roast chicken, coriander, and curry emanated from the kitchen at the rear of the building.

Barging ahead with purpose, Bailey marched into the kitchen. I followed.

Midge Martin, dressed in a snazzy lime green chef's coat, her frizzy hair held back in a stylish bandanna, bustled near her sous chefs, chopping green onions while pointing at preparations and giving commands. "More curry. More cumin. Where's the yogurt? You, new girl" — she aimed her knife at a lithe woman — "julienne more carrots."

"Yes, chef," the woman said.

From what I could tell, Midge was prepping for the tandoori chicken salad she'd told me about.

"Jenna," Midge said as she caught sight of me, "what's up?" Then she spied Bailey. Her forehead pinched with worry. "Is everything okay? Your dinner reservation is hours away."

Bailey said, "I need to ask you a question."

Midge sliced the knife through the air. "I can't talk. I'm way too busy."

"One minute. C'mon." Bailey hooked a thumb to follow her toward the walk-in refrigerator.

Midge rolled her eyes at me and mouthed: *What's with her?*

I didn't respond. I followed Bailey. As I did, I noticed framed photographs of Midge on her television show, Midge with TV talk show hostesses, and Midge with her daughter. None with her husband, of course. He'd walked out over ten years ago.

With a huff, Midge set the knife on the chopping block and trailed me.

When the three of us drew into a circle, Midge said, "What's the issue?"

"A witness saw you outside Your Wellness on Friday morning," Bailey blurted.

"A witness? To what?" Midge shook her head. "I don't understand."

"Kylie O was murdered upstairs," Bailey said. "What were you doing there, sneaking around?"

Midge's mouth drew into a thin line. "You can't possibly think—" She peeked over her shoulder at her staff and back at us. "I didn't kill Kylie, if that's what you're intimating."

"I repeat, what were you doing there?"

Midge huffed. "How dare you, Bailey. You know me better than that. I wouldn't hurt a fly, although I would destroy an army of ants."

Bailey tapped her foot. Waiting.

Midge jammed her fists against her hips. "Oh, I see. You caught Kylie and me going at it the other day, didn't you? Yeah, I remember spying you in the crowd. Kylie and I shared a few words. Big deal. Who didn't with her? She could be so caustic."

"Why were you outside the Boldine Building?" Bailey asked, as persistent as a hunting dog with its teeth sunk into its prey.

Midge narrowed her gaze. "If you must know, there's a new restaurant going in at the southernmost townhouse in the mini San Francisco units."

I knew the restaurant she was talking about. It planned to feature Asian fusion food.

"Katie—yes, your Katie—told me the chef was planning to serve up one of my exclusive recipes." She hooked a thumb over her shoulder. "So I went there to do reconnaissance. To check her out and size her up. I couldn't see much. Nothing, in fact. All the windows are covered with butcher paper. But then suddenly, the chef—who is also the owner, like me—burst out the front door. Astonished, I ducked to the left and acted as if I was peering into the jewelry store. That must have been when your witness saw me."

Bailey screwed up her mouth. "Go on."

"Subsequently, I have approached the chef, and she and I have made amends. She does not intend to use any of my recipes. Whatever Katie heard was a rumor. False."

"And what about the falling-out between your daughter and Kylie?" Bailey pressed.

"What falling-out?" Midge asked.

"Marigold was in a bake-off. At school. Her submission blew up. Kylie wrote about what happened. She ridiculed Marigold for the fiasco."

Midge tilted her head but kept mum.

"And then Kylie fat-shamed her," Bailey added.

I blinked, not believing my friend would bring up that particular point.

Midge's mouth dropped open. Her eyes pooled with tears. She sucked in air and wrapped a protective arm across her chest. "My poor daughter. Poor sweet Marigold." A tear leaked down her cheek. She swiped it with a knuckle. "What she suffered at the hands of Kylie O was horrific. There are no words to express my grief. And then Marigold—" She bit back a sob. "She and I are working through the issues, but it might take years for her to come to grips with what happened."

"So you held Kylie responsible," Bailey said.

"Sure I did, but I wouldn't kill her." Midge punched the air. "When I opened my restaurant, I received all sorts of bad reviews. I understood. People say horrible things. They always will. I advised Marigold that we women have to shore up when under fire. We have to have courage." She pounded a fist against her palm. "We are working through Marigold's issues. She's strong. She will survive. I did not kill Kylie. If that's all?" Midge raised her chin and breathed sharply through her nose. "Perhaps, in light of this personal and unwarranted attack, you'd like to cancel your reservation for tonight."

It wasn't a question. It was a command.

Chapter 13

As Bailey and I trudged back to the Cookbook Nook, I felt awful for having suspected Midge of murder and made a mental note to develop a spine. I would not—could not—let my pal or anyone else run roughshod over me again. Ever. I was nice, but not that nice.

When we entered the shop, Gran was ringing up a regular customer at the counter while touting the upcoming series of holiday cookie cookbooks we'd ordered. Aunt Vera was sitting at the vintage kitchen table fitting pieces into the food-themed jigsaw puzzle.

"Are you all right?" my aunt asked, abandoning a piece with five notches and following Bailey and me to the counter. Her silver caftan swished and caught Tigger's fascination. He pounced toward her. She nudged him with the toe of her slipper, but he wouldn't be dissuaded.

"Bailey . . ." I fanned the air. "Tito . . ."

"Didn't Jake call the police?" my aunt asked. "I thought that was the plan after last night's dinner."

"He contacted the precinct," Bailey said, sidling in beside Gran to sort through the morning's receipts. "But Cinnamon didn't respond."

"We ran into Jake at the hardware shop." I scooped up Tigger and gave his chin a scrub. "He said he would head to the precinct straightaway. That should clear things up."

"From your lips . . ." Bailey sighed.

I set Tigger on his kitty condo and assessed the shop. The bookshelves were a mess. "Did we have a sale?" I asked.

Aunt Vera chortled. "At least fifty customers have come in so far this morning."

"Fifty?" I gawped.

"That's my fault," Katie said as she waltzed from the breezeway carrying a tray of mini sandwiches, tacos, and tiny bowls of salad. Her chef's coat was lightly splattered with something pinkish. Her cheeks were flushed. "I invited a foodie reviewer from Monterey, who has a huge online presence, to cover us during the Food Bowl. She has declared the Nook one of her top ten. Isn't that wonderful?"

"Wonderful," I said, but inwardly sighed. Kylie O had tried so hard to protect her territory from Tito, and yet, an online reviewer had been able to make headway without so much as a ripple of conflict.

"By the way," Katie went on, "have you seen the line outside the café? Hoo-boy, are we going to be busy. It's winding all the way to the street."

I'd seen the line when entering. I hadn't put two and two together. "Gran, I'm sorry I was out when there was that much activity."

"No worries." She fanned the air. "Your aunt and I had it handled."

"Indeed, we did," Aunt Vera chimed.

Katie said, "By the way, get ready. We will be flipping customers like hotcakes, every hour on the hour. So eat up." She motioned to the tray. "You will need sustenance. I've brought you some tastings of everything."

Aunt Vera took a mini sandwich and bit into it. "Scrumptious."

"What you don't eat, I'll set in the breezeway." Katie regarded Bailey and me. "Explain the matching outfits and the long faces."

I quickly told her about our meeting with Principal Baker and added that Tito had not yet been exonerated.

"You two particularly need to eat." Katie thrust the tray toward me.

I chose a shrimp taco stuffed to the gills with shredded everything and took a bite. "Divine."

Bailey waved Katie off. "Not hungry. By the way, Midge Martin was seen at Your Wellness on the morning of the murder, but when I confronted her—"

"You confronted her?" my aunt squawked. "Jenna, how could you let Bailey—"

"I have no control over her," I countered. "Bailey is like a locomotive with no brakes."

Bailey smirked. "I am pretty forceful."

"You keep on doing what you're doing, young lady." Gran took one of Katie's treats. "A wife should stand by her man."

"Thanks, Gran." Bailey refocused on Katie. "Anyway, to answer your question, when I asked Midge why she'd been in the area, she claimed you told her the owner of the new Asian fusion restaurant was planning on serving up one of Midge's recipes, so she'd gone there to check it out."

"I never said anything like that," Katie protested. "I told her I thought the restaurant was going to be tough competition for her because they would be located close to one another and going head to head on creating clever recipes. She must have mistaken my meaning. I hate when people do that." Mumbling, she pivoted, set the tray in the breezeway, and returned to the café.

As I watched her go, I wondered whether Midge had mistaken Katie's meaning, or whether she'd deliberately lied to us to hide the real reason she'd been hanging outside the Boldine Building.

"Good morning," Cinnamon Pritchett said as she breezed into the shop, hat in hand, her uniform crisp. Her hair was slightly mussed. She must have ridden her bicycle over. I searched for it and saw it parked in the bike rack near Beaders of Paradise. "I have good news."

Bailey hurried to her, hands clasped. "About my husband?"

Cinnamon beamed. "Yes. Tito is officially in the clear."

"Jake did it!" Bailey jumped up and down. "He came through. Yay. Thank you. Bless you."

"Yes, Jake vouched for him," Cinnamon said. "Also, Flora Fairchild's phone tree worked. The gardeners for the Smiths saw Tito in the Celica and could identify him right down to the color of shirt he was wearing." She jutted her hand toward Bailey. "Congratulations are in order."

Bailey shook with her.

Cinnamon leaned in. "Between you and me, I never thought he did it."

"What about the lip gloss?" I asked. "Have you had that tested against the writing on the mirror?"

Bailey threw me a scathing look.

"The lab is still determining factors," Cinnamon said, "although they did find contaminating alleles."

"Speak English, Chief," Bailey said.

"Someone else's DNA," I said, "transferred by kissing."

"Don't worry," Cinnamon said. "It's probably a non-event with no specific outcome."

Bailey breathed easier.

Cinnamon placed her hat on her head and smoothed the rim. She nodded to Bailey. "Have a good day."

"You bet I will, Chief," Bailey chirped.

As Cinnamon strode across the parking lot to where she'd parked her bicycle, Bailey said, "Should we have told her about our chat with Midge, who now has a more substantial motive?"

"Cinnamon will be checking out Midge," I assured her. At least I hoped she would, given our conversation yesterday. "For now, let's revel in the fact that your husband is off the hook!" I hugged Bailey and she melted into me. "Do you want to call him?"

"You bet I do." She raced into the stockroom.

I clapped my hands. "Okay, everyone, let's get this place spruced up. Straighten the shelves. Fix the displays. If Katie is determined to turn the café's tables every hour, the next wave of customers will be bounding in here in a few minutes to make purchases."

Three hours later, when the shop was experiencing a lull, I decided to take a coffee break. Rather than enjoy it by myself, I swung by Latte Luck Café, purchased two espressos, and strode to Intime. Rhett would be in full prep mode for tonight's dinner, but I figured he could spare ten minutes for a kiss and a sip of something warm.

When I entered the bistro, the soft strains of Edith Piaf's "La Vie en Rose" was playing through the speakers. A few of the staff were singing along.

I made my way to the kitchen and found Rhett crooning into a wooden spoon. When he caught sight of me, his cheeks tinged pink.

"Sinatra, you're not," I joked.

He hurried to me and pecked my cheek. "What brings you around?"

"We missed you at our Sunday dinner. Thank you for the onion tarts. They were appreciated."

"About me canceling—"

"You don't need to explain."

"Yes, I do." Rhett clasped my elbow and guided me out of the kitchen to the foyer by the hostess's lectern. "You won't believe what happened."

"Try me."

"It turns out that my executive chef is pregnant and has been ordered off her feet."

"What?" I screeched and instantly covered my mouth. "Okay, that was an overreaction on my part, but, really? Why?"

"It turns out she's had two miscarriages."

"I've heard bed rest doesn't solve anything." I'd studied up on it while Bailey was pregnant. "It can make things worse."

"She's not willing to take the risk. So she quit."

I stroked his arm. "I'm so sorry."

"I'm sorry for us." Rhett clasped my hand. "I've got two new chefs coming in tomorrow for interviews. I will hire one of them. We won't have any downtime. Maybe, if they're both great, I can hire both of them. Plus, the investors have found a third manager, but she can't start for two weeks." His shoulders slumped. "I thought this enterprise was going to be easier."

I smiled. "Joan Didion said, 'Memory fades, memory adjusts, memory conforms to what we think we remember.'" My father often memorized quotes and asked all of his children to do the same. He felt they would come in handy when facing a personal trial.

"What you're saying is I'm living in a fantasy world?" Rhett asked.

I laughed. "No, I'm saying how quickly the mind forgets tribulations. Need I remind you how you toiled at the Grotto? Need I also mention a former boss of yours who happened to set her restaurant on fire so she could run off with all the art in order to recoup the money from the insurance company?"

Rhett rubbed his neck. "Got it."

"Forget the bad stuff; remember the good stuff." I caressed his arm. "No business is easy. You need to view things clearly and, sadly, not trust anyone you don't know well."

"We will get this resolved," he whispered and stroked my hair. "Before our wedding day."

"How about before our trip to Napa?" I grinned. "You know your folks will grill you like a shish kebab."

Rhett roared, a wonderful sound I hadn't heard in weeks. "Thank you for coming in. I needed to see your shining face."

"I needed to see yours."

We kissed tenderly and polished off our espressos in comfortable silence.

• • •

As I was strolling along the boulevard, heading back to the shop, I spied Alexa and her father standing outside the Boldine Building. Both were watching an electrician install a pair of security cameras above the front door.

I drew near and said, "Hey, Alexa. Eugene."

Alexa swiped a finger under each eye. Had she been crying? She centered the charm on her necklace, squared her shoulders, and forced a smile. "Hi."

"Hello, Jenna," Eugene said. "If only these cameras had been here the other day. Maybe the police would have seen who'd gone in after Kylie."

Or had entered before, I mused.

"How are you doing, Alexa?" I asked.

"I'm okay. Sad." She pressed her lips together. "Trying to make sense of everything."

"All of her clients have canceled for the week," Eugene said. "It's to be expected, but it's as if they blame her."

"That's not it, Dad." Alexa shot him a miffed look. "They don't want to be in the studio. They don't want to think about what happened. They don't want to picture it in their minds. It's not me they're rejecting. It's—"

"Your business will suffer," Eugene said.

"It's temporary. Do you hear me? Temporary." Alexa regarded me. "Once we have a memorial for Kylie, it'll be better. Don't you think, Jenna? You've experienced loss. Time heals, after all, like the saying goes."

"It does get easier," I said. "You'll still have memories, of course, but they're not as sharp or as painful." When I'd lost David, my husband, I'd mourned him for a long time. When he'd turned up alive a few years later, I'd hated him with a passion. When he'd died for real, the loss had been much easier to accept.

"I hope you're right," Alexa said.

"Have the police stayed in contact with you?" I asked.

"A bit. They're not saying much." She shrugged one shoulder. "Have you been in touch with them? I know you're really close to Chief Pritchett, and with Tito being the main—"

"Actually, Tito is off the hook. A witness came forward verifying his alibi."

"He is?" Alexa reached for my hand. "That's great."

"Great," Eugene echoed.

"Who do you suspect, Jenna?" Alexa asked. "You've solved other murders. Maybe we could bat around theories. You—"

"Honey, don't do this to yourself. Don't speculate." Eugene wrapped an arm around his daughter's shoulders and squeezed. "C'mon. Let me buy you a coffee. Nice seeing you, Jenna."

• • •

At six p.m., I closed the shop and, exhausted from ringing up more sales than I could remember in one day—the Nook's Food Bowl event had definitely been the driving force—I nabbed Tigger and headed home.

After feeding him a can of tuna, I set a homemade potpie in the oven. I'd made six of them a month ago and had frozen them for the coming winter months. A couple of years ago, I would have been stymied as to how to make them. My mother had done all the cooking while I was growing up. Now, thanks to Katie, I viewed recipes in smaller segments—five to seven ingredients—which made cooking manageable.

Next, I poured a glass of wine. I was too tired to paint, and way too tired to read, and way, way, way too tired to ponder my immediate future with Rhett, so I switched on the television to the Cutting Edge Cooking channel.

To my surprise, the channel was featuring a six-episode series of *Shredding.* In the opening segment, Midge, in her colorful chef's coat, was preparing a vegetarian chopped salad. First, she took a wedge of lettuce to task with a Wüsthof ten-inch blade. The wedge didn't stand a chance. In a matter of seconds, the lettuce was shredded. Next, she set in on a trio of cucumbers and followed that with red cabbage. Without looking as she chopped, she spoke to the audience. How she didn't slice off a fingertip was beyond me.

I watched the episode in amazement, knowing I would never feel as comfortable as Midge with a blade in my hand. Slow and steady would forever win the race for me.

When the episode concluded, I checked on the potpie. It required another fifteen minutes so that the crust would turn a warm golden brown.

Settling back on the couch, I clicked on episode two of *Shredding*.

Midge, in her lime green chef's coat and neatly fitting bandanna, was tackling a roast turkey that she would then shred to within an inch of its life and use in a turkey vegetable soup. Step by step, she took the audience through the proper way to truss a turkey.

"First, locate the center of your piece of twine, and then wrap both ends around the neck bone, in between the two breasts. See it here?" She pointed to the spot. "Second, tuck the wings under the bird. Like this." She demonstrated. "Third, pull the twine tightly and tie a knot to secure everything. Ta-da!"

As Midge gave the twine a hard tug, reveling in the way she'd conquered the dead bird, my stomach lurched. All I could picture was a killer stringing Kylie into the reformer and pulling the rope tightly around her neck.

I switched off the television and sat upright. How had the killer lured Kylie into submission? Had he or she knocked her out? Doped her? Had Kylie come in to work out, ready to punk Alexa with her brazen entry, but the killer, to her surprise, was lying in wait?

The killer had to have used the security code to enter the studio. Who, other than Alexa, would have known it? Viveca, of course. And Kylie, by Alexa's admission. Savannah might have known it, having learned it from Kylie. How would Midge have figured it out? Did she work out at the studio?

Or, on that fateful morning, had Midge spied Kylie entering the building, followed Kylie to the second floor, and raced into the studio before the doors had locked?

Chapter 14

I slept fitfully and awoke in a pool of perspiration. It wasn't the potpie's fault. It had been scrumptious. I blamed it on the extra glass of wine I'd consumed while I wrote down the theories that had been swimming around in my mind.

Parched, I downed two full glasses of water and took a fast run. Then I treated myself to an ice cold shower—chilly, but deserved—after which I threw on a chunky brown sweater and corduroys. There was a nip in the air.

Tuesdays were our single day off during the week. Seeing as the shop had met its monthly financial goal after yesterday's boon, I didn't feel the need to open the shop, even though it was the last day of the Food Bowl event.

Instead, I decided to indulge in one of my new passions, a crossword puzzle. I opened the daily delivery of the *Crystal Cove Courier*, found the section with the crossword, poured myself a strong cup of coffee, and moseyed to the back patio table. Tigger accompanied me and leaped into my lap.

I opened the section and laughed when I saw the crossword had been specifically designed for Food Bowl week. Knowing the answers should be a cinch—I was up to date on all my foodie knowledge—I set to work. Unlike my father, who did his crossword puzzles in pencil so he could erase, I did mine in pen. I didn't mind scratching out a wrong answer. I was not a perfectionist.

Clue 1 across was five letters: *offered at a culinary bookshop.* I smiled. How nice to have the shop acknowledged. *Books* wasn't the answer because the word *book* was in the clue. Hmm. Not saltshakers. Not cookie jars. Apron? I didn't write it down yet, and eyed clue 2 down: *a shop with tasty tomes, with 4 across.* Eight letters down, four across. *Cookbook Nook* was the correct answer. I wrote it in and studied 1 across again, ending in C. Could it be *magic* because we'd featured that event this week? I wrote it in lightly.

"Moving on," I said to Tigger.

He meowed.

"What am I doing, you ask? A puzzle to kick my brain into gear."

Food Bowl was its own answer, eight letters, no space. *Climb*, the answer for getting to the top of the Santa Cruz Mountains. *Music*, heard at Azure Park. *Paper*, what the *Courier* printed on. *Rooftop*, seven-letter word for where the fish fry would take place.

When I noticed the *e* in *Kylie*, the answer for food reviewer, crisscrossed the word *Shredding*, the answer for Midge's restaurant, and saw that the *S* in *Shredding* served as the last letter for the answer *pilates — one of three exercises suggested for the week*—I winced. The juxtaposition of the three words made me flash on Alexa's studio, the shredded paper, and poor Kylie, strangled to death.

Did Midge kill her? If not, who else had a strong enough motive?

Losing my appetite for completing the puzzle, I folded the paper, took it to the kitchen, and set it on the counter. I fed Tigger and popped a piece of sourdough into the toaster for me.

And then, craving a day without controversy or thoughts of death, I telephoned Bailey and asked if she, Tito, and Brianna wanted to accompany me to Azure Park for Food Bowl festivities. Bailey said she and the baby would love to, but Tito, thanks to being exonerated, was interviewing the band he'd planned to interview Friday. We agreed to meet in an hour.

• • •

Azure Park was the town's largest park, fitted with a sandy play area for children and loads of gorgeous trees for shade. At the north end of the park stood a permanent event stage. A huge arced tent protected the stage. Monthly, the stage featured live music. During Food Bowl week, bands were playing at night.

White tents circled the perimeter of the park, many of which had been rented by local restaurants wanting an additional venue for the week. In the center of the park stood café-style tables as well as small food vendor carts with clever names like Bone Sucking Sauce, Pita Wraps, Meat Moguls, the Grill Reaper, and Waffle Wonderland.

Bailey, with Brianna in her stroller, was waiting for me beside the Fruit on a Stick cart. When she caught sight of me, she raced to me and grabbed me in a bear hug. "My husband is so happy," she said. "Tito," she added, as if she'd needed to clarify. "He's on cloud nine." She released me and returned to Brianna. "Isn't Daddy happy? Yes, he is." She tickled her daughter's chin and adjusted the girl's pink giraffe-themed blanket.

"Yoo-hoo, Bailey!" a woman cried. "Jenna."

Flora Fairchild, walking with Pepper Pritchett, strode purposefully toward us. Both were wearing sweaters with beaded necklines over trousers.

"I'm so happy to hear the phone tree worked." Flora stroked her thick braid.

"What phone tree?" Pepper asked.

Flora explained.

Pepper said, "I heard Jake Chapman came forward as a witness."

"He did," I said. "Having Jake as well as the Smiths helped corroborate Tito's alibi."

Pepper flicked a finger. "I'm sure one was all my daughter needed."

Flora threw her longtime friend a sour look. "Yes, but the more the merrier. When you were a suspect, weren't you relieved when someone could verify your whereabouts? Wouldn't you have been thrilled to have had two or three come forward?"

Touché, I thought. Bringing up Pepper's run-in with the police was a mighty jab.

"Oh, look, hamburger sliders." Pepper strode away.

Flora pecked Bailey on the cheek. "Glad I could help."

"Me, too," Bailey murmured.

As Flora trotted after Pepper, I spotted Savannah Gregory, who was dressed in a billowing white Renaissance-style dress, paying for a treat at Pita Wraps. I excused myself from Bailey and hurried to her.

"Savannah," I called.

Savannah whirled around, and I bit back a gasp. I'd never seen her wearing so much makeup. Heavy base. Fake eyelashes. Too much rouge. Given her outfit, she reminded me of a woman in a bordello.

"Pretty dress," I said, stymied as to what else to say.

"Thank you." Savannah lowered her chin, avoiding eye contact.

"How are you?" I asked, keeping my tone in check. "Your mother told me—"

"Mom worries too much." Savannah received her pita wrap of

julienned ham, sprouts, and mustard tucked into a parchment cone, and then took a napkin from the dispenser and moved toward one of the unoccupied café tables.

I followed her. "I'm here with Bailey. Care to join us?"

"No."

"Um, I wanted to touch base. Thursday night you'd seemed so . . ." I didn't add *forlorn.*

"I'm fine." Savannah sat at the table and set her white macramé purse on the neighboring chair.

Although she didn't extend an invitation, I sat, as well.

"The police questioned me about Kylie," Savannah said, not making eye contact with me.

"Why?" I asked. Of course, I had my own reasons to wonder whether she'd had a hand in the murder. Blaming Kylie for her bad feet. For her weight. For her broken heart.

"Someone told the police they saw me Thursday night outside Intime, peering in at Kylie, as if . . ." Savannah hiccuped. "As if I was plotting against her."

I held up both hands. "Not me. There were lots of people roaming the streets that night."

"No, not you. I never suspected you. It could have been anyone." Savannah's shoulders rose and fell, but her chin and gaze remained lowered. "There were so many people out that night."

"Why would you have plotted against Kylie?" I asked.

Savannah took a bite of her wrap. "Supposedly, the police found a mean-spirited article written by Kylie about me at the crime scene." A tear leaked down her cheek. She mopped it with a napkin. "Kylie panned a cake I made in a review."

"The Alice in Wonderland cake."

"You saw the article?"

I nodded.

"Kylie could be cruel," Savannah whispered.

Apparently to everyone other than the Tinsdales.

"It was common knowledge that Kylie and I had been running buddies for a long time," Savannah added. "And many knew that I gave it up when my feet started to hurt. The police think that's my motive. Blaming Kylie for the reason my body fell apart. But it wasn't her fault."

Hmm. That wasn't what she had intimated on Thursday night.

"I mean, it was, but I didn't hold myself blameless. I need . . . more self-control." Savannah pushed her pita wrap aside.

"How are you feeling?" I asked. "Your mother told me you went home with a migraine Friday morning."

"I'm better. I was in bed for the longest time. Lights out. Ice on my forehead and the back of my neck." Savannah's forehead pinched, as if she were reliving the pain. "When I wasn't in bed, I watched cooking shows and tried out some new recipes. Keeping my mind busy takes my mind off the ache."

"Were you alone?"

"The police asked the same thing," Savannah said. "Yes, I was. No one can corroborate that I was there." She raised her chin and started to blink. Rapidly. Were the fake eyelashes giving her trouble? She pulled a compact from the outer pocket of her purse and studied her eyes. She tweaked the offending intrusion, took another look at her face, and sucked back a sob. "How's Alexa doing, do you know?"

"Actually, I ran into her with her father. She's worried about her business."

"I guess she'd have to be. I can't imagine anyone would want to train with her again." Savannah snapped the compact closed and returned it to her purse. "Mother said Alexa hasn't come in to the café at all. She's been a regular for the past couple of years, but—" She glanced to the right. "Speaking of my mother, there she is. By Bacon Blast. I've got to go. Thanks for checking on me."

Ponderously, Savannah rose from the chair and waddled across the park. Seeing her slow movements, I couldn't picture her being able to sneak into the Boldine Building, let alone overpower Kylie, who had been at the peak of physical fitness.

I rejoined Bailey, who was cooing to her daughter. "I'm wondering . . ."

"About?" Bailey asked.

"Savannah said something that made me question whether the killer had a peeve against Alexa, and therefore, killed Kylie at the studio."

"To what end?"

"To ruin Alexa's business."

Bailey's eyes widened.

I stared after Savannah. "Something was off about her."

"About Alexa?"

"Savannah. She was wearing a ton of makeup. I've never seen her with any on."

"Maybe she woke up with a bad case of acne. I wear a lot of foundation if a zit has reared its ugly head."

"Okay, so do I," I conceded. "When will that nasty plague go away, by the way? By the time we reach menopause?"

Bailey laughed. "One can hope."

"Even so, I don't apply makeup with as heavy a hand as Savannah," I went on. "She must have used a palette knife to put it on. Turpentine will be needed to remove it."

Baily roared. "You're mean."

"Being honest. She has such low self-esteem."

"Like me with this" — Bailey patted her abdomen — "and Midge's daughter and so many others. It's almost an epidemic." She pushed the stroller toward Waffle Wonderland. "I need sugar."

"Ahem. Sugar isn't going to help you get rid of the baby bump."

"Hush your mouth, devil woman!" Bailey pushed faster. Over her shoulder she said, "You know, maybe Savannah never learned how to apply makeup."

I swiveled and spied Savannah hugging her mother. Shari, who never wore makeup either, toyed with a ringlet around Savannah's face. Savannah wrenched free. Clearly, she didn't want to be babied.

Bailey ordered a Belgian waffle dusted with powdered sugar, and we settled at a new café table. "How's it going with you and Rhett?"

"Over the weekend, he lost his other executive chef."

"Oh, no. How could you not lead with that?" Bailey offered me a bite of the waffle.

I took it and hummed my approval. "Because it's not a big deal. The investors are providing funding for two more chefs and a third manager. It'll all come together."

Bailey twirled a finger in front of my nose. "You're acting very calm about it, meaning you are anything but calm."

"My aunt has told me that worry never solved any problem."

"Neither does putting one's head in the sand like an ostrich," Bailey gibed.

"That's a myth. Ostriches do not put their heads in sand. They would suffocate." I held up a finger. "They dig holes in the sand to protect eggs and such, and several times they put their heads in the sand to turn the eggs."

Bailey guffawed. "Someone has been watching the nature channel while her fiancé has been launching his business."

"Cut me some slack," I said. "Rhett and I are good. We love each other. He'll get it worked out, and then all will be right with the world."

"Oh, to be a dreamer for a day." Bailey covered her heart with her hand. "Being a realist is not nearly as much fun."

I cuffed her on the arm. "Knock it off. Besides, my aunt has bigger problems."

"With Sasha?"

"No. I think she and Sasha have worked things out. But I heard Appleby's son Steven—"

"Hold that thought." Bailey shot a finger at something behind me.

I pivoted. "Why? What—"

"Midge is going into the Shredding food tent."

"Yeah, so?"

"I want to talk to her."

"Bailey, cool your heels. We're *personae non gratae* with her, and Tito is no longer a suspect."

"So you say, but you never know with Cinnamon. She might come back around to thinking he is. Until the real killer is behind bars, I won't sleep." Bailey bounded to her feet and shoved the stroller, full steam ahead, toward the tent.

Here we go again, I thought, but I didn't slow down. I was destined to be her wingman, come what may.

The Shredding tent was busy with customers checking out bakers' racks filled with Midge's cookbooks, DVDs of her television shows, and jars of her homemade lemon–poppy seed salad dressing. Midge, in her signature lime green jacket, skirted the makeshift counter and nudged a young woman—her daughter Marigold—to one side. "Take a break," Midge ordered.

Like her mother, Marigold had frizzy hair and a winsome smile, but otherwise she didn't resemble Midge in the least. Her cheeks were gaunt and her skin pale, most likely from her battle with eating and purging. Her overall carriage was, as Principal Baker had described, somber.

"Ten minutes," Midge said. "You're on the clock for your work-study credits."

"Yes, Mama." Marigold removed her lime green apron and scurried out of the tent.

Midge asked the customer at the head of the line what she wanted to eat. On the counter sat cups of salads and premade shredded chicken-vegetable sandwiches on whole wheat, rye, or sourdough.

I whispered to Bailey, "If you want to talk to Midge, you'll have to wait your turn."

"Fine." Bailey aligned the stroller behind a gentleman in a running suit.

Stalwart friend, I stood beside her.

Under her breath, Bailey said, "Midge doesn't look guilty."

"I'm not sure what guilty looks like anymore." Over the past few years, I'd faced a number of murderous souls, most of whom had appeared perfectly normal to me.

Midge caught sight of Bailey and me and frowned. Did that make her guilty? Maybe she didn't want a repeat of yesterday's encounter at her downtown restaurant. With calm self-assurance, she dealt with the next customer. And the next.

When Bailey and I reached the head of the line, Midge glanced to her right. Was she hoping her daughter would return and take our order?

Forcing a smile, Midge said, "Jenna and Bailey, what a nice surprise."

Liar, liar. I could see the reluctance as well as hurt in her eyes.

"Ready for lunch?" Midge asked.

Bailey elbowed me, goading me to take the lead.

I glowered at her—wingmen shouldn't have to steer a conversation. Even so, I leaned forward and, keeping my voice soft, said, "Midge, we were chatting with Katie about what you said regarding the Asian fusion restaurant owner, and she denied it."

"Denied what?" Midge's voice rose in a cheery singsong fashion. Her work on television must have taught her how to fake an upbeat mood.

I said, "Katie denied telling you that the chef was going to copy your recipe."

"Oh, that." Midge lifted one of the salad cups and, in a bold voice said, "I think you'll like this, Jenna. Good choice. What else?"

"One of the sandwiches on sourdough," I replied, playing along, and added sotto voce, "so, we'd like to ask, what were you really doing near Your Wellness on Friday?"

Midge peeked to the left and back at me. "Jenna, honestly, now? I can't—"

"If you're innocent, let's put this behind us."

"I am innocent. I didn't—" Midge packaged up the sandwich while continuing to speak in a raspy whisper. "I'm not proud to admit this, but I was spying on my daughter Friday morning."

"Try again," Bailey said with a bite. "It was a school day."

"That's the point," Midge said. "She cut school, unlike today, which is a work-study approved day."

Bailey eyed me. "Why didn't Principal Baker tell us that?"

"We didn't ask," I said.

Midge gawped. "Why were you two talking with the principal?"

"That's who told us about the scathing articles Kylie wrote in regard to Marigold," I said, slightly embarrassed, "and we wanted to follow up on it."

"You had no right," Midge said.

Bailey squared her shoulders. "Yes, we did. My husband was a suspect in Kylie's murder. We needed to explore all angles."

"Was," Midge said. "Tito *was*."

A woman behind us cleared her throat, eager to purchase her meal and move on.

I smiled at her and said, "A minute longer, ma'am. Thanks for understanding." I refocused on Midge. "It must have upset you the way Kylie maligned your daughter."

"Kylie was vicious," Midge hissed. "I think she was jealous of anyone who could cook. Kylie couldn't. She didn't have an ounce of talent in her entire body. Over the past year or so, she lashed into me and so many others."

Like Savannah, I mused.

"To answer your question about why I was outside the Boldine Building," Midge continued, changing tack, "I was there because my daughter has a new boyfriend."

"An artist," I said.

"He's the grandson of the Boldines," Midge said. "I knew his grandparents had gone on a cruise. The boy's mother and his uncle had split town, too—they aren't foodies. Speculating that the kids might think it was a lark to sneak inside the jewelry store, seeing as they were already truant, I went to do a little reconnaissance. Except they weren't there. Frustrated but not thwarted, I drove to the young Boldine's house, which is where I found them. Of course, I can't tell anyone I was stalking them. If my daughter finds out?" Midge moaned. "We're already on shaky ground. She blames me for everything Kylie did to her. She thinks Kylie attacked her to get to me. Why Kylie wanted a pound of my flesh is still a mystery, but what she did to my sweet girl . . ." Midge fought tears. "The pain Kylie caused Marigold, making her self-esteem plummet, resulting in an eating disorder? Despicable. Deplorable. I will never forgive her, and I won't rue her death. But I do have a verifiable alibi."

"Verifiable?" Bailey said. "Try me."

I shot her a look to *cool it*. "What is it, Midge?"

Midge's eyelids fluttered. "Ever since you came to the restaurant yesterday, I'd wondered about whether someone had seen me outside the boyfriend's house, so I made a few calls this morning, and I found a neighbor who noticed me peeking in windows. In fact, she'd reported the incident to the police, so I should go to the police and admit—"

"Mom?" Marigold skirted the counter, surprising all of us. "What's going on? Why do you need to go to the police? What do you need to admit?"

Midge clutched her daughter's shoulders. "It's a small matter I need to handle. Start filling orders, sweetheart. We'll close up in an hour, as planned, and you can return to school." She cupped her daughter's chin with her hand. Marigold, like Savannah earlier, wriggled free of her mother's doting attention.

"I'm sorry, Midge," I said as I paid for our meals.

"Me, too."

"I hope you'll follow through and go to the precinct."

"I will."

Silently, I also hoped Midge and her daughter would go to counseling. After David's death, I'd met with a therapist. Having someone to whom I could air grievances had helped me a lot.

Chapter 15

Outside the Shredding tent, when Bailey and I finished our snacks—I enjoyed the sandwich; she ate the salad—she checked on Brianna in her stroller. "My daughter is down for the count. Want to take a walk?"

"Sure." I tossed our wrappers into a nearby garbage can. "How about a little window-shopping? Maybe we'll stop at Spellbinder." It was the mystery bookshop in town. I needed to replenish my to-be-read pile on the nightstand.

"Sounds good."

On Buena Vista Boulevard, as we were passing mini San Francisco, Bailey peered upward. I followed her gaze. The windows to Your Wellness were closed.

"Poor Alexa," Bailey whispered. "I can't help thinking about what you said. Is it possible someone killed Kylie in order to sabotage Alexa's business? Or was the killer someone who hated both of them? Is Cinnamon considering that angle?"

"I have no clue."

"Maybe we should visit Alexa," Bailey went on, "and give her some moral support."

"Where would we find her?" I asked. "Clearly, Your Wellness isn't open."

"Not necessarily." Bailey pressed the intercom to the studio. Alexa didn't answer.

"See? I told you."

"Maybe she's just not answering."

"We can't get inside without—"

"Catch the door!" Bailey said.

A deliveryman was leaving the building.

I managed to grab hold of the doorframe, told the bewildered man that our friend was expecting us, and allowed Bailey and Brianna to enter first. We took the elevator to the second floor and pressed the studio's doorbell. And waited. No one answered.

"Okay, this is a bust. When I'm right, I'm right." I moved to the elevator and pressed the Down button. The doors opened instantly.

"I know where Alexa lives." Bailey pushed the stroller onto the elevator and hit the number one. "I delivered cookbooks to her last week. She's living in the hills with her parents for another month until she gets her own place. It's not far from your father's house. Let's go."

"Bailey—"

"C'mon. Be a sport. An uphill trek will do me good."

The elevator doors opened. Bailey propelled the stroller forward, full steam ahead, through the foyer and onto the street. She veered right and continued the fast pace. At the dancing dolphins statue, she headed east, up the mountain. By the time we reached the Tinsdales' ranch-style home, I was perspiring but energized, and Bailey was beaming. Brianna, the darling child, was still asleep.

"Nice flower bed," I said.

The front yard was rife with red cyclamen, red lobelia, and white chrysanthemums. Little Miss, a red-tinged ornamental grass, created a lovely low border. The grass was perfectly trimmed. Beneath a stately maple tree to the right stood an all-weather bench and table. Through the front window, I could see Audrey, dressed in a paint-splattered smock and black leggings, working on a canvas featuring large-sized poppies.

"Leave it to Audrey to create a masterpiece in her yard, too." I pressed the doorbell. "I hope I'll have a green thumb. I've never maintained a garden."

"Maybe we should have called ahead," Bailey said when no one answered the door. "We're disturbing them."

"Too late to think of that. And I hear footsteps."

Eugene Tinsdale opened the door and smiled warmly. "Jenna, Bailey. What are you two doing here?"

"We were hoping to see Alexa," Bailey said.

"She's not here." Eugene swiveled his head and bellowed, "Audrey, when will Alexa be back?"

Audrey sauntered into the foyer, carrying a palette and an orange-dipped paintbrush. "Hello, girls. Alexa is working out."

"Not at the studio," Bailey said. "We went there first."

"No, no. Alexa is in the park near the junior college." Audrey aimed the paintbrush to the north. "She won't be long. She's doing an hour of pole work."

"Pole work?" I raised an eyebrow.

Audrey said, "Alexa claims pole dancing increases core and general body strength by using the body itself as resistance."

Eugene elbowed his wife. "You sound like a convert."

Audrey blushed and said to us, "I've taken up pole dancing. It's invigorating."

Eugene said, "As if you need to be more fit."

Bailey said, "Alexa has been trying to talk me into doing it."

"Try it," Audrey said. "It makes me feel sexy." Her cheeks tinged pink, as if she'd shared too much.

"Why would Alexa opt for the park?" I asked.

"There's a jungle gym," Audrey said.

"Yes, but there's a pole at the studio," Bailey countered.

"Alexa hasn't gone . . ." Audrey lowered her chin. "She hasn't gone inside since . . ."

Since the murder. I nodded, understanding. She could stand outside with her father and watch security lights being installed. Entering was another matter.

"Come in, ladies." Eugene beckoned us. "Would you like some tea?"

Audrey said, "How rude of me. Yes, come in. It's so nice of you to be supportive of Alexa. I'll clean up and meet you in a few. Eugene, put on a pot of water."

Eugene led Bailey and me to the living room, which was filled with a colorful array of furniture and what I presumed were Audrey's paintings on the walls. She taught all styles of painting, including surrealism, impressionism, and cubism, but given the works on the wall, she clearly enjoyed pointillism, using a technique of small dots of color applied in patterns to create an image. The artists Seurat, Signac, and van Rysselberghe were obviously her heroes. Seeing the Pacific Ocean and the coastline of Crystal Cove done in the pointillist style by such a talented artist took my breath away.

"Eugene, your wife has a gift," I said.

"I've told her the same, but she won't accept the compliment. She thinks she's a hack." He headed toward the kitchen. "I'll be right back. English breakfast okay?"

"Great," I said.

Bailey pushed the stroller next to the sofa and checked on Brianna. "What a snooze-hound. Should I worry that she's snoring?"

"Baby's snore," I said, matter-of-factly, as if I knew everything about babies. They did snore, didn't they? My cat did.

I roamed the room, eyeing Audrey's work and other items. Pictures of teenaged Alexa and Kylie at a gymnastics meet. Alexa and Kylie going to what had to be the prom with two very handsome boys. Alexa and Kylie in shorts and T-shirts tapping the bells at the top of a rock climbing wall.

"I see you're taking it all in, Jenna." Audrey ambled into the room. She had removed her smock, donned a silk bomber jacket, and had freshened her makeup. "Alexa had been a loner until she met Kylie, and then like that"—she snapped her fingers—"the girls bonded. I remember how they would talk until the wee hours of the night if they had a sleepover."

"They seem to have enjoyed competing against one another," I said.

"They did." Audrey removed four red-and-white Crystal Cove High School yearbooks, each emblazoned with the black Toreador mascot, from the lower shelf of the coffee table. "Alexa and Kylie said that competition made them reach for the stars. Sit, Jenna. Bailey, you, too. Have a look."

Audrey appeared to need a walk down Memory Lane. What harm could come from it?

As the three of us nestled on the ruby red sofa, Eugene entered the room carrying a tray filled with floral teacups, a matching pot of tea, and a bowl of sugar and four spoons.

"Help yourselves," he said, taking a seat in the royal blue club chair.

The doorbell chimed. "Can't be Alexa," Audrey said. "She has her own key. Would you answer that, darling?"

Eugene ambled to the foyer and opened the door. From my vantage point, I could see Viveca Thorn step inside, her hair tucked beneath a baseball cap, her baggy sweatshirt over leggings hiding her lithe figure.

Eugene said, "Viveca, what are you doing here?"

"Alexa contacted me. She said she can't afford to continue to pay me." Viveca sneezed and dabbed her nose with a tissue. "I came to pick up my final check."

"Alexa isn't here," Eugene said.

"That's all right. She said she left it in an envelope in the kitchen." She sneezed again.

This time, Eugene blessed her and went in search of the envelope. He returned with it. "Here you go. I'm sure Alexa will provide good references."

"If only . . ." Viveca began. "If only I hadn't gone to pick up sandwiches. If I'd stayed at the studio."

"Now, now," Eugene said, "you can't think like that."

"Maybe I could have prevented the murder."

"Or you could have been caught in the crossfire." Eugene petted her shoulder. "It's my belief that if a killer is determined to kill, the victim doesn't stand a chance."

"I suppose you're right." Viveca held up the check. "Please tell Alexa thank you for doing this."

"We Tinsdales honor our debts," Eugene said.

Viveca slogged out of the house.

Eugene closed the door and rejoined us in the living room, sitting in the chair he'd vacated. "I suppose you heard."

"Poor girl," Audrey said. "Everyone is suffering in the wake of Kylie's . . ." Tamping down emotions, she opened a page of the freshman yearbook. "Now, where were we?" She tapped a picture of the girls dressed in poodle skirts and teased hair. "This is Alexa and Kylie, age fourteen. Going out for Halloween. They had so much fun."

I poured myself a cup of tea and added sugar. "The other night, when Rhett and I ran into you two on Buena Vista, you said you couldn't think of anyone who might have killed Kylie."

"No one," Eugene said.

"Is there anyone who might have wished both Kylie and Alexa harm?" I asked.

Audrey gasped. "What are you implying?"

I mentioned the possibility that whoever had killed Kylie might have done so at the studio to destroy Alexa's reputation.

"Do you mean like a restaurant owner who Kylie might have reviewed badly but who also might have been one of Alexa's clients?" Eugene asked.

"That's an idea," Bailey said. "Or how about a rival from their past?"

Audrey shook her head. "They didn't have rivals."

"You said Alexa had been a loner," I stated.

"Yes, as a preteen, but when she met Kylie, she came out of her shell. Both of them were quite popular in high school and in college."

"They went to different universities," Eugene said.

"At any time did the two date the same boy?" I asked.

A smile tugged at Audrey's mouth. "Interesting that you should ask." She flipped the page. "This is Alexa with her boyfriend, Zach, who later became Kylie's boyfriend."

The caption below the picture read *Overachievers.*

"Where is Zach now?" Bailey touched the photo with her index finger.

"In New York," Audrey replied. "He's a successful stockbroker. Married to Marvin."

"Marvin?" I said.

"Zach's gay. He came out in his senior year." Audrey poured herself a cup of tea. "He and Marvin are married and have two children."

Eugene said, "I knew all along he was gay, but parents aren't supposed to have opinions."

"You did not know," Audrey chided.

That ruled out Zach wanting to hurt both Kylie and Alexa, I mused.

"Did Alexa and Kylie share other boyfriends?" I asked.

"A few. Tryce was the last one." Audrey glanced at her husband. "Do you remember him, darling?"

"How could I forget? 'Tryce this, Tryce that.' I think Alexa wrote a song about the boy." Eugene groaned. "When she dropped him like a hot potato—"

"Kylie swooped in." Audrey set her tea aside and picked up the sophomore yearbook. She opened to a page of Kylie in a white jogging suit hanging on the shoulder of a handsome track star. "Tryce was a beautiful runner."

Good runner or not, I wondered how Kylie had felt, always getting Alexa's seconds. Or had Alexa dumped Tryce because he'd fallen for her best friend?

"And where is Tryce now?" I asked.

"Living in Europe, married to a marathoner," Eugene said. "He owns a sporting goods company. Does quite well for himself."

"No bad blood between him and Kylie or Alexa?" I asked.

"Not a whit. He sends annual Christmas cards," Eugene said.

"Here we are. Junior year." Audrey opened the yearbook and showed us more pictures. Alexa and Kylie working on the school newspaper. Alexa and Kylie at an academic debate. The caption beneath that one: *The Winners.*

I took the yearbook from her and scanned a few pages, noticing one had been torn out. A ragged edge jutted from the interior of the spine.

Audrey noticed me fingering the edge and said, "Alexa tore that out after Funny Bunny broke it off with her."

"Funny Bunny?" I repeated.

Audrey tittered. "That was her nickname for him. Funny Bunny. What a card he was. The class clown. The page had a photo of Bunny yukking it up with a pair of his football buddies." Audrey sighed. "I can't remember Alexa ever laughing the way she had with him."

"Did Kylie date him?" I asked.

"No, never." Audrey shook her head. "She knew Alexa was as serious as a heart attack about him. The other boys didn't matter, but Bunny was special."

"Why did he break it off?" I asked.

"He became a vegan," Eugene said.

I gawked at Audrey. "Honestly?"

"Bunny was adamant about not eating meat, to the point of being a zealot. Alexa baited him mercilessly." Audrey turned to her husband for corroboration.

"But that didn't win him back," Eugene said. "Bunny had lost his sense of humor."

Audrey tsked. "A week later, Alexa tore out the page and ripped it to shreds."

I flinched. So did Bailey. Did Audrey not know about the shredded paper at the crime scene? Eugene seemed oblivious, too.

"Another lifetime," Audrey said, and closed the junior yearbook. "Alexa reached out to Kylie for emotional support, and Kylie for all intents and purposes—"

"Meant to come through," Eugene said softly.

Audrey sighed. "But she lost her parents around the same time, so she wasn't there for Alexa."

"I heard about their deaths," I said. "What a tragedy."

"It was." Audrey's voice caught. "The weather forecast predicted clear skies."

Eugene said, "The next thing you know, there were gale-force winds. Out of nowhere. The helicopter didn't stand a chance. Kylie's father was reviewing a site he'd wanted to build on."

"He built shopping centers," Audrey said. "We thought he was rich, but we learned, with his death, that he had nothing. He was hugely in debt. We helped Kylie a bit, but she needed grants to finance most of college. A year ago . . ." Audrey faltered.

Eugene said, "Bunny died."

"This time, Kylie was there for Alexa." Tears welled in Audrey's eyes. She took the yearbook from me, set it aside, and opened the senior yearbook. She flipped to the middle, turned a page, and gasped. Quickly, she closed the book.

"What's wrong?" I asked.

"Nothing."

"Audrey, let me see," I said gently, and pried the book from her hands.

I browsed a few pages until I saw what Audrey must have seen, a picture of Kylie as homecoming queen, with horns drawn on the tiara and the word *thief* scribbled beside Kylie's face. Why had Alexa defaced the photo? Had Kylie stolen money from her? Or a boy? Or the crown?

"Audrey," I said, "who was the homecoming king?"

Audrey studied the marred photo. "Hmm. I'd never noticed before. That's Bunny."

The front door slammed and Alexa bounded into the living room. "Mom, Dad, I'm—" Alexa stopped short and tugged the hem of her black workout shirt down over the matching leggings. "Hi, Jenna. Hello, Bailey. What brings you here? Ooh, is that your baby?" She rushed to the stroller and peeked in on Brianna. "She's so cute. She looks like you, Bailey. Don't you think?" Alexa stood up and gazed at the yearbook on my lap. "What are you doing, Mom?"

Her mother licked her lips. "I was showing the girls pictures of you and Kylie in high school, and, um, we stumbled on—" Audrey tapped the defaced photo. "Did you do this to the photo?"

"Oh, that." Alexa jutted a hip. "What a joke. Kylie had really ticked me off the day we got our yearbooks. She refused to sign mine until I apologized for saying she looked fat in her homecoming dress. Except she did, so I wouldn't. It wasn't flattering. Is an empire silhouette dress ever a good choice? It creates such a tummy pooch." Alexa demonstrated by sweeping her hand over her stomach. "So Kylie retaliated by breaking into my locker and taking my best pair of running shoes." Alexa's gaze swung from me to Bailey. "We had the same-sized feet," she added, in explanation. "So I wrote *thief* in my yearbook, and when she finally deigned to sign the yearbook, she saw what I'd written and went ballistic." Alexa snorted out a laugh. "It was so funny. She was as red as a —"

Alexa clapped a hand over her mouth. "Oh, crap, what is wrong with me? Mom?" She gazed at her mother, her eyes flooding with tears. "Mom? I'm sorry. She's dead. How could I say such horrible —" The floodgates burst.

Audrey bounded off the sofa and hurried to her daughter. She gripped her in a hug and patted her back. "I know, sweetheart. We all miss her."

Alexa peered over her mother's shoulder. "Kylie and me. We were besties. And rivals. For life. If only Tito hadn't had a lesson."

Bailey shot to her feet. "He didn't kill her, Alexa."

"I didn't mean to imply —" She blanched. "I know he's in the clear. Jenna mentioned it when we ran into each other yesterday. I simply meant that maybe Kylie wouldn't have come by the studio to confront him. Why else would she have been there?"

"To work out," Bailey said.

"Wrong place, wrong time?" I asked. "Could the killer have been after you?"

"Me? No. Not possible." Alexa's eyes widened. She gazed at her mother and father. "It's not, is it?" She sank into the other club chair and wrapped her arms tightly around her rib cage. "If the killer wanted to kill me, will he try again?"

"No, sweetheart, you're safe." Eugene strode to his daughter and clasped her hand.

I drew near to Alexa. "What have the police told you?"

She released her father's hand. "I didn't tell you this, Mom, Dad, but the police asked me for my alibi."

"They can't possibly think you're the killer," Audrey said.

"What utter nonsense," Eugene sniped. "You loved Kylie."

"Yes, but it was my studio. My equipment." Alexa placed a hand on her chest.

"What about the private client you met?" Audrey threw a helpless look at her husband.

"She confirmed that I was at her house." Alexa bolted from the chair and paced to the bay window. She pivoted. "But she couldn't confirm that I had a flat tire or that I'd fixed it myself. She'd left by then. I showed the police the tire that's still in my trunk, but that's not enough. They suspect me."

"Ridiculous." Audrey rushed to her husband and daughter. Over her shoulder she said, "I'm sorry, Jenna, Bailey. You'll have to go. Eugene and I need to confer with Alexa and decide whether we need to hire an attorney."

"I don't need an attorney," Alexa cried. "I didn't do this."

Chapter 16

"I'm here, Jenna," Harmony Bold rapped on the front door as she swept into the house. I'd left the door hanging open. "Hello?"

I entered the living room from the kitchen. I'd desperately needed a glass of water after the walk back from the Tinsdales'. Tigger trotted alongside me. He cozied up to Harmony and batted her leg with his tail.

"Are you allergic to cats?" I asked.

"Nope. I've got three." Harmony bent to scratch Tigger and stood up. "Where do you want to sit?" She raised her briefcase and portfolio. "We'll be going over party décor. I have quite a list of possibilities, and if we have time, photographers. I've got an hour."

"Let's settle in the kitchen." I led the way.

"Nice place," Harmony said, taking in the surroundings.

"It's a work in progress."

"So's my place, and I've been there five years." Harmony set her things on the antique white kitchen table, removed her navy blue blazer, and hung it on the slat-back chair.

"Coffee?"

"No, thanks. Let's get to it." Harmony flipped open the portfolio. "As you know, having so many friends who've recently married, choosing a color scheme is vital to the entire wedding. I like bold colors, like red, blue, and yellow, but others prefer pastels or even white."

I sat in a chair. Tigger leaped onto my lap.

"White is what Rhett and I had discussed for the décor," I said. "It's so romantic. We've even discussed serving all white food."

Harmony scrunched her nose. "What do you consider white food?"

I grinned. "Shrimp, calamari, white cheeses, tea sandwiches, cauliflower, turnips, oysters, mushrooms, garlic."

"Oh, yeah," Harmony snickered. "Let's serve plenty of garlic at your wedding. *Not.*"

"Exactly what I'd said when Rhett and I'd chatted about this before. But white food is elegant."

"You're set on this?"

I tilted my head. "Unless you convince me otherwise."

Today, I wouldn't make any firm decisions. I wanted to review all the choices with Rhett. I figured once he had his new staff on board, he'd be able to make more time for us. For now, Harmony and I were going to go through the paces. But, no matter what, taking a step forward was progress.

"Okay, let's look at white décor palettes." Harmony opened her book and flipped to a section tabbed *White.* "Here we go. White bistro chairs and tables. White clematis and roses and baby's breath. You realize there will be some green involved because of the floral choices."

"Yep."

"Spanish moss might be nice to add."

"Ooh, I like this." I traced a finger over a picture of a white table with white china, white placards, white flowers in hurricane candle glasses, lots of lit candles, and a white chiffon runner. "We're having an evening wedding."

"I know." Harmony flipped to another page. "Do you want your bridesmaids all in white?" She showed me a picture of a bride in a gorgeous white gown and her bridesmaids in sleek, long white dresses.

"Hmm. That is a lot of white. It's not like any of us are virgins." In fact, all the women who'd be in my wedding party were married.

Harmony grinned.

I worked my tongue inside my mouth. "Maybe we should consider using more green. It's one of my favorite colors. What do you think?"

"Emerald green is quite classy. So is asparagus, fern, and pear green."

"Asparagus?"

"Yep, it's a color. Any of those go nicely in a vineyard-like setting, such as Napa." Harmony browsed her book. She stopped on a page that displayed an image of a bride racing through a shower of white confetti. "Confetti or rice?" she asked. "Confetti is a lot less messy, in my humble opinion."

My insides jolted. The shredded paper at the crime scene had resembled confetti. Had the killer shredded multicolored paper with nothing on it—no words, no pictures—to confound the police?

"Jenna, are you okay?" Harmony rested a hand on my arm.

"Yes, fine. My mind went elsewhere. Rice," I said. "Let's go traditional. Next?"

. . .

"It's the last night of Food Bowl week," Lola said. "Can you believe it? Time whizzed by these past few days." She led my aunt and me to the rooftop of the Pelican Brief Diner. "Hasn't the entire event been wonderful? The restaurant has done double the business compared to this time last year. Word is that this is the hottest ticket in California right before the holidays." Lola, who had ceded all cooking duties to her staff, had dressed for the occasion in sequin-studded denim jacket and jeans. "How about you? Is the Cookbook Nook booming?"

"We knocked it out of the park on Monday," Aunt Vera said. She'd donned a sea-blue Nehru jacket over slacks and radiated confidence. "Katie's six-hour lunch event at the Nook Café was a huge hit, and nearly everyone wandered into the bookshop afterward to make a purchase."

"Which reminds me" — I tapped my aunt's arm — "we have to go over orders tomorrow. With Thanksgiving and Christmas coming up . . ."

"You're reading my mind."

"But tonight," Lola said, "it's all about me. Prepare your taste buds."

Like the restaurant below, Lola had set the rooftop with wooden tables and chairs and sawdust on the floor. Rustic but chic.

"Hello. Welcome!" The hostess, a perky California-born Latina who was dressed like a sailor — all the waitstaff wore nautical attire — said, "The bar is to your left; food stations everywhere." Like a flight attendant, she motioned with two fingers. "Smooth sailing. May the wind be at your back."

The sky was a pale blue with wisps of orange and yellow, thanks to the setting sun. There wasn't a hint of a breeze.

"Lola, the rooftop is packed already," I said. "Can it hold this much weight?"

There were at least fifty people in attendance so far. Most were hovering around the cooking stations closest to the ocean side of the restaurant. For the food or the view? Hard to tell.

Lola smirked. "Do you think I'd let you up here if it couldn't?" Before buying the diner, Lola had served as a full-time lawyer. A brilliant mind, she knew liability and every other kind of law, but ultimately she'd needed a change and had gone into the restaurant business, her second passion. "Don't worry. We won't cave in. Go. Be with my daughter. She's in a buoyant mood." Lola nudged me.

Bailey was standing next to Tito near the bar that was situated on the side of the roof near the boulevard. My pal radiated calm in a turquoise dress and matching shawl. Tito, in white shirt tucked into jeans, looked relaxed for the first time in a week. Each was holding a glass of white wine.

"Jenna!" Bailey called to me. "We hired Tina for the night. Come, celebrate."

My aunt said, "I'm going to chat with Jake and Z.Z. Have fun."

I strolled to Bailey and Tito and flagged down a waitress who was passing hors d'oeuvres. "Over here. Starving."

The waitress held out a tray of mini whitefish tacos. "Ahoy!" she said. "Don't miss the crabmeat morsels by Chef Phil. They're going fast. The cilantro adds just the right *yum*."

Chef Phil hailed from Carmel-by-the-Sea, down the coast. I hadn't yet dined at his restaurant, but if Rhett and I planned a trip south, it would be at the top of my list.

I took a fish taco and downed it in one bite. "These are fabulous. Could you bring me a glass of white wine?"

"It's self-serve," the waitress said.

As she moved on, my father, looking a tad more upscale than Tito—he'd thrown a linen blazer over his white shirt and jeans— strolled to me and pecked me on the cheek. "Daughter."

"Father."

"Did you have a good day off?"

I eyed Bailey, who squinted in Tito's direction. My guess? She hadn't told her husband about our visit to Alexa's house or the fact that Alexa was a suspect in Kylie's murder. I wouldn't spring that on my father right at this minute.

"I did," I said. "Bailey, Brianna, and I spent a delicious few moments at Azure Park."

My pal nodded. "The waffles were out of this world."

Dad said, "Make sure you tell Lola what a hit this soiree is. She has been fretting about it for a month." He squeezed my shoulder and raised the glass he was holding as he headed in Lola's direction. She was chatting with Z.Z. and Jake. "About our chess game, Jake," I heard my father say.

"So, Bailey . . ." I said. She and Tito were staring toward the boulevard instead of the ocean. "What's caught your eye?"

Tito shrugged. "Your Wellness. Actually, the Boldine Building, but you know what I mean."

The lights were off in the building, but a spotlight illuminated the front of the building as well as its rooftop.

"You're remembering the crime scene, aren't you, my love?" Bailey asked.

Tito grimaced. "I can't wrap my mind around what happened. Why was Kylie there? Had she gone in to wait for me, as Alexa implied? Or had she gone to chat with Alexa? The killer must have followed her. If we could figure out Kylie's intention, we might be able to drum up the culprit."

Bailey squeezed his forearm. "You're not pursuing this story, sweetheart."

"Maybe I should."

"There are other reporters who can. You stay clear."

"Eugene mentioned Kylie had been acting strangely lately. Not only did she argue with me in public" — Tito took a sip of his wine — "but it turns out she had taken on a few other reporters in recent weeks. She nearly had a knock-down, drag-out fight with Priscilla."

"Priscilla?" I asked.

"The crossword puzzle editor."

I presumed that was the woman in the crossword puzzle T-shirt who had almost plowed into me last Wednesday. I recalled seeing her name attributed to the Food Bowl–themed crossword I'd worked on this morning.

"What did Kylie argue with Priscilla about?" I asked.

"Apparently, Priscilla had canceled numerous running dates, and Kylie was giving her guff." Tito struck a haughty Kylie-like pose. "'If Priscilla wasn't serious . . .' 'If Priscilla wasn't up for more than the occasional jog . . .'"

Bailey said, "She could stick it where the moon don't shine."

"Exactly." Tito nabbed a fried shrimp from a passing waiter.

"Is Priscilla a person of interest?" I asked. Maybe she had decided Kylie's overbearing personality should be silenced.

Tito shook his head. "Nah. She's out of town. At a crossword convention in Los Angeles. She left Thursday afternoon. One hundred percent confirmed."

Bailey elbowed her husband. "Must eat."

Tito said, "Let me stake out a table, then we'll make the rounds." He kissed her softly on the forehead and went in search.

I stood staring at the rooftop of the Boldine Building. "I gather you didn't tell your husband about our going to Alexa's house?"

"No. I didn't feel the need — "

"What are you two gazing at?" a woman asked.

Cinnamon appeared on my left clad in a long-sleeved sweater and jeans. Her belly had a slight pooch. Finally. She took a sip from a glass of sparkling water and followed our gaze. "The Boldines canceled Alexa Tinsdale's lease," she said.

"Really? Alexa didn't mention — " Bailey jammed her lips together.

Cinnamon shot her a look. "When *didn't* she mention that to you, Bailey?" There was a bite to her tone. She focused on me. "Jenna, tell me you two didn't intervene."

"I didn't. We didn't. Okay, we did, but not in the way you mean." I was blathering. I hated when I did that. Cinnamon was my friend, but she was also the *law*. I liked to follow the rules most of the time. "We were concerned about Alexa, thinking how rough it must be for her, losing her best friend and possibly losing the business she'd built up over the past decade."

"We'd noticed the studio was closed earlier," Bailey said, "so we went to Alexa's house to check on her. She wasn't there, but her mother and father asked us in." She peeked at me to confirm. "They are so nice. They offered us tea and showed us lots of old yearbook pictures of Alexa and Kylie."

"A walk down Memory Lane," I added.

"Soon, Alexa showed up — she'd been working out — and she tried to shake off this one photograph . . ." Bailey wiggled a finger. "Not in a bad way . . . but . . ." She cleared her throat and glanced again at me, to bail her out.

"The photo was of Kylie as homecoming queen," I offered. "Posing with Bunny."

"Bunny?" Cinnamon raised an eyebrow.

"A boy. Funny Bunny was his nickname," I said. "He used to be Alexa's boyfriend, but then he dumped her when he became a vegan, and, well, he must have been voted homecoming king, so he was posing with Kylie. And Alexa sort of—" I stopped myself.

Stop blathering. Get it in gear, Jenna.

"Anyway," Bailey said, "during the conversation, Alexa said you, the police, suspected her of the murder. Is that true? I can't imagine—"

"We would like not to," Cinnamon said, "but her alibi is weak, and her fingerprints are everywhere."

"Of course they are," Bailey said. "It's her studio."

"Not so," I countered. "I heard the technician say the reformer had been wiped down. Plus, none of Kylie's hair had been found at the studio."

Cinnamon took another sip of water.

"Alexa said you met with the private client she'd met that morning," I went on, "and the woman confirmed Alexa had attended the appointment. Alexa also said she showed you the punctured tire that had delayed her. It was in her trunk."

"True, but there's a time frame where . . ." Cinnamon studied her fingernails.

Mentally, I filled in what she'd omitted: a time frame where Alexa, if she weren't fixing her tire, could have come back to the studio.

I said, "Alexa's parents are going to seek the advice of an attorney."

"They probably should." Cinnamon scanned the crowd. Hoping to spot an ally? An escape? Bailey and I weren't grilling her, but she clearly did not want to be having this chat with us.

"The family is torn up over losing Kylie," I added.

"Mm-hm," Cinnamon mumbled guardedly.

I said, "Since Kylie's parents are dead, I think the Tinsdales will be putting on the memorial."

"They've mentioned they would," Cinnamon allowed. "Alexa will probably take the lead on that."

"Well then." I spread my arms. "How could you suspect her if she's willing to honor her friend with—"

Cinnamon shot me a stink-eye.

I shifted feet. "I've got another question for you."

"I don't have an answer," Cinnamon quipped. "Unless it's about how you might balance better on your skates."

"You're a laugh riot."

A waitress moved toward our group. "Fried Asian kebab anyone? Gluten-free. It's been marinated in a tamari-based sauce."

We all took one. Two pieces of juicy tuna on a stick interspersed with mushroom slices and green onions. Fabulous.

When I finished mine, I said to Cinnamon, "Have your guys figured out what was printed on the shredded paper at the crime scene?"

"Nope."

"I'm assuming more articles?"

Cinnamon nibbled on her tuna, remaining as silent as a monk.

"I didn't touch any of it," I said—I hadn't; I'd used a tissue—"but I'd guess it was multimedia. Some photographic, some heavy bond paper, like the kind used for correspondence."

Cinnamon's nose flared.

"Did whatever it was include images of Kylie?" I asked.

"Stop, Jenna!" Cinnamon snapped. "Are you deaf? I'm not telling you anything more. Period."

My cheeks flamed with heat.

"Did Midge Martin talk to you, Chief?" Bailey cut in.

Cinnamon regarded her with outright contempt.

I put a hand on my pal's arm, but Bailey pressed on. "Jenna and I talked to Midge earlier. She has a strong motive to have wanted Kylie dead, but she has a solid alibi, so in case she's on your radar, we suggested that she contact you—"

"That's it. Bailey, no investigating. Do you hear me?" Cinnamon aimed her kebab at my pal. "And you, Jenna"—she jutted the stick at me—"rein her in."

"We weren't investigating," Bailey said. "We went to talk to her after we met with Principal Baker—"

"Why were you talking to Principal Baker?" Cinnamon snapped.

Bailey recoiled. Stammering, she said, "We'd heard a rumor about Kylie giving Midge's daughter Marigold a hard time. Principal Baker confirmed that Kylie had written scathing articles about Marigold. She added that because of the abuse, Marigold now has an eating disorder, so we thought Midge might have held a grudge against Kylie—"

"*Oof.*" Cinnamon flinched and listed to the right.

I steadied her. "Are you okay? You're ashen."

Her eyelids fluttered. "I'm feeling a little under the weather. I'm going home."

"Want me to take you?" I asked.

"I'm not a child. As for you two . . ." Cinnamon straightened her spine and lifted her chin. "We, the police, have got this. Tito is innocent. Move on, ladies. Good night." She pivoted and strode toward the exit, stopping briefly to say something to Lola.

As Cinnamon neared the stairs leading to the restaurant below, she peered over her shoulder at me. The message she sent was clear: *Tow the line.*

Rhett passed her and mouthed a greeting. Cinnamon waved to him but didn't say a word, which was very unlike her, proving she was ticked off at me and under the weather. A lethal combination.

"Hey, beauty." Rhett strode to me and bussed my cheek. "What's with the frown?"

"I'm concerned about Cinnamon."

"She seemed okay to me. You, on the other hand, look like you could use a glass of wine," he said. "I'll get it. Chardonnay?"

"Yes, please." I continued to stare toward the staircase. If only I knew what was on that shredded paper, maybe I could help Cinnamon piece the puzzle together.

Eugene and Audrey Tinsdale emerged at the top of the stairs. Eugene had dressed casually in denim; Audrey, sedately in a simple dark blue sheath. Perhaps she thought wearing a colorful outfit would be inappropriate now that her daughter was considered a suspect in her friend's murder. Alexa trailed her parents. In a sleek black jumpsuit, she appeared glum and pale. She moved behind them, toying with her necklace as if it were a lifeline, chin down, not making eye contact with anyone. So much for her motto: *Be brave, be bold.*

Eugene whispered something in his wife's ear and strolled across the rooftop to Tito. He clapped him on the shoulder. Tito smiled and they shook hands.

Audrey and Alexa remained huddled together, not moving toward either the food or beverage stations. I beckoned them. Looking relieved to have a destination, they strolled toward me.

"Were you able to meet with an attorney?" I asked.

"Yes. We'll see how that goes." Alexa glanced past me and said, "I'll miss working there, Mom."

"I know, sweetheart. Location, location." Audrey draped an arm over her daughter's shoulder.

"I put my heart and soul into Your Wellness." Alexa's voice caught.

"Your business is intact. You'll get all your equipment back. All the hardware, too. You'll find a new space and start anew." Audrey kissed her daughter's forehead. "New beginnings are vital for creativity."

"I'm not a creative person," Alexa protested.

"You are in your soul. Let's join your father." Audrey steered Alexa toward Eugene.

"Alexa, hold on," I said.

She turned back.

"Is there any other way into your building other than the front door and side exits?" I asked.

She peered at the sky, deliberating, and returned her gaze to me. "I don't think so. The restaurants at either end have a kitchen door, but those lead specifically to the kitchens and not into any other buildings. Why?"

"I've been racking my brain trying to figure out how the killer slipped in unseen."

Alexa shot a hand toward the building. "There were no security cameras at the time. Anyone could have gone through the front, if they'd timed it right."

"You're probably correct." Bailey and I had been able to enter, thanks to the courteous deliveryman.

Audrey nudged her daughter. "Let's go."

As they shuffled away, my heart ached for them. I remembered being a suspect in a murder. Until I was exonerated, people had treated me differently. But to have to start over completely, too? Alexa would need grit.

"Here you go." Rhett handed me a glass of wine.

"My hero." I took a sip. "How much time do you have?"

"The whole night."

My mouth fell open. "Are you kidding? Really?"

Rhett grinned from ear to ear. "Okay, an hour, but that feels like the whole night." He ran a knuckle along my jaw.

I shivered with desire. "I'll relish every minute."

"Listen, I had a very serious talk with the investors this morning. I told them I would quit if we didn't get this ironed out fast, and they promised they would by the weekend. They found a new executive chef, a real gem who worked at a high-end bistro in Seattle. She's already in place. And they pressed the new manager to move up her timetable and show up by the weekend or they'd find someone else." Rhett wrapped his arm around me and gave me a squeeze. "Aren't you proud of me?"

"Couldn't be prouder." I kissed him firmly on the lips. "Thank you."

"No, my love, thank you. You are my guiding light. I want a life, not a career. I'm excited about returning to the restaurant business, but if it ever begins to rule me, I'm out and headed back to Bait and Switch." Rhett lifted my chin with a fingertip. "You are my life."

A lovely chill ran down my spine. "I'm hungry."

"Me, too."

We feasted on stir-fried shrimp with shredded green onions, blackened halibut, and crispy pan-fried sole with a honey-sriracha sauce. Fabulous.

When we could eat no more, Rhett said, "Let's take a walk."

I was more than happy to oblige.

We left the party, crossed the street, and strolled toward the center of town. We didn't walk as far as Intime. Rhett was the one who suggested we avoid it by turning right and heading south along Ocean Avenue, the road that ran parallel to Buena Vista Boulevard and ended at Azure Park.

There was virtually no traffic. There were other, more popular arteries off Buena Vista leading to the park. Plus, Ocean Avenue featured mostly rental homes, half of which abutted the alley and backsides of the commercial buildings on Buena Vista.

A breeze kicked up and I started to sneeze. Rhett pulled a white handkerchief from his pocket. "Here. When you're done, give it back."

"I'll take it home and wash it."

"Don't be ridiculous. The restaurant will be more than honored to launder it." Rhett whisked it open and handed it to me.

The flicking motion reminded me of Tito's bandanna-banana magic trick. *Voilà.* How had he disposed of the banana? Had there been a pocket on the inside of his cape?

As I dabbed my nose, I caught sight of the backside of the mini San Francisco complex. All eight units were unlit, including the Boldine Building, but spotlights illuminated the back façade as they had the front façade. I noticed security cameras had been installed on the rear of the building, too. Even though there were no exit doors, there were windows. I gazed up at the windows for Your Wellness.

"What's wrong?" Rhett asked.

"I was wondering if the killer could have entered Your Wellness through those windows."

"How?" Rhett asked. "The exterior is smooth and there's no fire escape ladder."

"That's because they've been removed from most buildings. Bucky told me once that they proved more hazardous than helpful." I peered harder. "I suppose it's possible that Viveca, Alexa's assistant, didn't see everyone who entered or lingered at the front of the building that morning. She didn't spot Midge."

"Midge Martin?" Rhett asked. "Did she have a motive to want Kylie dead?"

"Yes." I explained quickly. "However, long story short, Midge has a verifiable alibi. Whoever killed Kylie went *poof.*"

"Poof?"

"Gone. Vanished into thin air." I gave him a quick recap of Tito's magic trick.

Rhett grinned. "Sorry I missed that one. Sounds fun."

I continued to stare at the Boldine Building. "Magic tricks are all about sleight of hand and misdirection. I'm guessing that a murderer thinks like a magician. Get in, get out, and disappear. Remain unseen and, therefore, remain innocent."

• • •

At two a.m., I awoke with a start after a nightmare about falling from the top of one large building after another. In the dream, I recalled thinking that Google Maps might help me learn more about the mini San Francisco structure. So I fetched my laptop computer, climbed back into bed, and opened the browser to Google Maps. I typed in the building's address and homed in. Closer, closer. I manipulated my view by tilting the image to 3D. The front of the building appeared the same as earlier. All lights off. Security cameras in place. Spotlights illuminating the façade.

I moved the cursor to provide a view of the rear of the building. Windows were opened at Your Wellness, but, as Rhett and I had noted, there were no ladders to access that floor from either the roof or from the ground. I spotted the two doors Alexa had mentioned at the opposite ends of the structure. A large square Dumpster-style garbage can stood outside each. Could the killer have hidden behind one of the Dumpsters and, when the coast was clear, sneaked in through a door, entered the ductwork, and crawled to the Boldine Building?

Knowing I could do no more, I closed Google Maps and went back to sleep. Tigger, sensing my distress, curled into my stomach.

More dreams plagued me. Of scaling and rappelling down mountains.

I awoke wondering if the killer had been able to reach the building's rooftop, would he or she have been able to rappel down to Your Wellness using a preset rope and sneak in through the opened windows. I made a mental note to discuss the possibility with Cinnamon. She'd reject me out of hand, of course, wanting no more interference from me, but I'd at least plant the notion in her head.

Chapter 17

Wednesday morning was sunny and deliciously warm for the season. In less than an hour I exercised, showered, dressed in a light sweater and capris, and ate a power breakfast of diced hard-boiled egg on avocado toast.

Keller showed up as I was gathering Tigger. "Hey, hey, Jenna. Beautiful day."

"Sure is. What's on the agenda?" I asked.

"That's something we need to discuss. Yesterday evening, on my way out, as I was stowing my tools and stuff in your garage, I discovered some dry rot."

I moaned. "That can't be good."

"It's not. Dry rot, which is also known as brown rot, is caused by fungi, which can ruin wooden structures. When dry rot occurs, the fungi break down cellulose and hemicellulose, the components that give wood strength."

"Okay." I wasn't a construction person. I'd never paid attention to what went into a house. Given Keller's propensity for detail, I feared I was about to learn. "Go on."

"Dry rot will affect timber that is damp. So, for this reason, removing the source of moisture should be the aim of any dry rot strategy." Keller slung a thumb into the pocket of his overalls. "If it's okay with you, I'd like to bring in a specialist and get the area dried out and repaired."

"What's the downside if we don't?" I asked.

"The wood will continue to rot, and ultimately the structure will crumble."

I rolled my eyes. The gift from my aunt was becoming a money pit. On the other hand, Rhett and I had savings, and we did love the location.

"Any business or home is an investment that will continue to require upkeep," Keller said.

"Do whatever you have to and keep a running tally of costs."

He offered a thumbs-up sign.

When I arrived at the shop, my aunt was already there, sitting at the vintage kitchen table, cradling a baby girl swaddled in a peach blanket. Aunt Vera was tickling the girl under her chin and cooing to her. Nearby stood Deputy Appleby and his daughter, Sasha. Appleby was beaming; Sasha was edgy and fidgeting with her fingers. I silently willed her to relax. The baby wasn't a china doll. She would survive my aunt's coddling.

"Good morning," I said. "What a beauty she is, Sasha."

"All babies are," Sasha murmured, like an unbiased mother.

"Not all." I recalled one poor child I'd met with bug eyes, a pumpkin-sized head, and porcine nose. Kids would not be kind to the boy as he grew up.

"Jenna," my aunt said, "we have to disassemble the window display and set up for Thanksgiving."

"On it."

On my way to the stockroom, I whispered congratulations to Appleby. I considered telling him what I wanted to say to Cinnamon but decided against it. He was enjoying a family moment. I set Tigger on his kitty condo and continued on.

We kept all our decorative pieces in marked boxes. In the Thanksgiving container, I had stowed a set of Plymouth Pumpkin dinner plates, a Fitz and Floyd horn of plenty cookie jar, a colorful duo of turkey saltshakers and pepper mills, and spools of orange and brown ribbon. The items would instantly beautify our annual window display. In addition, I'd decided somewhere around two a.m., after the Google Maps foray and before falling back to sleep, to create jars or baskets to sell in the shop. Each would contain a recipe and the necessary spices for seasonal dishes like turkey dressing, cookies, and Thanksgiving cider, the latter made with pumpkin pie vodka, cider, soda, and a cinnamon stick.

I lugged the box out of the stockroom and set it near the round table at the front. Then I fetched an empty carton into which I would deposit the items we'd used in the Food Bowl presentation. At the last, I chose a gorgeous jigsaw puzzle featuring a buggy arriving at an estate on a crisp, orange-toned evening, and swapped it with the puzzle on the vintage table featuring frisky cats in the bakery.

"Good morning, everyone," Pepper chimed as she strutted into the shop.

"You look positively perky," my aunt said.

Pepper was dressed in a bright orange beaded sweater over

white jeans. "My daughter said I needed to update my wardrobe. She said I'm starting to dress like a fuddy-duddy."

"Well, this outfit will silence those objections," Aunt Vera said.

"Who is this little gem?" Pepper asked.

"My daughter's," Appleby beamed. Proud grandpa.

"Hello, little girl." Pepper peered closely at the baby. "So lovely to meet you. I hope your mama will teach you to crochet and bead."

"I'm a klutz with crafts," Sasha said.

"I'm an excellent teacher." Pepper had no qualms about touting her talent. "Stop by the store sometime. I'll give you a free lesson. Once you've crocheted, you're hooked." She chuckled, enjoying her own play on words. "Jenna," she crossed to me, "I need a cookbook for my son-in-law's mother. She adores anything with nuts."

"I've got the perfect choice. *In a Nutshell: Cooking and Baking with Nuts and Seeds.*" I guided her to a shelf near the front of the shop and handed her the book.

Pepper flipped through the pages. "The pictures are pretty. Have you made any of the recipes?"

"The triple-ginger almonds are quite tasty."

"Done." Pepper headed to the checkout counter, but stopped to peek down the breezeway. "Any treats from Katie yet?"

I drew alongside her. "Nope. It's a little early. Check back around ten."

At the far end of the breezeway, a woman in a full-length white dress strode into the café.

"Say, Pepper, did you see that woman heading into the café? Was it Savannah Gregory?"

"I think it was. Poor thing," Pepper said, moving toward the register. "I fear something might have happened to sweet Savannah. Last Friday, I saw her ducking into her own house with a scarf over her face." She brandished the book. "Ring me up, will you? I don't need a bag. Just the receipt in case my in-law wants to return it."

I did and thanked her for her business.

Before Pepper left, she said, "You know, Jenna, the free lesson goes for you, too."

"As if I have time to crochet." I chuckled.

"It's quite calming. With your fiancé working all those long hours, you might enjoy the allure of a craft."

"I paint."

"Oh, that's right. I've heard your father extol your talent. Well, keep an open mind. When you're blocked on the canvas, perhaps crocheting would unblock you. Ta-ta." She hurried out.

I trailed her and paused at the breezeway wondering why Savannah might have hidden behind a scarf on Friday. Had she fought with Kylie before strangling her with the ropes of the reformer? Had she obscured her face to prevent someone from seeing *scratches* on her face? I hadn't noticed any when we'd chatted briefly at the park, but with all the makeup, how could I have?

Gran entered the shop while removing her cashmere, shawl-necked cardigan. "My, isn't everyone here early." She peeked at the baby and said, "You're a natural, Vera. She's sound asleep."

My aunt glanced up, a goofy grin on her face. "I'm enjoying every moment."

"Ladies," I said, "if you don't mind, I'm going to the café for a sec. When I return, I'll finish the display. If Bailey gets here, tell her where I've gone."

I didn't wait for their reply. I scurried along the breezeway and into the café. It was half full, most diners preferring to sit by the windows and take in the view. Outside, the ocean was a brilliant blue with a few whitecaps. Seagulls were having a field day diving into the water to hunt for their meals.

Savannah was sitting with her mother, Shari, at the far table, her back to me. The white dress Savannah was wearing stretched tautly at the seams. Shari was as slim as always in a silk sweater and skinny jeans.

A waitress set two cups of tea in front of them and moved on.

"Jenna." Shari hailed me. "Lovely to see you. Can you join us?"

"Why aren't you dining at Latte Luck?" I asked as I approached.

"If we eat there, the boss cajoles us to work," Shari said.

"Ahem. You're the boss," I stated.

"Exactly. I'm a taskmaster. Dining somewhere else is much more relaxing, and I love the croissants here." Shari indicated the empty chair. "Sit."

"Sure. For a minute."

Taking my seat, I gazed at Savannah, who lowered her chin. She was wearing a ton of makeup again, but I couldn't see any yellow-tinged concealer, like the kind models and actors used to cover blemishes. When working at Taylor & Squibb, our makeup artist had kept plenty of that on hand. Upon closer inspection, however, I did see what Savannah had tried to hide using normal makeup. Raised red welts. Not scratches. Had she run face-first into a beehive?

"Hi, Savannah," I said.

She whispered, "Hello."

"Darling," her mother said, "speak up. And don't be embarrassed. Jenna understands these things."

Tears pooled in Savannah's eyes. "Mo-om," she whined.

Shari clasped her daughter's hand and smiled warmly. "I'm sure Jenna has had a facial treatment or two." She addressed me. "My darling daughter went to have one last Friday morning. It went awry." Shari released her daughter's hand and frittered her fingers. "Tell her, Savannah."

Savannah mumbled, "No."

"Savannah reacted horribly to the needles," Shari said, "and now she's mortified by how she looks."

"Needles?" I asked.

"Micro needling, to be exact," Shari said.

I regarded Savannah again.

She raised her chin and met my gaze. "Micro needling helps remove scars and acne and rejuvenate the skin. I . . ." Air wheezed out her nose. "I'm embarrassed because I don't want anyone to think I'm vain, but with my bad diet, and picking at my face, and not drinking enough water, I've ruined my skin. So I went to the dermatologist and" — she swiped a hand in front of her face — "this is what happened. I look like a leper."

Shari said, "Ah, vanity, thy name is woman."

"That's not the quote," Savannah chided. "It's 'Frailty, thy name is woman.' Said by Hamlet, speaking about his mother."

"I stand corrected. My daughter the would-be English scholar." Shari offered a sympathetic smile. "The doctor swears Savannah will be fine in a week or so."

"It's her fault," Savannah said. "Her nurse forgot to tell me not to use any anti-inflammatories before the treatment, so I reacted badly."

I said, "When you told me yesterday that you were home Friday morning with a migraine —"

"I did go straight home after seeing the doctor. I wasn't lying about that."

"You said you baked and watched cooking shows. Was that true?"

Savannah shook her head. "I couldn't very well bake through tears."

Shari said, "Savannah is at a loss. Her diet plan isn't working. She can't exercise because of the pain in her feet."

"And baking and icing at Latte Luck isn't helping me," Savannah cut in. "I adore sugar. I probably need to change jobs."

"Nonsense," Shari said. "You need someone to help you learn more self-control."

I thought about the weight counselor Midge's daughter, Marigold, might need and wondered whether that kind of doctor would be able to help Savannah, who suffered from nearly the opposite problem.

"Maybe you could do exercise that doesn't require putting weight on your feet," I suggested. "You could talk to Alexa Tinsdale. She could set you up with a regimen using—" I stopped short of saying *using the reformer.*

"Alexa," Shari said. "That's a brilliant idea. You like her, Savannah."

Her daughter nodded glumly.

I rose to a stand. "Savannah, I hope you'll tell the police the truth about your visit to the dermatologist."

"The police?" Shari's voice skated upward. "Why would they need to know—"

"That's why I wanted to meet for tea, Mom. I'll fill you in." Savannah addressed me. "I will. I'll even have the dermatologist verify what happened. She likes to document everything. Her assistant took photographs. Before and after." Savannah made a face. "Talk about ugly."

I returned to the Cookbook Nook feeling happier for Savannah, certain that she hadn't killed Kylie.

Before starting in on the Thanksgiving display, I removed the items from the Food Bowl one. First, I placed the mandoline, grater, and potato peeler into the empty carton. While I did so, I thought about Kylie. With Savannah and Midge exonerated and Tito in the clear, who did that leave as the likeliest murder suspect?

"There you are," Bailey said as she pushed through the break in the stockroom drapes. "Where have you been?"

"Didn't Gran or my aunt tell you?" I shot a look at Gran, who was organizing the children's cooking kits. Her face reddened. I said, "Don't worry about it. My mind is a sieve, too." To Bailey I said, "I was in the Nook."

"You and Rhett cut out early last night." Bailey knelt beside me, her capris rising above her knees. She pushed up the sleeves of her long-sleeved Crystal Cove *Love, Love, Love* T-shirt and said, "Let's make this stuff disappear."

"Poof," I whispered and sat back on my heels.

Bailey gazed at me. "What's with the funky look in your eyes?"

"Last night, Rhett and I took a long walk. We were on Ocean Boulevard, when we paused behind the Boldine Building." I told her about the opened windows at Your Wellness. "We didn't see a fire escape ladder or any other way for the killer to have entered that way." I added that I'd awakened at two a.m. thinking Google Maps might help me discover another entrance. "Other than rappelling from the roof or crawling through ductwork, no such luck."

"Face it," Bailey said. "We're not cut out for this deducing stuff. Hopefully, Cinnamon and her team are doing a bang-up job and will resolve this soon."

"You know, statistics say that if a murder doesn't get solved within seventy-two hours, it might not get solved."

"Don't be Debbie Downer. Here. Take this." Bailey handed me the food processor and its blades. "Be careful. Those are sharp."

I stored them in the box and then began wrapping each of the porcelain fruits and vegetables in tissue. "Want to come to my place for dinner tonight?"

"Absolutely. Can we bring Brianna?"

"You bet."

"What's on the menu?" she asked.

"What would you like?"

She held up a veggie slicer. "Something that hasn't been shredded."

Chapter 18

When I paint, I often outline my idea on a large sketchpad before I address a canvas. When I'd worked at Taylor & Squibb, in order to visualize the concept, we'd storyboarded our ideas—storyboarding was a graphic way to depict ideas with accompanying words, laid out in sequence.

After I prepared an antipasto platter, set the chicken shish kebabs to marinate in a spicy red sauce, and decanted a bottle of pinot noir, I decided to go with a mash-up of a sketchpad and storyboard—some pictures, mostly words—to help me visualize the crime scene and come up with other ideas of who might have killed Kylie. I knew it wasn't my job, but it was plaguing me, and I figured Cinnamon might appreciate my help—*might*—if her investigation stalled.

I set up my easel in the kitchen nook and flipped open the sixteen-by-twenty sketchpad. Tigger toured my feet, making wailing sounds, asking what I was doing.

"Thinking," I said to him.

More squalls.

"First, a sketch of the crime scene." I drew the studio, with the entry off the corridor and the windows at the front and rear of the building. The ballet barres to the left. The glass-enclosed office to the right. The wall of handheld weights and such between the office and lavatory. The pole for pole dancing in the far left corner. Cubbies to the right of the entry. Six reformers, set in two rows.

Kylie, I noted, had been killed on the far left reformer. The crumbled and shredded paper had been scattered around that unit.

Tigger's tail crooked into a question mark.

"I agree, kitty," I said. "Who killed Kylie Obendorfer?"

I wrote the question in pencil beneath the crime scene sketch. I didn't have a photograph of Kylie, so I couldn't post a picture the way police did on TV shows. Instead, to visualize her, I drew a caricature of her, highlighting her blonde locks.

In my mind, there were three suspects with an axe to grind— Savannah, Midge, and Tito—but all of them had been exonerated.

Alexa said the police suspected her, so I wrote her name and sketched her face. I jotted *flat tire* beneath her name and *loved Kylie*. Then I added *motive?*

"Who else?" I said to Tigger.

He mewed and scampered off to chase the bird toy Gran had given him.

"So much for being Watson to my Sherlock, cat," I gibed.

I thought about Alexa's parents. Eugene had provided an alibi. Why? Did he feel he'd needed one? I recalled the spat he'd had with his wife at the café. Discussing Kylie had clearly upset Audrey. Had Kylie really planned to leave her job? Had she truly found an investor, as Alexa had suggested? Had she intended to buy out Eugene?

I wrote Eugene's name on the board and added Audrey's beneath it. I tapped the tip of my pencil next to her name. Audrey had been quite solicitous when Bailey and I had visited the house, showing us yearbooks and chatting up Kylie like she was family. Her sorrow had been real. Was I missing something?

Beneath Kylie's caricature, I wrote *investor. Who?*

I thought again about the shredded paper. Maybe the red and black ink wasn't writing or an image; it was just the color of the paper. Maybe that was why Cinnamon had acted circumspect about the contents.

After creating a column on the right and giving it a header—*Evidence*—I jotted *shredded paper* and *crumpled articles*, then I created a bubble in the upper left and scribbled: *Did killer or Kylie bring paper to scene? Does that matter? Articles involved Midge, Eugene, Savannah, and Tito. Who else?*

"Knock, knock, Jenna. It's Tito, me, and the baby," Bailey shouted, letting herself in through the front door.

"In the kitchen," I replied.

"The house is looking good." Tito pushed Brianna in her stroller through the archway. "I like the sea-blue color of the living room."

"That's the original color," I said. "We haven't had time to paint everything yet."

"Well, I like it."

"We're going neutral, but first we have to address a few problems. A leak and some dry rot."

"To be expected," Tito said. "Unless you buy brand-new, every house has hiccups."

Tigger abandoned the bird toy and bounded to the baby. He stood on his hind legs to get a closer look and meowed.

"Yes, Tig-Tig, she is pretty," I said in response. "But, *shh*, she's sleeping."

Bailey set a bottle of sauvignon blanc on the island. "We brought this."

"I decanted a bottle of pinot noir." I pointed to it. "I'm serving spicy chicken kebabs."

"Red it is." Bailey stowed the white wine in the refrigerator and poured some of the pinot into three glasses, then she studied the sketchpad. "You've been busy."

"So busy that I forgot to set out the appetizers. At least I preheated the grill." I hurried to the refrigerator, removed the platter of provolone cheese, salami, and olives, and set it on the counter. I placed some cocktail napkins near the platter. "I hope you don't mind simple food."

"I adore simple food," Tito said, pairing a cube of cheese with a slice of salami.

Next, I removed the pan holding the marinated shish kebabs from the refrigerator. "Let's go outside. You relax while I barbecue. Tito, bring the cheese platter."

Bailey pushed Brianna out, anchored the wheels of the stroller, and tucked the blanket beneath the baby's chin, after which she took a seat at the patio table. "What a week."

"You're telling me." I brushed the grill with olive oil and set the kebabs on top.

Tigger did a figure eight around my ankles.

"Move, kitty." I nudged him with the heel of my sandal. I didn't want spicy tomato sauce dripping on him.

Getting the message, he leaped into Bailey's lap and begged for a cuddle.

Bailey scratched Tigger's ears. "Having seen your sketchpad, I can see you're mulling things over. I'm trying to think of other suspects, too."

"Kylie's parents are dead," Tito said, "and she didn't have any siblings."

"Was there anyone else with whom she was on the outs?" Bailey asked.

"Other than the folks she riled at the newspaper and a few restaurateurs?" Tito shrugged. "Who knows?"

I said, "I'm sure Cinnamon is following those leads."

"You know" — Bailey sipped her wine — "Audrey Tinsdale talked about all the boyfriends Kylie inherited from Alexa. Did she have a current one?"

Tito said, "If so, he hasn't surfaced. I haven't seen her with anyone in at least a year."

While rotating the shish kebabs a quarter turn, I thought of Savannah, who'd had a crush on Kylie. Had she caught Kylie flirting with someone? Had— No, she was innocent.

Tito leaned forward on his elbows. "Jenna, I saw your board inside. You don't honestly think Audrey had anything to do with Kylie's death, do you? She's such a sweet lady."

"Yeah," Bailey said. "Remember how torn up she was when she was showing us those yearbook photos?"

I nodded. "I can't come up with a motive for her. On the other hand . . ." I told them about the spat I'd witnessed between Eugene and Audrey at the café, and Audrey saying *you can't trust her* in an acid tone. "When I asked Eugene about it, he told me that the woman in question was Kylie. He explained that Kylie was getting ready to quit her job."

"Why would that upset Audrey?" Tito asked.

"Maybe she felt all employees should be loyal to Eugene while he was undergoing financial struggles," Bailey theorized.

Tito said, "Or maybe Audrey thought Kylie was playing Eugene, not really leaving but saying she would so she could angle for a raise."

I shook my head. "The vibe I was getting was that Audrey wanted Kylie to leave sooner rather than later. When Eugene said Kylie needed a little more time to get her affairs in order, Audrey shot to her feet."

"Poor Audrey," Bailey said. "She must be on pins and needles with Eugene having to sell a lifelong business, not to mention the police considering Alexa a suspect."

"They do?" Tito raised an eyebrow.

"It's her studio. Her fingerprints." Bailey nudged Tigger off her lap. "They won't rule her out."

"Someone must have seen her changing her tire," Tito said. "Maybe Flora could start a phone tree on her behalf."

"Great idea." Bailey took a sip of wine.

"I can't imagine the conversations behind closed doors at the Tinsdales' house." I twisted the kebabs another quarter turn. "Is Audrey accusing Eugene? Is he blaming her? With Kylie leaving, I asked Eugene if he would be letting go of others, namely Tito. He told me Tito was solid."

Tito exhaled his relief. "Good to know."

"Unless Eugene sells," Bailey reminded him.

"True." Tito paired another piece of cheese with salami. "What will I do if—"

"*Shh.*" Bailey placed a finger against his lips. "We do not talk about what-ifs, remember?"

I revolved the shish kebabs one more time. "Remember how I told you that Kylie had sought out an investor so she could buy the paper?"

Bailey folded her arms. "Maybe that's why Kylie wanted to leave, so there would be no conflict of interest when she came back with an offer."

"Except she didn't come back with an offer," I said. "Do you think someone killed her so she wouldn't be able to invest?"

"What are you implying?" Tito asked.

"I don't know. Something doesn't fit the scenario." I removed the shish kebabs from the grill. "I'll be right back." I bustled into the kitchen, plated our dinners, and returned in minutes.

As I set the plates on the table mats, I muttered, "That darned shredded paper."

Bailey said, "What about it?"

"Cinnamon won't say what was on it."

Tito said, "I don't blame her. That's police business."

"Who brought the paper to the crime scene?" I asked, voicing the question I'd noted on the sketchpad. "Kylie or the killer?"

"The killer, of course." Bailey leaned forward, her gaze riveted on her husband. "And I've got a theory about who that might be."

Tito said, "Don't keep us hanging."

"Viveca Thorn might have worked at the studio for only a month, but what if she had a previous history with Kylie that we don't know about? Kylie got around. She did reviews up and down the Central Coast."

I whistled. "That hadn't occurred to me. Viveca knew Alexa had left for a private session. Maybe she texted Kylie and asked her to come to the studio."

"And erased the text." Bailey tapped the table.

I darted inside and jotted Viveca's name on my murder suspect board with a list of possible motives: *Loved same person? Business deal gone wrong? What else?* Then I returned.

The baby stirred. Tito tended to her. *"Shh, cara."*

Using a knife, I slid the shish kebab meat off the stick onto my plate and sliced a piece in half. "Back to the crumpled paper. They contained articles."

Tito moaned. "Don't remind me."

"There was a picture of Kylie and Eugene in one," I said. "At the NNA convention."

Bailey said, "The chicken is perfect, by the way. Really moist."

"Thanks." I forked a piece of chicken but didn't eat it as the memory of Audrey and Eugene's argument hit me again, full force. The way Audrey had bounded to her feet when Eugene said Kylie had needed to get her *affairs* in order. "Gosh, you don't think . . ." I swung my gaze from Tito to Bailey.

"Think what?" Bailey peered at me earnestly.

"You don't think Eugene and Kylie had an affair, do you?"

Bailey gasped. "Kylie was his daughter's age and Alexa's best friend."

"Like that makes a difference," I said snidely.

"I know someone who went to the convention," Tito said. "I could ask around."

I set down my fork. "What if the crumpled article about the two of them was brought to the studio to slut-shame Kylie?"

"Brought by Audrey?" Tito asked.

"I doubt Eugene would have wanted the affair to be out in the open."

Bailey winced. "What if Kylie brought the article to threaten Eugene, saying she'd tell Audrey, but he killed her?"

Tito pushed his plate away. "And he wrote the words on the mirror?"

I frowned. *You should have reformed.* What had the killer been implying?

"When Rhett and I ran into Eugene and Audrey the other night," I said, "I remember Eugene giving us his alibi, unsolicited. Neither of us had asked for it. Audrey confirmed it, but she came across stilted, as though she were lying on his behalf."

"Where did Eugene say he was?" Bailey asked.

"They — he and Audrey — had met with one of Audrey's students, a trust fund baby who wants to invest in the newspaper."

"Have the police followed up on that?" Bailey asked.

"I didn't mention it to Cinnamon," I said. "She wants me to stay out of her investigation."

"I could check it out." Tito offered. "Do you have a name?"

"I don't."

Bailey rubbed her knuckles along Tito's jaw. "I know I told you not to pursue this story, but you will find out, won't you, my love? Yes, I know you will. You are a brilliant investigative reporter."

Chapter 19

I tossed. I flailed. I had nightmares about confetti, which morphed from docile shredded paper into machine-gun fire and cannonballs and bombs, all of it peppering the mural I had yet to paint on the wall. I awoke with my besieged brain trying to spell the word *strafing*.

Tigger, who usually stayed by me through thick and thin, had positioned himself on the second pillow, far from my writhing body.

"Sorry, buddy." I scratched him under the chin. "Mama had bad dreams."

I threw on my running gear and jogged on the beach barefoot, trying to figure out why I'd dreamed about explosives. I drew to a halt when it dawned on me that learning the truth about Kylie's relationship with Eugene might be explosive and could destroy the Tinsdale family. I couldn't make assertions that weren't true. Would Tito find out what had really happened?

As I was making a U-turn near the Pier, I spied Audrey Tinsdale and a nice-looking man carrying easels down the nearby steps to the beach. The two were talking intimately, heads quite close together. A notion occurred to me. Was Audrey the one having an affair and not Eugene? I recalled Audrey saying that pole dancing made her feel sexy. She also told her daughter that new beginnings were *vital for creativity*. Was she ready to fly the nest? If that were the case, did that remove her from my suspect list? I mean, why kill Kylie O if she was ready to leave her husband anyway?

Audrey whirled around and, catching sight of me, frowned. Had she felt me staring at her? Did she intuit that I considered her a suspect?

I waved cheerily. Audrey responded in kind.

Edgier than I'd felt in months, I raced home and took a steaming hot shower. By the time I'd dressed in jeans, a T-shirt with the word *Thankful* in puffy letters written on it, and a super-soft hoodie, I felt better. Slightly.

I telephoned Cinnamon at the precinct. She wasn't in yet. It was too early. I didn't want to ring her cell phone, so I left a voice mail sharing the ideas Bailey, Tito, and I had conjured up about Viveca

Thorn, as well as my thoughts about the opened rear window and the possible entry to the studio via ductwork. I didn't add that we'd wondered whether Eugene had had an affair with Kylie or that I'd seen Audrey with another man minutes ago. I could tell her all of that when she returned the call.

If she returned the call.

Praying our illustrious chief of police would contact me sooner rather than later, I sat at the kitchen table and nibbled an English muffin topped with mascarpone and jam. A little sweet paired with a smidgen of protein was just enough to get me going. If I had an appetite later, I would beg Katie to make me a healthy lunch.

When Cinnamon didn't touch base, I gave up on my vigil and slogged to the Cookbook Nook. I set Tigger by the children's table and made a pot of coffee. Caffeine would be a much-needed beverage today. Then I queued up heartfelt music, starting with "The Thanksgiving Song" by Mary Chapin Carpenter. What we could all use today, per the songwriter, was the gift of loving kindness. Amen.

Twenty minutes later, Gran and Aunt Vera arrived, Gran dressed in a pumpkin-colored cashmere dress and my aunt in a bronze caftan.

"Don't the two of you look ready for the season," I said. "I'm setting out all the new titles we have for the holiday, including *All Time Best Holiday Entertaining* by America's Test Kitchen."

"I love that one," Gran said. "I've tried the Brussels sprout salad with warm bacon vinaigrette. Delish."

"I've got my eye on the *brie en croute*," I said. "The picture of it, with the cheese oozing out the center, is amazing." I aimed a finger at her. "Also, we will be receiving a shipment today of aprons and children's cooking sets."

"On it." Gran saluted and stored her purse by the register.

My aunt drew near and studied my face. "Darling, what's wrong?"

I forced a smile. "Nothing."

"Don't kid a kidder. Your eyes are squinty and your skin is sallow." She clutched my elbow and led me to the vintage kitchen table. "Sit and talk."

"There's no time—"

"There's always time to find peace in your heart. We don't have customers. What's rattling you?"

I told her about last night's dinner conversation. "I know you care for Eugene, but we have to find out the truth. Did he or did he not have an affair with Kylie, and if so, did he kill her to quiet her?" I added that I'd seen Audrey with another man on the beach this morning. I didn't want to read anything into it, but said that something Audrey had implied yesterday made me wonder.

My aunt fingered her phoenix amulet. "The cards never lie," she whispered.

"What do you mean?"

"Remember Eugene's reading? The cards said intense love or intense hate could be involved. What you describe — the possibility — involves both love and hate."

I sighed.

"You have to tell Cinnamon what you suspect," my aunt added.

"I left a voice mail for her to call me."

"A message is not good enough. You must have a one-on-one chat. I realize she keeps you at bay, but, in the past she has appreciated your help. If she tells you that she has already delved into the Tinsdales and ruled them out, you can rest easier."

I strode to the counter and dialed the precinct. The clerk advised me Cinnamon wasn't available and wouldn't be. She had been rushed to Mercy Urgent Care the moment she'd entered the precinct. I asked why, but the clerk couldn't reveal that. I ended the call, my stomach roiling with concern.

"What now?" Aunt Vera asked.

"Cinnamon. Urgent care. I'm going." I grabbed my purse.

"What happened?"

"I don't know."

• • •

Mercy Urgent Care was one of two decent-sized clinics in the area. The place smelled Lysol clean. Doctors and nurses strode purposefully along the halls.

I asked if I could see Cinnamon Pritchett but was told to wait in the waiting room.

Wood-framed vinyl chairs and tables set with magazines lined two of the walls. A muted television with closed captioning was airing on CNN. Vending machines peddling snacks and hot beverages stood against the far wall. A somber orchestral piece I didn't recognize was playing softly through a speaker.

I hadn't been sitting a minute when a nurse I'd met last December entered and told me to follow her.

She led me to a room. The door was ajar. "Chief Pritchett is in there," she whispered.

I slipped inside and was surprised to see my father and Bucky, Cinnamon's handsome firefighting husband, both in jogging outfits, sitting in chairs to the left of the bed in which Cinnamon lay propped up and alert, a few gadgets attached to her arms and chest.

"How could you not call me?" I asked my father as I hurried to the right side of the bed and clasped Cinnamon's hand.

Dad started to speak, but I hushed him.

"Your gown is less than flattering," I said to Cinnamon. "Pale blue isn't your color."

"Ha-ha," she said wearily.

"Are you okay?" I asked. "Is the baby —"

"I'm fine. The baby is hunky dory. I had a lot of nausea and started vomiting, so now I'm dehydrated."

"What brought it on?" I asked.

"It's normal for some. I'm here so they can fill me with fluids and send me home."

Bucky stood, towering over the bed. "Home," he said. "Not to work."

Cinnamon smiled beatifically. "I heard the doctor. I'm not deaf, like Jenna."

"What's that?" I cupped my hand around my ear. "Couldn't hear you."

"Deputy Appleby will take charge of everything, darling," Bucky added. "You relax."

"Don't boss me around, mister." Cinnamon aimed a finger at him. "Not if you know what's good for you."

I breathed easier. She hadn't lost her edge.

Bucky grinned.

"Shouldn't you be at work, Jenna?" Cinnamon asked. "How did

you know I was—" She paused and pursed her lips. "Let me guess. You contacted the precinct with a tip that you would only deliver to me."

My father suppressed a smile. A few years ago, he would have chided me, but now he understood my passion to seek the truth.

"Actually, yes," I said.

Dad couldn't help himself. He roared.

"Don't, Cary," Cinnamon warned.

Dad mimed buttoning his lips.

"I was picturing the crime scene, and the shredded paper," I began, "and that got me to thinking about the crumpled article that featured Eugene and Kylie, which made me flash on a conversation Rhett and I'd had with Eugene and his wife when we ran into them on Buena Vista Boulevard. We were all enjoying a bite at one of the vendors. Out of nowhere, Eugene blurted his alibi for Friday morning."

"Out of nowhere?" Cinnamon smirked.

Bucky petted her shoulder. "Give it a listen."

She batted his hand away. "Just because you're starting the academy, darling, do not think you know more than me."

I gazed at Bucky. "You're giving up firefighting?"

"I'll do both, but living with a cop has been a challenge. I figure I should get into the business, if I know what's good for me. I'll learn the lingo. I'll be able to offer my two cents without getting a tongue lashing." Bucky had the most easygoing temperament of anyone I knew. He was a giver and lover, a perfect balance for someone as structured and Type A as Cinnamon. "You should join me, Jenna."

I grinned. "As if."

Cinnamon said, "He's got a point. Maybe you should. Then you could become legit, too."

"Very funny." I smirked. "I love my job."

"Then why are you trying to do mine?" Cinnamon quipped.

Bucky petted her shoulder. "Easy, tiger."

"Go on about Eugene, Jenna." Cinnamon twirled a hand. "Neither he nor his wife have been on my radar."

"Even though Eugene's picture was included in one of the crumpled articles?" I asked.

"I told you. I asked Mr. Tinsdale about that. He said he was there when Kylie received her award. That was it. He didn't have a clue why the article was among the mess. He suggested that perhaps the killer had left the article to point us toward the convention attendees." Cinnamon twisted to adjust the pillow on her bed and settled back down. "Appleby and I thought that was a worthy lead, so we've been in contact with many of them, but we've come up empty. Your turn."

I filled her in on the possibility of an affair between Eugene and Kylie.

"Are you kidding?" my father asked. "Eugene is Kylie's boss and twice her age."

Cinnamon rolled her eyes. "Honestly, Cary, what century do you live in? Haven't you been paying attention to the news? Men in power and the MeToo Movement? Abusing and using women who hope to climb the corporate or creative ladder is a timeworn theme and often a good reason for murder."

"Of course, it's just that" — Dad opened his hands — "I know Eugene. He's a fine man. He's worked alongside me on Habitat for Humanity houses." My father often donated his time to charitable causes.

"Not all people who volunteer are saints," Cinnamon chided.

"Firemen are," Bucky countered.

"Good try!" Cinnamon started to cough.

The nurse said, "Okay, everyone out. Now. Chief Pritchett needs her beauty rest. So does the baby."

Bucky kissed Cinnamon on the cheek and exited with my father.

Before I could leave, Cinnamon clasped my hand. "Tell Appleby everything you know, Jenna."

I flinched. Had I heard her correctly?

"Yes, I'm deputizing you, but don't let that go to your head," she went on. "This is a one-off. We have nothing to go on. We need help with this investigation. I'm willing to bend a little."

"About the shredded paper, can you tell me what was on it?"

"My techs are trying to piece it together. It's been a chore. Whoever sliced and diced it did a royal job on it. A professional shredding machine was used." Cinnamon squeezed my hand hard. "Again, this is hush-hush between you, me, and Appleby."

"Why?" I asked.

"Let's just say the baby is making me do it. Okay?" I smiled. "It's our secret."

• • •

When I returned to the Cookbook Nook, Bailey charged me, gleeful and worried all at the same time.

"How is Cinnamon?" she rasped.

"Dehydrated but fine."

"Phew."

"She told me to —"

"Me, first." Bailey gripped my forearms. "Tito is at the café with Eugene. Tito told him he wanted to talk business. Eugene agreed to meet."

"Okay."

"Tito wants you to stop in. He has some news. He figures you should hear it, so you can tell Cinnamon, if it proves helpful." Bailey nudged me. "Gran, your aunt, and I have the shop under control. Go."

I rushed down the breezeway while smoothing my hair with my fingers. What had Tito learned? Did it warrant having Deputy Appleby present? No, I'd listen and then contact Appleby.

Tito and Eugene, both dressed in suits, were sitting at a table for four in the far corner. Most of the other tables were occupied. A few single customers were browsing through cookbooks they'd borrowed from the built-in bookshelves.

I weaved through the tables and said, "Hi, Eugene. Tito. How are things going?"

"Join us," Tito said.

I signaled the waitress. She drew near the moment I sat. I asked for a glass of water and a refill on coffee for Eugene. She returned within seconds with the order.

When she left, Tito said, "Eugene and I were discussing the sale of the newspaper. As you might imagine, he's quite upset about having to do so."

"I am." Eugene toyed with the knife in his place setting, flipping it repeatedly. "However, I informed Tito that we might have an investor after all."

Tito sipped his tea and regarded me over the rim. "It's Peter Pomerance."

Eugene gaped. "How did you—"

"Jenna told me you'd reached out to one of Audrey's students, who happened to be a trust fund baby," Tito replied. "I checked out Audrey's website. She put up pictures of her students' work. I saw one by Peter and thought, *Aha*. His grandfather had been in the newspaper business. Peter was bound to have an affinity for it. So I contacted him, and he confirmed my guess."

I'd met Peter once, at a function at the Aquarium by the Sea. Nice man. A crossword puzzle aficionado. Not the man I'd seen on the beach with Audrey.

"Jenna said you and Audrey met with him the morning Kylie was killed," Tito went on.

Eugene gawked at me. Had he thought I wouldn't mention our conversation to anyone? "Yes, that's right," he stammered.

"Wrong. Peter wasn't in town that day." Tito folded his arms on the table. "He was in San Francisco presiding over a board meeting. He spent the night in the city Thursday."

Eugene swallowed hard. "I must have been mistaken."

"Audrey, too?" I asked. She'd confirmed their appointment.

Eugene stared daggers at me. "My wife . . ." He addressed Tito. "What do you want to know?"

"Sir, there was a crumpled article about the NNA convention at the crime scene. In it was a photo of you with Kylie." Tito tapped the table. "That prompted me to reach out to a few of my buddies who attended the convention."

I said, "Tito, I spoke with Chief Pritchett. She said the police questioned many of them and came up empty."

"Not all. Not *my* guys. Anyway"—Tito sat back, resting his hands on the table—"one of my buddies said he thought there was something going on between you and Kylie."

"No." Eugene thumped the table so hard that his silverware bounced.

"A picture is worth a thousand words," Tito said.

"Don't be glib, young man," Eugene said. "The police asked me about that article. I told them the photograph commemorated a moment of celebration. Kylie had won a Food Critics Society award."

"Was that all the photo commemorated?" I asked.

Eugene blinked. "What are you implying?"

"When you had dinner at Intime on Thursday night, Kylie teased you, saying, 'What happens at the NNA stays at the NNA.' Your wife didn't look pleased." I sipped my water and nudged the glass out of the way. "Then, early Friday morning, you and Audrey argued here, after which she stormed out, and you told me you'd been discussing Kylie quitting her job. But that wasn't true, was it? Audrey guessed you and Kylie were having an affair."

Eugene moaned. "We weren't. That's a lie. We . . . Okay, yes. We did have sex. Once. At the convention. It was horrible and something I'll regret until the day I die . . ." He moaned, realizing his bad choice of words again. "Kylie." He shook his head. "She was always such a nice girl, although a bit of a challenge. Dogged and driven. She and Alexa invariably tried to outdo one another. Get the best grades. Date the same boys."

Faster, faster was Kylie's motto. *Be brave, be bold* was Alexa's.

Eugene worked his tongue inside his mouth. "A year ago, my wife and I . . . our marriage was struggling. We started couples therapy." He rotated his knife nervously on the table. "Out of nowhere, Kylie started coming by my office more often. She said she was a good listener. I'm not sure where she got the idea Audrey and I were . . ." He released the knife. "Alexa might have told her about the problem, I suppose. Anyway, I assumed Kylie was trying to befriend me, you know, take sides, because I was her boss." He traced his finger along the edge of the table. "But then, a few weeks later, she began lashing out at me. Demanding things. A higher salary. A bonus every few months. I told her the newspaper couldn't afford that and asked why she'd turned on me. She'd laughed scornfully. 'Family,' she said over and over. 'Your high and mighty family.' I didn't understand. And then, a few weeks ago, at the NNA convention, she . . ." He sighed. "I'm not exactly sure what happened. I drank something. After that, I was putty in her hands. We had sex."

"Did she drug you?" I asked.

"Possibly. I've never been much of a drinker. Kylie led me to her room and seduced me and took pictures. She vowed she would show them to Audrey if I didn't pay her what she was worth."

Eugene licked his lips. "As I said, Audrey and I were at odds, but I didn't want a divorce. So, to keep Kylie quiet, I gave in to her demands. I paid her what I could every few days. That seemed to appease her."

"Did you reveal any of this to your wife?" I asked.

"Not at the time, and then a week ago, when Kylie told me she was quitting, I thought that was the end of it."

"Why was Kylie leaving her job?" I asked.

"To pursue something new, she said. She didn't tell me in what field."

I said, "Alexa believed Kylie wanted to buy the newspaper. She said Kylie told her she'd found an investor."

"She'd what? She'd found a . . . a what?" Eugene let out a caustic laugh. "Man, that's rich. How stupid could I be? I" — he thumbed his chest — "had to be the investor. I was paying her hush money. Oh, crap."

Yes, that made total sense.

I said, "Don't be so hard on yourself."

"Who else can I blame?" Eugene lowered his chin. Tears trickled down his cheeks. "I'm not sure why Kylie zeroed in on me. I'd never done anything but treat her with respect."

Tito cleared his throat. "Sir, I hate to say it, but extortion is a pretty good motive for murder."

Eugene vehemently shook his head. "I didn't kill her. You've got to believe me."

"Does Audrey know everything now?" I asked.

Eugene peered from beneath his moist eyelashes. "Yes. Last Friday morning I told her. Every last detail. We exchanged words. We were rehashing it the other day when . . ."

When I'd overheard them.

I tapped the table with my index finger. "The killer included that article with the photograph of Kylie and you to point a finger at you."

Eugene nodded.

"Or to implicate Audrey," Tito suggested.

"No. Oh, crap, you don't think—" Eugene hiccupped. "Audrey had nothing to do with this. Nothing."

I said, "Sir, I'm sorry, but if you and your wife weren't with Mr. Pomerance, then neither of you have an alibi."

"Audrey does. She went to see our therapist. She went there directly after our fight. She met with him this morning, too. He'll corroborate her whereabouts."

"Sir, I saw Audrey earlier," I said. "She wasn't with her therapist. She was on the beach with a nice-looking man."

"That's him. The therapist. He gives her an hour of therapy, and she teaches him to paint. When money runs low, you learn to barter. *Quid pro quo,* isn't that what it's called?" Eugene scrubbed a hand along the side of his head. "Audrey lied about our meeting with Peter to protect me."

"So you don't have an alibi?" Tito asked softly. Compassionately.

"I was alone. At home." Eugene's shoulders rose and fell. After a long moment, he gazed at Tito and then me. "If it helps, I was online talking to someone. A woman. I'm not proud to admit it, but with all our troubles, Audrey has locked me out of the bedroom. I've turned to online dating sites to . . . chat."

"Will this woman testify on your behalf?" Tito cut in.

"I don't know. She's married, too. I'll ask her."

"I think the police would keep your communications confidential," I said.

Eugene blotted his nose with his napkin. "I wish I could turn back the clock. I wish I could get the photos Kylie took. I wish I'd never hired her. If only I could make things right with Audrey. I was such a fool."

Chapter 20

Eugene paid the bill and slogged out of the café.

Tito walked with me through the breezeway to the shop. "You know," he said, "my pal from the NNA convention said Kylie was bragging about how she kept all the scathing restaurant reviews she had yet to post in a safe at her place. The photographs with Eugene might be in there."

"Uh-uh, yeah, not," I said, getting his drift. "We are not going after them."

"Whoa!" Tito held up both hands. "That's not what I meant. I'm saying you should tell Cinnamon."

"She's in the hospital, recuperating from dehydration."

"I'm sorry to hear that."

"And it's Eugene who should tell the police."

"Don't you think if Eugene had known about the safe" — Tito thumbed toward the Nook Café — "he would have brought it up?"

"Why didn't you mention it?"

Tito shrugged. "I didn't want him doing something stupid. Call it professional courtesy."

"The photos and any other evidence Kylie kept will point a finger at him."

"I know," Tito said, "but if Eugene's alibi pans out, he'll be in the clear. No matter what, the police should know about the photos. Maybe Kylie was blackmailing someone else."

Tito's parting words made me realize it was time to visit Deputy Appleby and bring him up to speed. Had Cinnamon alerted him to my visit? Would he be welcoming or dismissive?

I advised my aunt and Bailey where I was headed and hurried to the precinct.

I found the deputy by the water cooler, downing a cup of water.

"Got to keep hydrated," Appleby said, as if Cinnamon's bout in the hospital had converted him to live a healthier life. "How can I help you?"

"When I saw Cinnamon at Mercy, she asked me to assist the investigation. I know that doesn't sound like her, but —"

"Save your breath. She texted me." Appleby beckoned me to follow him.

We sat in his office, a simple white room with a tidy metal desk and no plants. He had set a few framed family photos on the bureau abutting the wall.

Over the course of the next fifteen minutes, I told Appleby everything I'd told Cinnamon—about Viveca, the opened rear window at Your Wellness, and the possible entry to the studio via ductwork. I added that I had neglected to tell Cinnamon about Savannah and her alibi for Friday morning. "If that can be proven, then she's exonerated. Do you know if she's contacted the precinct?"

"Not to my knowledge."

"How about Midge Martin?" I summarized her motive and alibi. "She promised to stop in."

"Midge did come by. I never considered her a suspect, although Cinnamon did. We had a lot of restaurateurs on our list. All ruled out."

"Good to know." I concluded by sharing the details of Tito's and my chat with Eugene, his brief, sad affair with Kylie, and the photographs she'd taken to extort him. "What if Kylie was blackmailing others? A friend of Tito's said Kylie talked about having a safe in her home. If so, there might be incriminating evidence in it. Have you or your team searched her place?"

"We did, for clues about her life and friends, scouring her computer, cell phone, and email for possibilities. We combed her place of business, too." Appleby swiveled gently, back and forth, in his chair. "Miss Obendorfer had very few friends. She didn't live a big life, no major trips or vacations. However, she owned a lot of clothes, some high-end jewelry, and a few pieces of art. Like the rest of us, she'd racked up a ton of bills. Two of her credit cards were maxed out. She'd received a number of default notices."

"Did you see anything about Kylie collaborating with an investor?"

Appleby shook his head.

"Did you find a safe?"

"No, but thanks to Mr. Martinez's intel, we should look."

"How about going over there now?" I said. "I'll help you hunt for it."

The deputy regarded me slyly. "Why don't you do what Cinnamon suggested and join the force? Then you could—"

"Actually, Bucky is the one who suggested it." I smiled. "Would it help to say I'm considering the idea?"

Appleby roared. "Yeah, like your aunt or father would ever let that happen."

I leaned forward. "Please, Deputy, your chief gave me permission to help. I'll keep my involvement on the down low. I won't tell a soul if you don't."

Appleby shrugged. "Let's go." He fetched the key for Kylie's place and said he'd drive.

• • •

"Here we are," the deputy said as we pulled up to a set of garden apartments near the junior college, the building built in a circle so each of the twelve units had a separate courtyard entrance.

"Deputy, look." I pointed.

Alexa was walking along the path leading to Kylie's gate.

Appleby parked and clambered out of the vehicle. For a big guy, he was fast. I hurried after him.

"Miss Tinsdale, hold up." Appleby hailed her.

Alexa whirled around, a bouquet of gerbera daisies in her hand. "Officer. I mean, Deputy." She tugged the hem of her bomber jacket and smoothed it over her black jeans. "How can I help you?"

"What are you doing here?" Appleby asked.

"Paying my respects," Alexa said. "Since Kylie has yet to be buried — my parents and I will work out those arrangements, when your department releases her body — I thought it fitting that I lay flowers at her doorstep." She held up the bouquet and set it next to the gate, where other bouquets and trinkets lay.

I'd always found it interesting that people would set memorial items for the dead out in the open. Did they know the deceased? Did they leave them there to console themselves or to remind others to mourn? Apparently, Kylie O had more admirers than I'd imagined.

"Since you're here, Miss Tinsdale," Appleby said, "and considering how well you knew Miss Obendorfer, can you tell me whether she has a safe in her home?"

"I don't have a clue. We didn't socialize a lot after she moved to this location. I reached out" — Alexa fingered the hair feathering her face—"but she'd changed. She'd grown inward. She wouldn't talk about whatever was bothering her."

I recalled Eugene saying Kylie had seemed different over the past year. Had money or career been the issue? What would have caused her to let a lifelong friendship wane?

"Did she break up with a guy?" I asked. "Is that why she moved?"

"I honestly . . ." Alexa's eyes moistened. "Didn't you already search Kylie's place, Deputy?"

"We did."

"Wouldn't looking for a safe have been standard protocol?"

"Not necessarily."

"Well, I'm sorry I can't help." Alexa spread her arms. "If you'll excuse me, I have an appointment." She started down the path.

"One more thing, Miss Tinsdale." Appleby pivoted. "I have a question about your assistant, Viveca Thorn."

Alexa whirled around. "What about her?"

"Is there any possibility she might have had a prior connection to Kylie?"

"No way. Uh-uh. You can't think she . . ." Alexa shook her head. "Viveca moved from San Francisco a month ago. I hired her through an agency. She has no friends here. She didn't know Kylie at all. I'd rule her out."

"What did Miss Thorn do before working for you?"

"She was a receptionist at a national gym chain."

"Is it possible Miss Obendorfer belonged to that gym?"

"As if." Alexa snorted. "Kylie wouldn't step foot into a place riddled with sweat and germs if you paid her. Other than my place, of course. She—" Alexa's breath caught in her chest. Tears leaked from her eyes. After a long moment, she said, "If you don't mind, I'm late."

Appleby bid her goodbye, and Alexa hurried to her Honda Accord parked at the curb.

I eyed the bouquet of daisies she'd left and bent to read the note: *Rest in peace ~ A.* Simple. Not seeking emotional acclaim.

"Should we take all these flowers inside?" I asked.

"No, leave them for the building manager to handle."

I followed Appleby into the apartment.

Books and magazines occupied most of the living room, stacked in corners and piled on bookshelves. A few oil paintings adorned the walls. A glass-and-metal desk faced the bay window. Numerous half-edited reviews lay on the desk beside the desktop computer. At first glance, a few of them were scathing while others were quite complimentary. Were there more languishing in a safe?

Photographs hanging on the wall nearest the desk showed Kylie with Alexa, Kylie with a young man or two, and Kylie with the Tinsdales. There were many photographs of Kylie winning awards. I didn't see any photos of people who might have been her parents. There were no pets and no plants. Nothing to take care of. The lack of *life* saddened me.

"Jenna, in here," Appleby said, having strolled into the bedroom ahead of me.

I strode through the doorway. The room wasn't large. There was barely enough room for a queen-sized bed and the reformer workout machine Alexa had mentioned.

Appleby was standing beside a safe in the center of the floor, a small area rug and wood panel shoved to one side, a painting by Audrey propped against the bed. "We didn't think to look under the rugs."

I pictured the rug covering the stain in my bedroom. I hadn't thought to move it, either.

"How did you open it?" I asked.

"I recalled seeing a safe-like code written on the back of that painting when we'd searched the other day but hadn't thought much about it at the time. I figured it was probably a gallery code regarding price. There are a couple of things inside the safe. I'd like you to witness as I remove them."

Appleby donned Latex gloves, knelt down, and aimed the flashlight on his cell phone into the recess. He removed a lilac-colored envelope. "One letter," he announced and set it on the floor beside his knees. He reached in and removed a heart-shaped locket. "One necklace." He checked the backside. "There's an etching. *Love B.*" He popped it open. "No picture inside." He closed the necklace and set it atop the envelope, and reached into the safe a third time. He produced a small photo album. "That's it."

"Nothing else?"

"Nope. No compromising photos. No extortion memos."

Had Eugene been the only one Kylie had blackmailed, or had he lied about that?

Appleby rested his rump on his heels and flipped through the photo album. He twisted it in my direction and continued to turn pages. "Recognize anyone?"

I shook my head. "Wait. There." I gestured to a picture of a teenager. "I've seen him before. I'm not sure where."

"Anyone else?"

"Yes. There. Stop. Savannah Gregory. As I said at the precinct, Savannah and Kylie used to be friends. They ran ten-Ks together until" —I pressed my lips together— "their friendship ended."

"Got it." Appleby rose to his feet and set the items on the bed. He opened the envelope and pulled out a folded sheet of lilac-colored paper. He read it and clicked his tongue. "Well, well."

"What does it say?" I tried to get a peek.

"It's a love letter."

"From?"

He displayed it to me. In big loopy letters, it read:

> *Dear Kylie, you will always have my heart.*
> *No matter what you do to me, I will never stop loving you.*
> *~ Savannah*

Appleby's cell phone jangled. He tapped off the flashlight app and scanned the screen. "I should get this."

I motioned for him to proceed.

"What is it, son?" Appleby asked.

A woman responded on the other end, speaking so loudly that I could hear her diatribe.

"He's drunk!" she yelled. "Ran off the road . . . So furious with you . . . Said he wanted to commit you. You're getting married, Marlon? Are you nuts?"

"Slow down, Sue," Appleby said, and whispered to me, "My son's wife." He spoke back into the phone. "Where is he now?"

"Mercy Urgent Care. He's never this bullheaded. You've got to do something."

"I'm on it. I'll be right there."

Appleby ended the call. "Jenna, we're done here. Please don't tell your aunt about this call. My son . . . I'll handle it."

As he raced out of the house, taking the items we'd discovered with him, I pondered the love note. Why had Kylie kept the letter? Had she returned Savannah's love? No. Not possible. She and Alexa had swapped boyfriends throughout high school.

Don't be naïve, Jenna.

Maybe along the way, Kylie had realized she wasn't into men and liked women. Maybe she'd made an overture to Savannah. On the other hand, Savannah had told me Kylie had mocked her. Had Kylie's dismissal sent Savannah over the edge?

Chapter 21

Latte Luck Café was packed with people. I slipped inside and skirted the line. I searched for Savannah and was surprised to see her behind the cash register, stuffing a wad of money into a customer's to-go bag. The customer was someone I recognized, the local dermatologist, Dr. Bellini. She had gorgeous skin and a stoic demeanor. I was pretty certain that she worried smile lines would mar her face. After the doctor slotted the to-go bag into her purse, she ordered a coffee to go.

I stood transfixed. Had I just witnessed Savannah paying off the doctor to lie for her?

The doctor accepted the coffee and waved a two-finger goodbye to Savannah, who headed back to her icing station.

I swooped up to the counter. "*Psst*. Savannah."

She lumbered toward me. Her face seemed better. The welts were nearly gone. "Hi, Jenna, I can't talk. I have three cakes to ice."

"Give me one second." I hitched my chin toward the retreating figure of the doctor. "Was that Dr. Bellini?"

Savannah nodded.

"Why were you giving her money?"

"I . . . I was paying my bill. I couldn't pay last week because I get paid bimonthly."

"You didn't pay with a credit card?"

"I don't ever use credit cards. I went into debt in my early twenties, and once I bailed myself out I promised myself I'd never charge anything ever again. Why do you ask?" Her eyes widened. "You don't think—" Her mouth dropped open. "You do. You're wrong. I was not doing anything illicit. I was not paying her hush money. Promise. Go after her. Ask her." She shot out a hand. "Please, believe me."

"Savannah, the police searched Kylie's apartment." I hesitated.

Would Appleby frown on me telling Savannah about the letter? I had to make a snap decision. He was out of pocket with his son and Cinnamon was in the hospital. She'd asked me to assist in the investigation.

"The police," I continued, "found a safe. In it was a love letter. From you to Kylie."

Savannah blinked. "I never wrote her a letter."

I recited what it said.

Savannah pressed her lips together. "I never wrote that."

"The letter was written on lilac paper."

Savannah shot out a hand. "That proves it. I don't own anything lilac. I hate anything pastel. Oh, sure, I wear this stupid pink apron and I make cakes with pastel colors, but after a day of pink this and baby blue that, I—" She bit back tears. "Everything I own is white, Jenna."

White weddings. White clothing. White, white, white.

"Since my twenties," she whined, "I've been a blank slate."

"Would you do something for me?" I asked.

"Sure. Anything."

"Would you write your name on a piece of paper."

A few years ago, for fun, I'd taken a handwriting analysis course. I'd wanted to see what my signature said about my friends and me. My signature, which was bold and ascending, said I was creative and optimistic. Bailey's signature—she used large capital letters—showed she was capricious. Spot on.

Savannah hesitated, but after a moment she tore a piece of paper off an order pad and scrawled her name. She held it out for inspection. Her letters were small and tight, which I recalled meant she was thrifty and rational. Most importantly, her handwriting looked nothing like the words that had been written on the love letter. Nothing.

• • •

The rest of the morning sped by, with customers streaming in to inspect the Thanksgiving cookbooks we'd set out. It seemed everyone wanted to cook a new side dish. They were tired of the same old sweet potatoes, corn bread stuffing, and bean casserole. One of the fan favorite cookbooks was the *Barefoot Contessa Family Style: Easy Ideas and Recipes that Make Everyone Feel Like Family*, with recipes perfect for the holidays, including saffron risotto with butternut squash and parmesan-roasted asparagus.

Around two p.m., while Gran was manning the register, Bailey was dusting shelves, Aunt Vera was breaking apart the jigsaw puzzle, and I was rearranging the front display table, Tina scurried in with Brianna in her stroller.

"Hey, everyone! What a beautiful day." Hair in a ponytail and dressed in a red skate dress and Keds, Tina reminded me of a cheerleader. She wheeled Brianna to Bailey. "Your little girl is the best-est girl in the whole world. She started to say Ti-Ti today. Say it, Brianna. Ti-Ti."

"No, she did not." Bailey set down the feather duster and removed Brianna from the stroller. "Ma-ma," she cooed. "Ma-ma is your first word, baby girl. Say it, Ma-ma."

Brianna started to cry.

"So much for being the best-est girl in the world," I joked.

"Not my problem." Tina winked at me and strode to the counter. "How's it going, Gracie? Miss me?"

"Not much," Gran said.

"Ha! Yes, you do. I've heard rumors."

"Not from these lips." Gran blew Tina a kiss and finished packing a customer's purchase.

Tina sauntered to me. "So, Jenna, I've got a question, is there a new sports challenge in town?"

"What do you mean?"

"For days I've been seeing people exercising everywhere. Running, jumping. When I was walking Brianna earlier, I spied girls doing cartwheels for the entire length of Azure Park." Tina spread her arms wide. "I even saw Alexa climbing a building, and Flora riding a recumbent bicycle toward the top of the mountain."

"Really?"

"Yep, and I heard the toy store owner scaled the lighthouse a couple of days ago. That had to have been a sight." She tittered. "So, is there a challenge? You know, like, what's the most unique sporting thing you can do?" Tina lifted a popular cookbook from the display table, *The Pioneer Woman Cooks: A Year of Holidays: 140 Step-by-Step Recipes for Simple, Scrumptious Celebrations*, and flipped through it. "Scalloped potatoes and ham? Yum!" She showed me the accompanying picture and returned the book to its proper place. "Is there a cash prize for the challenge? If there is, I'm thinking of paddle boarding from the Pier to Santa Cruz and back. Doesn't that sound like fun?"

Not to me. I was not a paddle boarder on the ocean. On a quiet lake? Maybe.

"I don't know of a challenge," I said.

"Rats." Tina clicked her fingers. "Hey, maybe I could start one. Do you think Mayor Zeller would be interested in that as a theme week? I could help her organize it."

"Do you have time to do that?" I asked. "You're going to school, working as a nanny, and—"

"I'm only young once. I might as well do it all while I can." Tina's giggling was infectious.

I smiled until something she'd said struck me. "Back up a sec, Tina. When did you see Alexa climbing a building? Today?"

"No, the other day when I was delivering dinners for Shredding." Tina tapped her chin while thinking. "Over a week ago. I was delivering food for Midge Martin on the street behind the building. The street that ends at Azure Park."

"Ocean Avenue."

"Right. Alexa was wearing this really cool aqua blue camouflage jumpsuit with a hood. She almost blended into the building's façade."

"Which building was it?"

"The Boldine Building, where her studio is."

"How did you recognize her?"

"She swiveled her head to look at me. Maybe she felt me staring. Her eyes are so distinctive." Tina fluttered fingers beside her own.

"Go on."

"Alexa continued upward, to the rooftop. She took a breather and then descended and slipped into the studio through the window."

Rooftop. Seven-letter crossword clue for where the fish fry would take place, I mused.

Tina said, "I thought Alexa might have been practicing for whatever the challenge was but keeping it secret until she conquered it."

"How was she climbing?" I asked. "There aren't any stairs or ladders."

"Freestyle. Like a rock climber. I saw a Dumpster at the base, so maybe she gave herself a boost so she could reach the bricks on the second floor."

Of course. The first floor of the building's façade might have been smooth, but the second floor featured brick. Because it was painted the same color as the rest of the building, neither Rhett nor I had noticed. Bricks would have provided plenty of fingerholds.

Tina glimpsed her watch. "Oh, I've got to go. Class in twenty minutes. Bye, Bailey. Bye, Brianna. See you tomorrow, sweet thing."

I hurried to Bailey and said, "Did you hear that?"

Bailey was rocking Brianna and wiggling one of the baby's fingers. "What?"

"Tina said she saw Alexa scaling the Boldine Building."

"No surprise, I suppose. Alexa is an exercise nut." Bailey chuckled. "She's also jumped out of a perfectly good airplane, and she loves to bungee jump."

"No, you're missing the point. She was wearing camouflage, to match the building."

"Okay." Bailey signaled for me to continue.

"What if Alexa lied about having a flat tire on the morning Kylie was killed—she punctured the spare tire to cover the lie—and she doubled back, clambered up the building, slipped in through the opened window and hid in the studio until Kylie entered, and then attacked her?"

Bailey's mouth fell open.

I said, "Alexa could have killed Kylie and escaped without anyone seeing her."

"Why would Kylie have come there?" Bailey set Brianna in her stroller.

"Because Alexa texted her and asked her to meet."

"Except there weren't any messages on Kylie's phone, remember? The police checked."

"Alexa could have erased it."

Bailey mulled that over. "Why would Alexa kill Kylie? She loved her like a sister."

Earlier, outside Kylie's apartment, Alexa had said she hadn't been inside Kylie's place. She'd said they hadn't socialized a lot after Kylie had moved to that location. Why? Had they had a falling-out? Were Alexa's tears for her friend fake?

"What if their friendship went *poof*?" I flicked my fingers.

"Poof?"

"Because Alexa found out that her father and Kylie had a brief affair."

"They what?" Bailey's voice skated upward.

"Eugene admitted as much to Tito and me at the café. I didn't tell you because I had to meet with Deputy Appleby."

"Secrets," Bailey said. "Everyone has secrets."

"Kylie tricked him. It was—" I rotated a hand. "That's not what matters right now. Eugene said Kylie was blackmailing him. The deputy and I went to Kylie's to look for evidence of the extortion."

"Did you find it?"

"No." I clutched my pal's elbow. "Stick with me on this. What if Alexa knew Kylie had instigated the affair and blamed Kylie for creating a wedge between her parents?"

Bailey blinked. "Hold it. Aren't Audrey and Eugene together? They seemed happy when we went to visit Alexa."

"They're in couples therapy," I said. "I'm not sure the marriage will survive."

"Oh, man." Bailey moaned softly. "Even so, why would Alexa kill Kylie, her *bestie*, because of that? The message on the mirror said, 'You should have reformed.' Had Alexa warned Kylie to back off the thing with her dad?"

"The message." I snapped my fingers. "Remember how Alexa hugged Tito when he came into the studio? What if she wrote the message and dropped that tube of lip balm in his pocket?"

Bailey gasped. "Why wouldn't she have gotten rid of it after killing Kylie?"

"Because she needed a patsy. You or Tito or even Viveca could have been her fall guy."

Brianna started to whimper.

"*Shh,* sweetheart." Bailey pushed the stroller back and forth. "Jenna, we need to tell—"

"The police?" I rolled my eyes. "Cinnamon is in the hospital, and Appleby had to rush to an emergency with his son."

"What emergency?" my aunt asked, walking toward us.

I blanched. "I wasn't supposed to tell you, Aunt Vera." I petted her arm as I laid out the issue between Appleby and his son. "Marlon said he'll handle it and not to worry. So, please, don't *worry*."

"We should go to the precinct," Bailey said.

"Good idea." I moved to the counter to fetch my purse and drew to a halt. "Alexa was at Kylie's when I went there with Deputy Appleby. She told us she'd come to deliver flowers as a tribute, seeing as Kylie wasn't yet buried. What if that was a lie? What if she took files out of Kylie's safe to protect her father?"

Bailey whistled.

My aunt said, "I saw Alexa when I was at Latte Luck a bit ago. You know me and my brownies. Shari makes the most amazing ones on Thursdays. Anyway, Alexa was rolling a suitcase into the Boldine Building."

"A suitcase?" I raised an eyebrow. "Do you think she's planning on leaving town?"

"I wouldn't have a clue, dear." Aunt Vera *tsk*ed. "I read tarot cards, not minds."

Bailey said, "Alexa's lease is over. She has to give up the space. Maybe she's cleaning out her office."

"Or maybe she put whatever she filched from Kylie's place into the suitcase so she could dispose of it." I grabbed my purse and cell phone. "I'm going over there."

"To do what?" Bailey asked.

"I'm not sure."

"Dear, even though Cinnamon is under the weather, you'd better call her," my aunt said.

Bailey pushed the stroller toward my aunt. "Vera, I'm going with Jenna. Will you watch Brianna? She might need a bottle."

"Absolutely."

• • •

Bailey and I flew out of the Cookbook Nook and headed toward the mini San Francisco complex. On the way, I phoned Mercy Urgent Care and asked for Cinnamon's room. The connection rang and rang. Maybe she'd been released, or she had been taken to another room for a test.

I hoped everything was okay and dialed her cell phone, leaving the following message: "Chief, I think Alexa Tinsdale might be the killer after all. I'll explain when I see you. FYI, minutes ago, Alexa was seen entering the Boldine Building. Bailey and I are going there, and we'll watch the exits until someone from your team arrives."

When I ended the call, I dialed the precinct. Appleby was still out and unavailable. I asked if there was anyone I could speak to. The clerk transferred me to the officer on duty, except he didn't answer. I reached his voice mail, too. Swell. I left him the same message I'd left Cinnamon and, frustrated, stabbed End on my cell phone.

I hoped Bailey and I wouldn't take heat from the police for doing our citizenly duty, but I knew I was a dreamer. Cinnamon might have given me permission to help with the investigation, but no good deed went unpunished. At least I could claim, by taking Bailey along, I'd considered safety in numbers.

Apparently the Boldines had returned from their vacation. Customers were entering the building when we arrived, most veering into the jewelry store, which was having a preholiday sale on diamonds.

"Let's go to the second floor," I said to Bailey.

"Whoa. Hold on." She grabbed my shoulder. "Your message to Cinnamon was that we'd watch exits."

"What if Alexa escapes the way she did the other day?" I strode to the stairs. "Through the open window?"

Bailey raced after me. "Wait! What's our plan?"

"If Alexa is still inside? Be cordial. Stall. Someone from the police department will show up." I took the stairs two at a time to the second floor.

Bailey followed, huffing and puffing. "I really am out of shape," she wheezed.

"You can start skating with Cinnamon and me once a week."

"Speaking of Cinnamon, call her again. Maybe—"

The door to Your Wellness opened. Alexa poked her head out. "I thought I heard voices. What are you two doing here?" Her face was placid and emotionless. No smile.

I cleared my throat. "I was concerned about you, after running into you at Kylie's. You were so distraught." Which, if I was right about her guilt, had been a total lie. "My aunt saw you enter the building earlier, so since business was slow for us, Bailey and I decided to make a social call. I'm so sorry you have to give up this space."

"Yes. It's awful. The Boldines . . ." Alexa pressed a hand to her chest. "I get why they ended the lease. I wish they'd give me a second chance. C'mon in."

I stepped inside and my gaze instantly went to the tower-style reformer with its retractable rope system.

Alexa followed my gaze. "If only I'd been here. For Kylie. I feel so guilty."

"You shouldn't blame yourself," I said, though I was thinking: *Sure you should.* "Anything new on the business front?"

"Not a peep from my students. I'm sunk."

Bailey said, "Alexa, is it okay if I grab a cup of water? Those stairs did me in."

"Sure."

Bailey made a beeline for the water cooler located outside the glass-enclosed office. She hesitated and gazed over her shoulder at me. Deliberately, she hitched her chin to the right. I spotted what she wanted me to see. Alexa's suitcase. Inches inside the office door. A black overnighter, its top open and resting against the office door. From this distance, all I could see on top was what appeared to be a manila envelope and a book.

I turned back to Alexa. "Traveling?" I asked, keeping my voice easygoing.

"Yes. Heading to Oregon for the weekend. Between you and me, I can't wait for a change of scenery."

"I can't imagine what you've been going through this past week." I licked my lips. "You know, I could use a glass of water, too." I ambled in that direction, to get a closer look inside the suitcase.

Alexa rushed ahead of me and clapped the suitcase closed. Her face changed. Hardened.

"Going with anyone to Oregon?" I asked, acting as if her bolt to conceal had been a non-event. "A special someone?"

"No boyfriend, if that's what you mean." Alexa heaved a sigh. "He dropped out of my life a year ago."

"I'm sorry to hear that. I had no idea."

"Good riddance."

The edge in Alexa's voice made me shudder.

"Look, ladies, I've got a flight to catch," Alexa said, "so if you don't mind, I'm kicking you two out."

Bailey took a step toward us and tripped. On purpose? Her cup of water went flying. She landed on her knees and reached for the suitcase. She flipped open the lid. "What a klutz!" she groused. "Sorry about that."

I peeked into the suitcase. The manila folder was inscribed with the words *Eugene $$$*. Beside it lay a yearbook with *Kylie* written on the cover in black marker pen. I flashed on the sketch I'd made of the crime scene and my notes about the shredded paper. Some of the bond-style paper had red and black ink on it. Could it have come from a Crystal Cove High School yearbook? The Toreador mascot was black; the school's color scheme was red and white. Alexa had defaced a page in her yearbook and had torn out another. Her mother had said the missing page had been a picture of Bunny yukking it up with some football buddies. Had that been the truth? Could that page have contained another picture of Bunny and Kylie? Had Kylie, and not veganism, been the root of Alexa and Bunny's breakup? Was that yearbook picture among the shreds?

Bailey scrambled to her feet. "Sorry, Alexa. I'll get some paper towels. I've been so clumsy ever since delivering the baby."

"That's a lie, Bailey Bird Martinez," Alexa growled. "I'm your trainer. I know what you're capable of."

"Yes, but—"

"That's it." Alexa lunged to her left and grabbed a double-handled resistance band from the collection on the wall. "I know what you two are up to." She whisked one end with whiplike accuracy at Bailey, catching her on the arm. Bailey wailed. "And you, Jenna." Alexa loped to her right, toward the entrance to the studio, while wiggling the resistance band as if it were a cobra. She whisked the band in my direction. The handle whizzed by my ear but missed hitting me.

Given the opening she'd created, I darted past her to the weights wall and grabbed a three-pound barbell.

Alexa cracked the band again. It caught me on the thigh. I bit back a yelp.

"I knew you were nosey, Jenna," Alexa said, "but I had no idea you were stupid."

I positioned the barbell chest-high. I wasn't quite sure what I would do with it. I was an ace with a Frisbee, but I couldn't put a shot worth a darn. Heaving a barbell had to be the same kind of move. Dumb. Even so, Alexa kept her distance.

"You robbed Kylie's safe, didn't you?" I asked. "Right before Deputy Appleby and I showed up. That's where you found your father's file."

Alexa glanced in the direction of the suitcase and returned her focus to me.

"Kylie was blackmailing him," I continued, "but then you knew that, didn't you?"

"She might have mentioned it."

"You stowed the contents of the safe in the trunk of your car right before Deputy Appleby and I drove up," I said, edging to my right. "You'd brought flowers to cover your tracks, in case a neighbor saw you in the vicinity."

With Alexa's focus riveted on me, Bailey edged to her right.

"Is that Kylie's senior-year yearbook?" I knew it was. I recognized the date from the one her mother had shown us. "Did Kylie deface pictures the way you did in yours?"

"No."

"So why take it?" I asked. "Maybe someone who loved her would want it."

"Like family?" Alexa said snidely. "She didn't have family. That's why she glommed onto mine."

"But she didn't succeed," I said. "Your parents adore you."

"Don't kid yourself. They adored her, too. My father perhaps a little too much," Alexa said with a bite, cutting a sharp look in the direction of the folder with her father's name on it.

"You and Kylie were besties, you said."

"Things changed when she took Benjamin from me."

"Who's Benjamin?" I asked.

"Who *was* Benjamin?" Alexa corrected.

"He's dead?"

"Yep. He died a year ago last week."

I gulped. Had Alexa killed Benjamin as well as Kylie? How?

Silently, Bailey grabbed a barbell like the one I'd taken.

"Tell me about Benjamin," I said, keeping Alexa's gaze trained on me.

"Bunny was my fiancé."

Bunny? Of course. Audrey had said Alexa had been as serious as a heart attack about Bunny . . . Benjamin.

"How long were you and Benjamin engaged?" I asked.

"Since high school."

She was lying. Her mother had been clear about the breakup.

"Is his picture in Kylie's yearbook?" I gestured to it. "Can I see what he looks like?"

"No!" Alexa hissed.

Bailey inched more to her right, keeping eye contact with me.

"Alexa, I happen to know Bunny, I mean, Benjamin, dumped you." The statement was cruel, but I pressed on. "Your mother said it was because he became a vegan, and you teased him mercilessly."

"That's not why he—" She sliced the air with her free hand. "How petty would that make him look? We broke up because Kylie stole him from me." Her voice turned raspy, tight. "She stole all my boyfriends."

"Your mother said Kylie wouldn't have done that. She knew you were mad about Bunny."

"That didn't matter to Kylie. She wanted to defeat me at all costs."

Lifelong rivals, I mused.

Eugene had said Kylie changed a year ago. When Benjamin died?

I noticed Alexa's necklace. Seeing it conjured up an image of the crime scene. Kylie O hadn't been wearing the locket she'd had on when she and Priscilla the crossword puzzle lady had nearly run me over. Was it a locket with *Love B* etched on the back?

"Did you kill Kylie because of Benjamin?" I asked, praying the police would show up and end this madness.

"I didn't kill her."

"Yes, you did. You scaled the building, climbed in through the opened window, and hid in the studio. When Kylie entered, you attacked."

"Get real." Alexa scoffed. "There are no ladders or stairs on this building."

"A witness saw you practicing your freestyle climb. She didn't think anything of it. She thought there might be some kind of sports challenge coming up." When Alexa didn't argue, I laid out my theory. "You set a meeting with Kylie on Friday morning. I'm not sure how you convinced her to come, seeing as the two of you were at odds. She'd maxed out her credit cards. Did you promise her money? It doesn't matter. She showed up."

Alexa didn't blink.

"After killing her, you left without leaving a trace. There were no security cameras to record your actions." I lowered the barbell and started to swing it — a little back, a little forward. "Did Benjamin give you a necklace etched with *Love B* on it?"

Alexa cracked the resistance band.

I dodged to my left. "No, of course not. He gave it to Kylie, didn't he? They were in love. Since high school. That must have driven you crazy. After you killed her, you tore off the locket and put it and a phony love letter from Savannah in the safe at Kylie's apartment."

"Savannah. What a loser." Alexa's lip curled up in a snarl.

"Everything you've done has been misdirection." I patted my chest. "'Don't look at me, police. Look over there, at *them*.' You brought the crumpled articles to the crime scene to implicate others in Kylie's murder. Even your own father. Was Benjamin's yearbook photo, the one with him clowning around with his buddies, on some of the shredded paper at the crime scene?"

"Why would I have included one of him?" Alexa sniffed. "That would have incriminated me."

True. Even so, I was certain a picture of Benjamin — *Bunny* — was among the shredded paper. To rub his death in Kylie's face.

"How did Benjamin die?" I asked. "Did you kill him?"

Bailey slipped up behind Alexa.

"No. He died in a car crash." Alexa's lower lip started to quiver. "I'd planned to win him back, but Kylie made that impossible. A year ago, he was on his way to see her. It was late, and he was tired from work, but she ordered him to drive anyway. All the way from San Francisco. She was selfish that way. He fell asleep at the wheel and ran off the road, and in an instant, he was dead."

"I'm so sorry."

She went silent.

"I don't understand one thing," I said. "Why didn't you kill Kylie then, when Benjamin died? What wait until now?"

Alexa pursed her lips. "When he died, she begged me to forgive her. Begged me to love her again. To trust her. My mother and father begged me, too." Tears leaked down her cheeks. "So I did. I would be the bigger person, I told myself. But then I learned that she'd lied to me again."

"About your father?"

"No!" Her scream was bloodcurdling.

"About having an investor to buy the *Courier*?" I asked.

"Shut up! Let me finish."

Bailey blinked. She mouthed something. I couldn't make it out.

"I discovered" — Alexa shot her free hand forward — "that Kylie planned to open her own studio. Exactly like this one. Can you believe it? When I asked her about it, she smiled and said she was going to put me out of business."

"Why would she do that?"

"Because I had a happy family and she didn't. Don't you see? She was sick. Twisted."

Alexa was the twisted one, but I didn't say it out loud.

"Who was her investor?" I asked.

"My father, of course."

Eugene had guessed correctly.

"By extorting him, Kylie said she could start anew." Alexa raised her chin. "I told her over *her* dead body. She was screwed up in the head. A hot mess. I told her she needed to change, but she refused."

You should have reformed read the message on the mirror. Alexa had warned her; Kylie hadn't complied.

Bailey raised the barbell. I knew what she planned to do. Knock Alexa out. But if she accidentally killed Alexa, she could go to jail for manslaughter.

I shook my head.

Alexa noticed my action. She spun around and elbowed Bailey, who stumbled backward.

I charged Alexa, barbell first, and rammed her into the wall of equipment.

At the same time, the door to the studio flew open.

Cinnamon strode in, wearing civilian clothes, gun aimed. "Alexa

Tinsdale, don't move." She glowered at me. "And you, Jenna? Really? This is not the reason I needed to get my sorry rear end out of the hospital bed."

"No? It seems to have worked." I smiled with relief.

Chapter 22

Cinnamon hauled Alexa to jail. Neither Alexa's father nor mother, after learning the truth, would pay for her bail. So much for devoted family.

A week later, family and friends met at my father's house for Thanksgiving dinner. Katie and Keller had done most of the cooking. I'd made the *brie en croute* recipe that I'd found in the Ina Garten book. Bailey had brought sweet potato soup. My aunt and Marlon Appleby were not in attendance for the occasion. Days after Alexa's arrest, they had gone to Las Vegas to elope. Appleby's son had shown up to protest, but he'd arrived an hour after they'd said "I do." According to a text from my aunt, Appleby had told his son to *Stuff it — his life, his decision.* His ultimatum had not gone over well.

"How are you?" Rhett asked as he handed me a glass of chardonnay.

"Breathing deeply."

It was a warm night. Many of us had gathered on the terrace to enjoy a glass of wine and take in the view of the ocean. Katie's little girl, Min-yi, was dutifully checking out Brianna in the living room. Tito had fashioned an enclosed area where both children could play without bumping into or breaking things.

"You look incredible." Rhett kissed my cheek.

"Thanks." I'd slipped into a copper brown sweater, matching corduroys, and closed-toed flats. Dangly gold earrings completed the ensemble. "You *smell* incredible."

"New cologne. Like it?"

"Yum."

Rhett had been very attentive since my run-in with Alexa. He hadn't wanted me out of his sight. Granted, *wanting* and *getting* a wish were virtually impossible, given his schedule at work, but all of the new hires were working out, and because they were, we'd agreed to follow through with our trip to Napa in early December to see his folks. While there, we would meet with Harmony and review every aspect of our June nuptials, right down to wedding gowns, tuxedos, and boutonnieres.

Rhett slung an arm around my waist and faced the ocean. "Nice view."

"The nicest."

"Get a room, you two." Cinnamon, casual in a sweater over leggings tucked into boots, sauntered up to me and addressed my father, who was rocking in the slat-backed rocker, a glass of whiskey in his hand. "Cary, what are we going to do about your daughter?"

"We?" My father winked at Lola, who was sitting beside him in the companion rocking chair. "I have nothing to do with what my grown daughter does. She makes her own decisions."

"Thanks, Dad," I murmured.

"And if I recall, you gave her carte blanche to help in this investigation," he added.

"Who told you that?" Cinnamon stared daggers at me.

"Not I!" I raised a hand. "Mum was the word."

"I believe your deputy shared the news with his intended, my devoted sister," my father said and grinned. "C'mon, admit it, young lady, Jenna did help you suss out this murderer."

"Suss." Cinnamon huffed. "What kind of word is *suss*? We would have come to the same conclusion."

"When?" I demanded. "When Alexa was on the flight to Argentina?" Going to Oregon for a hiking vacation hadn't been Alexa's true itinerary. A passport and ticket to Buenos Aires had been tucked into the outside pocket of her overnight case.

"Her parents are heartsick," Lola said.

"And well they should be." I sipped my wine. "Not only did Kylie pull the wool over their eyes, but their daughter had been a ticking time bomb since high school."

Rhett said, "I heard they're getting divorced."

"Yep," I said. "When Peter Pomerance said he'd buy the newspaper, Eugene and Audrey finally admitted to one another that Alexa was the reason they had stayed together. Separation will be good for them. Both need new beginnings. I hope they can find peace."

Bailey and Tito joined us on the terrace. "Speaking of Peter Pomerance, he's offered Tito the position as newspaper editor, and he's taking it."

"Hear, hear!" Rhett raised his glass in a toast. "Congratulations."

Tito blushed. "I hope I'm up to the task. I might need to get my head examined."

Rhett chortled.

"Speaking of getting one's head examined," Cinnamon said, "did you hear Midge Martin canceled her TV show, and she's hired another chef so she can spend more time with her daughter? Both are starting therapy."

"'Tis the season for healing," I said. "Savannah and her mother are going to dual therapy, too."

"I heard food is therapeutic," my father said, rising to a stand. "When's dinner? I'm starved."

As if on cue, Keller and Katie appeared in the sliding glass doorway. Both were wearing aprons over their outfits emblazoned with *Eat, drink, and be thankful.* "Turkey's on," they said in unison.

"About time." Dad offered a hand to Lola and pulled her to her feet.

As Rhett and I were passing into the living room, Keller waylaid us. "Guys, listen, I don't want you to worry. I'm going to finish doing everything in your house, but—" He worked his tongue inside his cheek.

"But?" I asked warily.

"But then I'm hanging up my paintbrush."

"Why?"

"I've decided I am not my father's son. I love making ice cream. If I do any second job, it'll be running Taste of Heaven for my mom."

"Good for you." Rhett patted Keller's arm. "Great decision."

I offered a supportive smile. "We're pulling for you. We both know that a person has to do what inspires him, not necessarily what pays the bills."

Rhett clasped my hand. "Amen."

Recipes

Bird's Nest Salad
Cocoa Bliss Balls
Coconut Haystack Cookies
Mini Crab Cakes
Honey-Lemon Vinaigrette
Pretzel Haystacks
Pumpkin-Chocolate-Coconut Muffins
Shredded Grilled Cheese Sandwich

Bird's Nest Kale Salad
(Serves 6)

From Katie:

If I must say, this is one of my new favorite salads. It has so many delicious ingredients plus plenty of protein. I also love the fact that you can change it up by using a different dressing. In the mood for sweet? Use the ginger dressing. Salty? Use the peanut dressing.

6 eggs, soft-boiled
6 ounces kale, chopped
6 ounces baby spinach
6 ounces carrots, peeled, julienned
3 ounces peanuts
4 ounces shitake mushrooms, stems removed, sliced
1/2 cup peanut dressing or ginger dressing (recipes follow)
Salt and cracked pepper, to taste
Shichimi, to taste (Japanese 7-spice mixture)
1 cup crispy wonton strips

Soft-boil the eggs by bringing a pot of water to boil, then lowering the temperature to simmer and adding eggs (in shells). Simmer for 5 minutes. Remove from heat and set aside until warm to the touch, then peel off the shells.

In a mixing bowl, add kale, spinach, carrots, peanuts, shitake mushrooms, and peanut (or ginger) dressing. Season with salt and cracked pepper, to taste.

For each salad, set combined vegetables in the center of bowl and create a small "nest" or hollow in the center. Place the warm soft-boiled egg in the nest. Sprinkle each egg with a dash of shichimi.

Arrange crispy wontons around the salad. Serve immediately.

Peanut Dressing

1/4 cup creamy peanut butter
1 tablespoon toasted sesame oil
1-1/2 tablespoon soy sauce
1 tablespoon rice vinegar
2 teaspoons honey
1 lime, juiced, yields about 1 tablespoon juice
1/2 tablespoon freshly grated ginger
Water, as needed

Put all ingredients into a blender and blend until smooth. Refrigerate.

Ginger Salad Dressing

1/2 cup minced onion
1/2 cup peanut oil
1/3 cup rice vinegar
2 tablespoons water
2 tablespoons minced fresh ginger
2 tablespoons minced celery
4 teaspoons soy sauce
2-1/2 teaspoons sugar
2 teaspoons lemon juice
1/2 teaspoon salt
1/4 teaspoon black pepper

Put all ingredients into a blender and blend until smooth. Refrigerate.

Cocoa Bliss Balls
(Yield: 12–16 balls)

From Jenna:

Katie will claim these are her famous bliss balls, but because it's a 5-ingredient recipe, I'm sharing the recipe with you. I love having these little morsels on hand in my refrigerator. I adore a burst of protein that isn't a shake or energy bar.

1 cup cashews
3/4 cup pitted dates, chopped
1/4 cup unsweetened cocoa powder
1/8 cup raw honey
Splash of whole milk or almond milk

In a blender, combine cashews, pitted dates, cocoa powder, and raw honey, and blend until incorporated. Add a splash of milk and blend again. The mixture should hold together but not be sticky. If it is, add a tad more cocoa powder. If it's too dry, add another splash of milk.

Roll the mixture into 1-inch balls, about the size of walnuts. Store in an airtight container. Refrigerate. These keep a very long time.

Coconut Haystacks
(Yield: 18–24 cookies)

From Katie:

These are super easy and fun for children to make. I can't wait until Min-yi is old enough to bake with her mama. The hardest part is not to eat the entire batch in one sitting. At the end of the recipe, I've added a chocolate option. If you don't like chocolate, try white chocolate or even butterscotch chips. Enjoy.

5-1/2 cups sweetened flaked coconut
1 14-ounce can sweetened condensed milk
2 teaspoons vanilla extract

Heat oven to 325 degrees F. Line baking sheets with parchment paper. Spray the paper with nonstick cooking spray.

In a medium bowl, combine the coconut, sweetened condensed milk, and the vanilla extract. Blend well.

Using a cookie scoop or a spoon, drop mounds (about 1 tablespoon each) of the coconut mixture onto the parchment paper. Leave about an inch between them.

Bake the cookies for 10–12 minutes, until lightly browned. Remove from the oven and set the cookies on a rack to cool.

Chocolate Version

If desired, you can dip the cookies "foot," or base, after baking, in melted chocolate. To do so, melt 1 cup of semisweet chocolate chips with 2 teaspoons of butter. Dip the cookies in and set on parchment paper to cool.

Or . . . you could drizzle the melted chocolate over the tops of the haystacks. Have fun!

Mini Crab Cakes
(Gluten-free or regular)
(Yield: 16)

From Lola:

I love serving fish to my customers, whether baked, broiled, grilled, or fried. One of my favorite appetizers to serve is crab cakes — all the flavors of crab in bite-sized portions. Serve with homemade aioli, and voilà. These can be made using regular panko or gluten-free panko. I'm partial to Ian's gluten-free panko, but any will do.

2 6-ounce cans lump crabmeat
1/3 cup Panko (use gluten-free if necessary)
1/4 cup red onion, finely chopped
1/4 cup parsley, minced
1 large egg, beaten
1 clove garlic, minced (you can omit if you have a garlic issue)
1/4 cup mayonnaise (I use Best Foods, which is gluten-free)
1/4 teaspoon Old Bay Seasoning (found at the fish counter at your grocer)
1/4 teaspoon salt
1/4 teaspoon pepper, ground
1/2 cup panko, extra for dredging the crab cakes
2 tablespoons olive oil

Aioli

1 cup mayonnaise (see above re: gluten-free)
2 cloves garlic, crushed
2 tablespoons parsley, minced
1 teaspoon lemon juice
1/8 teaspoon salt
1/8 teaspoon pepper, ground

To make the crab cakes:

Combine all the crab cake ingredients in a medium mixing bowl.

Shape mixture by tablespoonfuls into small cakes. Dredge with the extra panko. (They will be soft. It's okay.)

Heat olive oil on medium-high in a large sauté pan. Sauté crab cakes in oil until golden brown on both sides, about 4–5 minutes a side. Serve with aioli sauce.

To make the aioli:

Combine all ingredients in a bowl and mix well. Refrigerate what you don't use.

Honey-Lemon Vinaigrette
(Yield: 1 ¼ cups)

From Jenna:

This is a go-to salad dressing for me. It's my mother's recipe. It works on just about every variation of salad. I keep it in the refrigerator at all times. The honey is the magic.

Zest from 1 lemon
1/4 cup fresh lemon juice
1 tablespoon apple cider vinegar
1 teaspoon Dijon mustard
1/2 teaspoon kosher salt
1/8 teaspoon black pepper
1/4 cup honey
3/4 cup vegetable oil

Put all ingredients into a blender and blend until smooth. Refrigerate.

Haystacks
(Yield: 30 cookies)

From: Katie:

This is another great recipe for children. It is a no-cook recipe. You will need a microwave. I like using white chocolate melting wafers instead of white chocolate chips because they hold together better. Also, note, don't use the natural kind of peanut butter. It's too oily. The cookies will not firm up well. I prefer Jif brand, but many mothers like Skippy. You decide.

12 ounces white chocolate melting wafers
12 ounces butterscotch chips
1 cup peanut butter (not the natural kind)
12 ounces pretzels

Prepare a baking sheet by lining it with parchment paper.

In a medium-sized bowl, mix the white chocolate melting wafers and butterscotch chips and microwave for 30 seconds at a time. It should take 3 zaps. Stir in between each round.

Remove the bowl from the microwave and stir in the peanut butter and pretzels.

Using a cookie scoop or large spoon, drop mounds of the cookies (about 2 tablespoons each) on the parchment paper. Let sit until fully hardened, about an hour.

If you store these in an airtight container in the refrigerator, they'll be good for about a week. You can freeze them but make sure they are airtight.

Pumpkin-Chocolate-Coconut Muffins
(Gluten-free version)
(Yield: 24)

From Katie:

I don't mean to boast, but these little goodies are Keller's favorite muffin, and that's saying something, because he's an ice cream guy through and through. Insider tip: I knew two of his favorite flavors were chocolate and coconut, so I experimented and won him over. He has even said he wants to try making a complimentary pumpkin-chocolate-coconut ice cream. What do you think? I say go for it.

1-1/2 cups gluten-free flour
1/2 teaspoon xanthan gum
1 teaspoon baking powder
1 tablespoon whey flour
1 teaspoon ground cinnamon
1/2 teaspoon ground ginger
1/8 teaspoon ground nutmeg
1/2 teaspoon baking soda
1/2 teaspoon salt
1 cup pumpkin puree
3/4 cup granulated sugar
1/2 cup coconut oil, melted and cooled
2 large eggs
1 teaspoon vanilla
1-1/2 cups shredded coconut
1/2 cup semisweet chocolate chips

For the topping:

1/4 cup shredded coconut
1/4 cup semisweet chocolate chips

Preheat oven to 350 degrees F. Line a muffin pan with paper liners. Spray them with nonstick cooking spray. Set aside.

In a medium bowl, whisk together the gluten-free flour, xanthan gum, baking powder, whey flour, cinnamon, ginger, nutmeg, baking soda, and salt. Set aside.

In a large bowl, combine the pumpkin puree, sugar, melted coconut oil, eggs, and vanilla. Gradually add the dry ingredients to the pumpkin mixture. Stir until combined. Add in the coconut and chocolate chips.

Fill each of the muffin cups about 3/4 full. Sprinkle with additional coconut. Bake muffins for 20–22 minutes until a toothpick comes out clean. When you remove from the oven, top with additional chocolate chips. They will melt as the cupcakes cool on a rack for 20 minutes. Seal in an airtight container.

Shredded Grilled Cheese Sandwich
(Yield: 2 sandwiches)

From Aunt Vera:

This is one of the sandwiches Katie served for the Nook Café's Food Bowl event. It's simple in nature and one of my favorite sandwiches. I love the idea of baking the parmesan on the outside of the bread to give it a nice crunch. If you don't want to, then incorporate the parmesan on the inside of the sandwich. The more cheese, the better, in my humble opinion.

4 slices bread
4 tablespoons butter
4 tablespoons cream cheese
6 ounces cheddar cheese, shredded
6 ounces parmesan cheese, shredded, divided

Butter each slice of bread on one side. Spread the cream cheese on the other side of the bread. *(Note: The cream cheese side is the inside of the sandwich; the butter side is the outside.)*

To assemble: Top two slices of bread, cream cheese side up, with shredded cheddar cheese and half of the parmesan cheese. Set the other slice of bread on top of the sandwich and press slightly.

If cooking on a stovetop: Heat a large skillet over medium heat for about 2 minutes. Sprinkle the remaining parmesan cheese on the skillet. Set the two sandwiches on top. Cook the sandwiches on the skillet for 4 minutes, until golden brown. Flip the sandwiches, using a spatula, and cook another 2–4 minutes. You can compress the sandwich with the spatula. Turn the sandwich one more time. Press down with the spatula, and remove the sandwiches from the pan. Let cool about 2–3 minutes, and serve.

If cooking on a panini or sandwich maker: Sprinkle the remaining parmesan cheese on the griddle. Set the 2 sandwiches on the cheese and slowly lower the top of the sandwich maker. Cook for a total of 4 minutes. Remove sandwiches from the griddle and let cool 2–3 minutes, then serve. *Beware, the insides might ooze out the sides. If the lid is too heavy, you might want to consider resorting to the stovetop method.*

About the Author

Daryl Wood Gerber is the Agatha Award–winning, nationally bestselling author of the French Bistro Mysteries, featuring a bistro owner in Napa Valley, as well as the Cookbook Nook Mysteries, featuring an admitted foodie and owner of a cookbook store in Crystal Cove, California. Under the pen name Avery Aames, Daryl writes the Cheese Shop Mysteries, featuring a cheese shop owner in Providence, Ohio.

As a girl, Daryl considered becoming a writer, but she was dissuaded by a seventh-grade teacher. It wasn't until she was in her twenties that she had the temerity to try her hand at writing again . . . for TV and screen. Why? Because she was an actress in Hollywood. A fun tidbit for mystery buffs: Daryl co-starred on *Murder, She Wrote* as well as other TV shows. As a writer, she created the format for the popular sitcom *Out of This World*. When she moved across the country with her husband, she returned to writing what she loved to read: mysteries and thrillers.

Daryl is originally from the Bay Area and graduated from Stanford University. She loves to cook, read, golf, swim, and garden. She also likes adventure and has been known to jump out of a perfectly good airplane. Here are a few of Daryl's lifelong mottos: perseverance will out; believe you can; never give up. She hopes they will become yours, as well.

To learn more about Daryl and her books, visit her website at DarylWoodGerber.com.

Made in the USA
Las Vegas, NV
30 November 2021

35661795R00132